Blushing in the Big Leagues
Copyright © 2023 R.S. Grey

Published: R.S. Grey 2023
authorrsgrey@gmail.com
Editing: Editing by C. Marie
Proofreading: Red Leaf Proofing, Julia Griffis
Cover Design: R.S. Grey

READING ORDER

This book can be read as a complete standalone.

However, this book shares characters with *Three Strikes and You're Mine*. If you're planning to read both, *Three Strikes and You're Mine* should be read first. Happy reading!

BLUSHING
in the
BIG LEAGUES

a forbidden lovers romantic comedy

USA TODAY BESTSELLING AUTHOR
R.S. GREY

ONE

TATE

AS RIDICULOUS AS IT SOUNDS, it all started with a silly dare.

I'm putting the finishing touches on my mascara when one of my roommates lays this gem on me: "We triple dog dare you to hook up with someone tonight."

Wow. So original. If we were in eighth grade, the dare would be accompanied by tittering laughter, blushing cheeks, and a speed-dial call to some punk named Jason. But we're not middle schoolers. We're adults in our mid-twenties with careers and ever-intensifying skincare routines. I contribute to a 401k. *I am not susceptible to ridiculous dares.*

"Is that even a real thing?" I ask Daphne.

She's the one who issued the dare. I thought she was otherwise occupied—she's been lying on my bed in her underwear (no boundaries with this one) watching a makeup tutorial on YouTube and trying to convince herself that today, finally, she might master the art of winged eyeliner—but I was wrong. Apparently, she grew bored with the video and moved on to a more interesting topic, i.e. my love life.

She's looking at me now like I've just asked her if cheese *really* belongs on pizza. "*Yes,* it's a real thing! There are compounding levels of dare seriousness. A *triple* dog dare is an escalation of a double dog dare, obviously."

"*Obviously,*" I retort.

My other roommate, Sophia, steps out of my closet. She was in there rifling through my clothes, trying to decide if she should swap her outfit and wear something different to the party we're about to attend. She shouldn't bother. She looks great in her white dress.

Her problem is she's bored. She's been ready to leave for half an hour. Always on time, she's the mom of the apartment, which would make Daphne the petulant toddler, and me...somewhere in between. The spunky middle child? The type-A oldest daughter? Who knows. I'm a fiercely competitive, goal-oriented people pleaser. I am not whimsical like Daphne or as serious as Sophia. I do, however, enjoy a challenge, which is maybe why Daphne has dared me in the first place. She knows me too well.

I touch up my mascara one last time and then twist the cap closed. "So what happens if I complete the dare?"

I'm imagining a trophy with my name carefully engraved on it. A three-tier cake in my honor.

I catch their private glance in my mirror; their barely restrained smiles say it all. Sophia and Daphne are sisters. Occasionally, they share a secret language I'm not privy to.

"Uhhh...you get to enjoy a night of raucous lovemaking?" Sophia responds.

Daphne sits up and emphatically adds, "You get laid, Tate. *Laid.* You need it. Everyone agrees."

"Who's *everyone*?"

Sophia grunts. "You don't believe us, do you?" She affects a serious tone as she continues, "All those in favor of Tate getting banged tonight say 'aye.'"

Daphne and Sophia both raise their hands. "Aye."

"Those opposed say 'nay.'"

"*Nay,*" I respond drolly.

"The ayes have it, and the motion is carried." She bangs her fist on my bed like a gavel.

"Hilarious. Both of you."

I zip my makeup bag closed and step back to assess my look. I've poured myself into a black mini dress that I'll pair with a vintage Knicks bomber jacket and black heeled ankle boots. I've let my chestnut brown hair do its thing. It's long and prefers to be unkempt at all times. If I try to straighten it completely, it curls. If I curl it, it decides to go pin straight. People have told me it's sexy, so I try to just roll with it these days.

My makeup, hair, and outfit actually all look good, which means in the next week I'll have to pay for it somehow. That's just the way it is; you can't have it all. Tomorrow, watch, I'll wake up with a pimple the size of Mount Vesuvius.

"Look at her, Soph: a bombshell. You make me so proud." Daphne applauds from her perch on my bed.

I tap a pretend watch on my wrist. "You getting up anytime soon? We're supposed to be there already."

She groans and dramatically log-rolls off the bed. "Okay fine! *Fine!* I'm going. It should only take me like thirty minutes to figure out this winged eyeliner."

"*DAPHNE!*" Sophia and I both chide in unison.

"I'm kidding! I'll be ready in five. Go crack open a bottle of wine to take the edge off before we leave because that dare is happening, my friend. Mark my words. An hour from now, you're going to be doing the splits on top of some Henry Cavill lookalike. I know it."

———

IT'S Tuesday night in New York City and we're heading to a random apartment. In the normal world, people don't party this hard on a Tuesday, but we aren't in the normal world. We're beholden to the whims of major league baseball and its somewhat erratic schedule. Spring training wrapped up yesterday down in Florida and the Pinstripes are back in New York after a long month away, which means, tonight, we celebrate.

There are lots of names for women who chase professional athletes, and I refuse to repeat any of them. Quite frankly, more power to the ladies who go after what they want. I'm stuck around the guys for a very different reason. It's more like...I can't escape them. My brother's a veteran pitcher on the team. Sophia's boyfriend, Josh, also plays. His best friends, Dustin and Nick, are now *my* good friends. We're all together *all the time.* At this point, I might as well be the team's resident little sister.

When Daphne and Sophia issued their dare earlier, they knew it wouldn't involve anyone from the Pinstripes roster. I will never date a professional baseball player and they know that. The reasons are complicated but sound.

Don't get me wrong, it has nothing to do with the sport itself. I love baseball. I've been surrounded by it my entire life. I'm the product of a collegiate baseball coach and a small-town Texas beauty queen. I had a bat glued to my hand when I was still toddling around in diapers, a big bow stuck in my hair while I was catching fly balls in the outfield. I was carted from ballet to the ball field and back again, endlessly.

My dad had his hands full with his job at the University of Texas *and* coaching my older brother who showed real talent from a very early age, but that didn't mean I could escape the mandate. Oh ho ho, *no way.* The sky is blue, the sun rises in the east, and the Allens play baseball, end of story. In kindergarten, I was the only girl on an all-boys T-ball team. Those little shits harassed me endlessly, especially if I made an error on the field, so I learned *not* to mess up. I hit better than any of them could. I figured out how to throw the ball hard enough that I once gave ol' Tommy Nichols a black eye. From that day on, I was a walking legend.

Eventually, my baseball career came to an end in middle school in favor of dance (much to my dad's dismay), but I was still part of the world. My brother was already getting noticed by major league scouts. Our weekends were spent at baseball tournaments. Our summer travels always included a tour of that city's professional stadium. Fall ball, winter ball, spring ball—baseball was all I knew.

So it should come as no shock that my first kiss happened in a dugout. My first boyfriend asked me out underneath a set of bleachers. My first date involved stadium peanuts and nachos and nine innings where our attention never once strayed from the field. I can't even remember the guy's name, but I do know Joseph Vargas pitched a no-hitter that game.

My issue with baseball guys begins when they make the transition into the majors. Aside from the fact that their schedules are horrendous, their priority is *always* the game, and their egos are obscenely inflated—most of them have this unyielding urge to go crazy the *second* they sign on the dotted line on their MLB contracts. And I get it. For most of their lives, these guys have been focused on honing their craft and putting in the work to play professionally. Once they do, all bets are off, especially when it comes to women and how many they choose to date at once.

Anyway, the point is, when it comes to dating baseball guys, it's plain and simple: don't do it. Look elsewhere. A cafe, a park, a retirement home—*any* other place will do.

Daphne and Sophia don't agree with my poor assessment of professional baseball guys. Sophia is crazy about her boyfriend, Josh, and I will say, he's one of the good ones. An outlier, if you will. They've been together for years and he's never so much as *sniffed* in the direction of another woman. He puts her first, always. Also Daphne, while single, has made it very clear that she would be willing to entertain any Pinstripes player who happens her way. *Just ask my brother.*

Unfortunately for her, he's been officially off the market for a while.

Once we're in the elevator in a swanky high-rise in Midtown, I look over at my friends. "There are going to be other guys here tonight, right? Not just our group?"

That was the promise. This isn't supposed to be another standard get-together with all the usual suspects. I've done that a million times, and while fun, nothing unexpected ever happens with our group. Josh and Sophia fawn all over each other. Dustin and Daphne get on each other's nerves. Nick regales us with a story that is either funny or gross or outright idiotic. Rinse and repeat.

"Yes," Sophia insists. "This isn't even a baseball party, really. It just so happens that the guys will be here."

"Whose place is this anyway?" Daphne asks, using the mirrored surface of the elevator to check her teeth for lipstick stains.

"Some tech mogul. He's the one who got Josh and Dustin to invest in that baseball app that took off last year. He's apparently pretty nice. The guys like him. I don't know... I was told there's going to be catered food and an open bar so I didn't ask too many questions."

"Sold," I tease with a wink. "And who knows? If the tech guy is hot, maybe he'll be the one I hook up with tonight."

I'm talking out of my ass, mostly just stringing them along at this point. I'm not going to hook up with someone just to complete a dare. Sure, I could use a little action. It's been...a while since I've had sex, and Sophia and Daphne have clearly caught on to that fact. However, I'm not a love 'em and leave 'em kind of girl. I'm the exact opposite. I consider all things from all sides, contemplate every side effect and consequence. I read the fine print. Hence why my friends think I need a silly dare to jumpstart my love life, but they're wrong.

I'll admit, I'm partly to blame for this misunderstanding. For the better part of the last few years, I've been focused on my career. Graduating with my nursing degree and establishing myself as an RN took precedence in my life probably for a little *too* long, but now seeing my brother happily engaged and knowing Sophia's not far from the altar herself has been a big wakeup call. I have to shift gears. I love love as much as the next gal! I want a boyfriend! I even think I've figured out exactly what I'm looking for in a partner. Why is that important? Oh, *simple*. The idea of letting the universe orchestrate my love life seems absolutely ludicrous. Leaving room for fate? No ma'am. Spontaneity? Never heard of her.

My plan for my perfect guy includes (but is not limited to) the following criteria. Obviously, we've established that he can't play baseball. Outside of that, I'd like him to be kind; smart; attentive; a hard worker; tall; handsome; someone who can sleep on the left side of the bed because I prefer the right; someone who gets along with my friends, but not like *too* well, not in a creepy way; dog lover; brunch lover; book lover; and for brevity's sake, I'll skip past a fair number of other requirements to emphasize that he must, most importantly of all, make me feel safe and steadfast in our relationship.

It's really not that much! There are probably ten guys at this party who could fit the bill. For all I know, hot tech guy himself could be my soul mate!

We discuss him on the way up to the top floor. Well... Daphne discusses him, and by discuss, I mean she chants "Hot tech guy! Hot tech guy! Hot tech guy!" like she's a frat bro about to do a keg stand.

When the elevator stops and the doors sweep open, we arrive in an ultramodern apartment. It's so blindingly white that I feel bad walking on the marble floor in my boots.

A large foyer gives way to a living room filled with art and décor and people. *People!* I sigh in relief. Scanning the crowd, I see a lot of unfamiliar faces. In fact, I don't see any of our friends. A rare occurrence, for sure.

"Come on," Sophia says. "Josh said he's here somewhere."

We stick together, moving through the crowd, looking for Josh. But oops, would you look at that? We land at the bar instead and take our time perusing a custom cocktail list.

"Ooo, I might get a French martini."

Daphne's not even looking at the cocktail list. She's leaning back against the bar, watching the crowd.

"Found him," Daphne proclaims proudly.

"Josh?" I ask, trying to follow her line of sight.

"*No.* I found the hottest guy here."

I eye her skeptically. "How do you do that so fast?"

She shrugs, nonchalant about it. "It's a gift."

I shouldn't indulge her, but I'm mildly curious. Daphne has good taste. "Where is he?"

"Over in the corner, near the glass windows. He's talking to two other guys. Ignore them—they aren't important."

Her instructions make it easy for me to find the person she's referring to quickly enough. Glass windows in the corner...three men talking...then *wham*. The sight of him hits me like a Mack truck.

Wow, she's good. He's without a doubt the hottest guy at this party. How do I know? Because he's the hottest guy I've ever *seen*. Tall, tan, clearly in shape. He has luxuriously thick black hair and a sharp jawline. His full lips say, *Kiss me.* His sultry eyes say, *If you dare.*

Before I fall deeper into his devastating good looks, I turn away and accept my drink from the bartender.

"Nice," I tell her.

My remark seems casual enough, but it's not. Looking away was absolutely necessary. The tight tug that man elicited in my low belly was way too intense. A warning, loud and clear. Knowing absolutely nothing about him beyond how he looks, I'm certain he would not fulfill my list of requirements for a boyfriend. He'd be nothing but trouble. He would wreak havoc on my carefully laid plans.

Daphne hasn't looked away from him yet, even as she puts in her order for a gin and tonic.

"*Daph*," I hiss. "Don't be obvious."

"I'm not." She says this while waving coquettishly in his direction.

My eyes bulge and I reach out to take her hand and yank it down out of the air.

"Are you insane?" I snap despite knowing the answer.

Certifiably.

Against my better judgment, I glance back shyly over my shoulder to find the guy is looking at Daphne with an uncertain expression, like he's trying to figure out if he knows her. Then his gaze shifts to me and—*the skyscraper is falling.* Or at least it feels like it. I'm plummeting toward my death as his eyes lock with mine. He doesn't look away when he should. In fact, his eyes narrow and his jaw tightens as our gazes hold steady.

Butterflies take flight in my stomach as Daphne releases a long, steady exhale.

"Hot damn. That man wants you."

TWO

TATE

DAPHNE'S outlandish assessment pulls me back to reality. I blink and look away from the stranger, refocusing my attention on my best friend. She's grinning ear to ear, staring at me with a mischievous twinkle in her blue eyes. She's gorgeous tonight, but then again, she's always gorgeous. Like her sister, she has bright red hair that's impossible not to notice and fair, almost porcelain skin. But where Sophia can be slightly guarded, Daphne has these expressive eyes that seem to telegraph every single thought, always. And right now, I know she's up to no good.

I hold up my hand to stop her before she can even start. "I don't want to hear it."

She steamrolls right past my rejection. "Him. That's your guy."

"I don't even know him!"

"That's the point!"

Once we have our drinks, we start to weave through the crowd again. I trail behind Sophia, leaving Daphne to chase after me. She's going on loudly enough that soon, I'm sure the entire party will know about the dare she's issued.

"I bet that's the tech guy. This is his house. I have a gut feeling about it."

She's relentless.

"Good. Trust your gut, stroll right on over, and introduce yourself."

I keep walking, but she's hot on my heels. "I would, don't get me wrong. I mean, he is all kinds of sexy. He has to be Latin or something. That *tan*. That *dark hair*. That dreamy bone structure. *Mamma mia*."

I can't help but laugh at her flamboyance. "So what's stopping you?"

"I'd be standing in the way of fate," she says with a little wink.

Now she's really lost it.

Fortunately, Sophia finally spots our group of guys. They're sitting around a coffee table, sipping beers. Josh looks up to find her in the crowd and he immediately pushes to stand, cutting through anyone and everyone to get to her. Blind to the rest of the world, he wraps his arms around her waist and scoops her up for a soul-searing kiss.

No one even says anything about it. There's no taunting, no *oohs* and *ahhs*. The guys know there's no point in yanking Josh's chain about his infatuation with Sophia. He readily admits it himself. The two of them are sweetly, passionately, a-little-nauseatingly in love.

The kiss lingers long enough that I turn and look at Daphne. She rocks back on her heels and rolls her eyes like we might be here a while.

Josh finally releases her, and he laughs. "I've missed you."

They haven't seen each other in two weeks because he's been down in Florida with the team for spring training. Sophia visited him in mid-March, when the elementary school where she works was on spring break. Even still, two weeks without each other was apparently too long.

They kiss again, and Daphne tosses up a hand.

"Okay, just go around them, Tate. We'll be standing here all night."

We weave past the lovebirds to get to the guys. The gang's all here. Josh—the one currently suction-cupped to Sophia—is lanky and tall with short blond hair and a big smile, Nick has a dad bod he proudly rocks and is the most fun-loving person I've ever met, and then there's Dustin. Oh Dustin…

He stands up to greet us, ruffling my hair so I'm forced to punch his shoulder hard enough that he pretends to wince. Then he nods his chin toward Daphne.

"Sup, Price?" he asks, using her last name because he knows it annoys her.

Daphne rolls her eyes, ignores him, and cuts past us to join Nick.

The two of them are always like that, oil and water.

"Why do you do that?" I ask him with a chiding tone.

He smiles and his dimples pop. "Do what?"

Dustin McDowell—Pinstripes first baseman and MLB bad boy—is extremely attractive, and he never fails to wield his good looks anytime it suits him. Now, for instance, he thinks my knees will buckle and I'll turn to putty at his feet, but Dustin doesn't affect me. He never has.

"You could try being nice to her for once."

He frowns like the idea doesn't sit right with him. Then he slides a hand through his brown hair. It's in need of a trim, and I'd tell him that if he were being nicer to Daphne.

"It's a two-way street."

I snort at his childish remark and move to the couch, taking the seat next to Nick.

Dustin steals the seat next to Daphne, but before he can say anything to her, she turns her back to him and gifts her full attention to Nick. "So, how'd it go down in Florida?"

It's a question that was on my mind too.

I feel bad I didn't keep track of their spring training this year. I'm usually the Pinstripes' number one fan, but my plate has been overloaded with work for the last month. One of our nurses has been out on maternity leave. Management was going to bring in a travel nurse, but her contract fell through, and well...I volunteered to pick up the slack. Lesson learned. I worked at the hospital nearly every day in March, and when I wasn't at work, I was helping take care of my niece, Harper. My brother's fiancée, Chloe, has become a huge help with her, but I still try to spend as much time with my niece as possible, especially when Luke is away with the team. Yesterday, he called me to check in and sounded so excited to be reunited with his family. I can only imagine how sweet that reunion was.

"Florida was good. Beach. Sun. *Ladies*." Nick grins. "Can't beat it. And Navarro was as insane as everyone promised he would be." He shakes his head like he can't fully believe it himself. "The guy's unstoppable. He broke the all-time record for number of home runs in a preseason game."

Daphne whistles, impressed. "I'm glad he's on our team."

I frown, trying to come up with the name in my head. I know the 26-man roster like the back of my hand and there's no Navarro on it. Did the Pinstripes take on a new player? God, I'm behind. I usually catch every game, or I at least watch the game highlights afterward. The guys would give me a hard time if they knew how little I've been keeping track lately.

Still, I'm curious. The name is vaguely familiar. "Grant Navarro? From Miami?" I ask.

Dustin laughs. "Yes, *Navarro from Miami*." He shakes his head. "You been under a rock?"

I smile sheepishly. "Yeah, actually. Hospital's been crazy."

His eyes soften as he takes pity on me. "We got him just before the start of spring training. His rookie contract was up with Miami, and he was about to go to Los Angeles before we scooped him up."

"Lucky us," Daphne says with a waggle of her eyebrows.

"Lucky *him*. Did you hear what we dished out to get him?" Nick puffs out a breath like it was no small sum. Clearly, there were quite a few zeroes involved in Grant's Pinstripes contract.

"A fuck ton more than we dished out to you, Williams."

Nick shoots Dustin his middle finger.

After having met their make-out quota for the hour, Sophia and Josh deign to join us. We scoot around on the couches to make more room and Dustin offers Daphne his spot, but she declines, staying right where she is beside Nick.

Dustin looks at me and shrugs as if to say, *There. I tried. You happy?*

As the night wears on, my dare falls on the back burner. We all sit around catching up, and it feels just like any other night aside from the fancy setting and hand-crafted cocktails. I missed the guys while they were down south. I forgot how much they make me laugh. At one point—at Josh and Dustin's insistence—Nick lifts his shirt to reveal a new tattoo he apparently got one night down in Miami. "I love mommy" is written obscenely big across his lower back, each letter at least an inch tall. The whole phrase is slightly left of center, so that the I is at his hip and the Y is only slightly past his spine.

"Nick!" we exclaim as our hands fly to our faces.

"NO!"

"*WHY?!*"

He shrugs and looks over his shoulder, trying to see it for himself. "I wanted a tattoo for my mom. I think it's cool."

"You're supposed to get something discreet," I tell him, barely able to look at it. I wince. "The dumb little heart with an arrow through it…"

"Yeah, and why did they do *mommy* instead of *mom*?" Daphne shudders. "That makes it weird!"

Dustin howls with laughter. Apparently, that part was his doing.

Nick is wholly unperturbed by our reactions. "I like it, and I can confirm the ladies don't mind it one bit."

I reach for my drink, needing a *long* sip to recover from this conversation, but my cup is all ice. Womp womp.

Daphne catches my eye and holds up her empty glass.

"Another?" she mouths.

I nod and stand to join her. Surprisingly, Sophia hurries after us.

"Leaving your man so soon?" Daphne taunts.

"Gotta keep him wanting more," she teases as we get swallowed by the crowd. "Besides, I want to have a front-row seat for when the guy from earlier finally makes a move on Tate. I was watching him while we were all over there on the couches. He was *totally* checking you out."

I hum in disbelief. "Uh-huh."

"I'm serious. *He was.*"

I'm actually inclined to believe her. Sophia's not one to embellish something like that. Daphne on the other hand...

"So here's how I have it planned in my head," Daphne starts.

"Planned?"

"Yeah, I've been strategizing all night. Give me your jacket." She starts yanking it off me before I even have time to react.

"What? *Are you crazy? Stop.*"

She doesn't stop.

"It's part of my outfit," I insist.

"Yeah, okay, the jacket is perfect if you're trying to look cool, but you're not. You are going for sex kitten, aka classed-up lady of the night, so that means we need to show off the assets."

She points between my boobs to emphasize her point.

I roll my eyes. "Subtle."

She ignores my sarcasm and continues her mission.

"You're going to yank my arm off," I protest. "Jesus. Would you knock it off?"

With a final huff of exertion, she succeeds in getting the jacket off me. Then she folds it over her arm, standing back to assess me. "*Fine.* You want to give up? Be my guest. I saw some blonde smokeshow sidle up to Mystery Man a few minutes ago. You probably missed your opportunity anyway."

My neck nearly snaps in two with my attempt to look over at the guy. I'm not kidding; I'm a barn owl twisting my head around to see if she's serious. He's not in his corner anymore. I know because I've been tracking his every goddamn movement. *Yeah, that's right—Sophia wasn't the only one stalking him.* He's at the bar now, waiting on his drink. His buddies from earlier are gone. The blonde has left his side too, but she's not far. She's chatting with some friends nearby, keeping close watch on him with visions of hot, *hot* sex dancing in her gaze. She wants him, clearly.

"He's probably into blondes," Daphne remarks offhandedly.

I know perfectly well what she's doing, and yet it manages to stoke my competitive nature all the same.

"Yeah, it was a dumb dare, anyway, Tate," Sophia adds. "Don't feel bad."

Don't feel bad?

Are they joking? They really don't think I'll do it?

Fine.

I shove my empty glass in Daphne's hand and start toward him. On my way, I tousle my hair, check for anything lurking between my front teeth, and ever-so-strategically tug down the top of my dress. Blondie's eyes widen when I come into her periphery. I almost feel bad. I mouth a "Sorry" as I pass her, and I truly am sorry on some level. She might be his soul mate and here I am, standing in the way of that. But this is only for one night. After that, she can have him.

When I make it within reaching distance, I tap on his shoulder—his massive, well-defined shoulder that's in line with my face. He's at least a foot taller than me. It didn't seem like such a massive leap from a distance, but up close, I'm suddenly intimidated by his size.

It's too late to scurry away now though because he's turning around and my *GOD*, he's a vision. His black hair is styled expertly, slightly longer on the top, short on the sides. He has heavenly brown eyes, the color of honey—only honey is sweet, and *he* is nothing of the sort. He's a threat personified. Bad decisions morphed into a devilish body. His features don't hide, they demand attention: chiseled cheekbones, strong jawline, piercing eyes.

Once I find my voice buried deep down beneath the layers of shock and awe, I ask the only question I care about. "Are you single?"

He wasn't expecting this question, just like he wasn't expecting me to boldly tap him on the shoulder. His surprise shifts to curiosity. His eyes spark as he scrutinizes me.

"Yes" is all he says before I press up onto my toes and give him a half-second warning: "I'm going to kiss you. I hope that's okay."

And then I am.

Kissing him, in front of everyone.

It's brief. Tentative lips meeting a surprised mouth.

Heaven.

He doesn't have enough time to recover and kiss me back properly before I'm already pulling back, smiling like a deviant.

"I'm sorry I had to drag you into this. Don't look over my shoulder, but there are two redheads watching us right now and their jaws are probably on the ground. Oh god, I wish I could see them."

He looks despite my warning.

"They're watching," he confirms, amusement evident in his tone. I'm glad I didn't offend him with my kiss.

"Good. Now, there's a blonde nearby. She's pretty and probably extremely nice. Do you want me to leave so you can talk to her again?"

His eyebrows furrow like he's having a hard time keeping up with me. To be fair, this is the weirdest conversation I've ever had too.

"No," he replies with a tone that sounds like he's rising up to meet my challenge.

Good. I didn't ruin her chances with him. I would have felt bad about that.

His gaze flits down to my lips and I wet them instinctively. Is that hunger lurking in his pale brown gaze or a trick of the low lighting?

"I have a dare I'm supposed to accomplish," I go on, trying to fill him in as fast as possible before he calls security and has me banished from the building.

"A dare?" he asks with a raised brow.

I like that he doesn't outright laugh at the absurdity of all this. He's playing the game, following my lead.

"A *triple* dog dare."

He hisses like we've found ourselves in extreme circumstances. "Let me get you a drink. I just ordered a bourbon neat. You want something?"

"That. I'll take that."

He turns to ask the bartender for another and passes me his in the meantime. When he slides the glass into my hand, sparks fly like we're made of live wires. I'm surprised smoke doesn't plume out of my ears. *Of course it would be this way.* What did I expect? I took one look at this man and knew he had the capacity to turn my world upside down if I let him. But I won't. Tonight, I'm keeping my wits about me.

Right after this bourbon.

I down the drink in one go like it's a shot, which it's definitely not. I barely contain the urge to sputter and cough as it burns going down. Meanwhile, he's watching, completely captivated. *I wish.* More like he's trying to track my movements and guess my next move, protect himself from the brunette psycho.

I press the back of my hand to my lips and compose myself as best as possible. "Okay, are you still with me, or are you planning your escape?"

Another guest walks up to get to the bar, and Mr. Fuck Me Sideways politely moves me to the side with a possessive hand on my arm. *Ooh la la.* Assertive. I like that.

"I'm still with you. I think." His forehead creases. "So was the dare just to kiss a stranger? Because you've accomplished that."

"Not exactly." I feel my face starting to flood with color. Thank god I'm tan. "I'm supposed to hook up with you."

I do not miss the muscle in his jaw tightening at this news.

"But obviously that's not going to happen," I blurt out, sidling up closer to him, both to keep my next words from being overheard by the strangers nearby and because this way, it looks like things are heating up between us. I can barely contain my delight knowing Daphne and Sophia are probably losing their minds right now. "*However*...my friends don't need to know that. Like right now, they think we're having an intimate conversation. You're looking down at me like I've really caught your interest."

His mouth quirks with amusement. "Am I?" he taunts.

"*Yes.* Very good. You're playing your part to a T." I pretend to scrutinize him. "Have you done this before?"

His mouth finally spreads into a smile that has the power to take possession of my heart right here and now. Oh my...*god.* This guy. He's going to make some lucky lady really happy one day.

"So what do you think? Are you willing to help a girl out?"

It wouldn't be hard for him to back out now. It would be a seamless transition. He was a willing participant in my half-baked plan up until now. Any sane person would exit stage left, but not him. He throws back his bourbon the same way I did, quick and to the point. I watch his Adam's apple bob as he drinks it down, and it's like I'm watching porn. That's how my body is reacting to something as simple as him swallowing. Lord help me.

Then, as if we've had this in the works for weeks, he drops our empty glasses on the bar, takes my hand, and starts leading me through the crowd. He's suddenly a man on a mission, and my blood spikes with alarm.

Oh! We're moving!

Only now does my brain come up with all the reasons why this is a horrible idea. For starters, I don't even know this guy and have just invited him to whisk me away!

This is how those *Dateline* documentaries start! Keith Morrison's script will read "Tate could always light up a room" while my bad prom pictures flash across the screen.

What kind of idiot am I?!

But we're already slipping down a hallway. Thankfully, it's not *completely* deserted. There's a short line of people waiting for the bathroom and a few others admiring a black and white abstract painting. They wouldn't have noticed us except I make sure they do.

"Great piece!" I say pointedly. That way they remember me for when the police need information on my whereabouts.

I'm being dramatic, and quite frankly, if this is how I have to go—in the arms of Adonis—well then sayonara, cruel world. It was nice knowing you!

The handsome stranger pushes open a door on the right, and rather than stumbling into a bedroom, we find ourselves in a state-of-the-art home gym.

"Does this work?" he asks, dropping my hand to walk inside.

He doesn't pull me in after him. He lets me hover near the door, watching him for a second, giving me the power to make the decision for myself.

I peer back over my shoulder to see Daphne and Sophia have surreptitiously followed behind us. They're at the end of the hall, giddy. Sophia claps and gives me an enthusiastic thumbs-up and Daphne mimes a blow job, so there's that.

Trying to play it cool, I flick my hair over my shoulder and step inside, closing the door behind me.

"It's perfect."

What in the world have I gotten myself into…

THREE

TATE

I LEAN BACK against the door and tentatively watch as the stranger walks deeper into the room. He doesn't bother to inspect any of the workout equipment. He seems confident in here, like he owns the place. Maybe he *does* own the place. Maybe Daphne was right; maybe he's the tech mogul and this is his house. I could ask, but then that would bring us back down to reality. Names, jobs, logistics—it all feels so mundane. I only have a few more minutes of playing this silly game and then it ends and I'm right back to living my simple everyday life.

He sits down on a black padded workout bench, facing me.

I take him in, not bothering to hide my assessment. After all, he's doing the same to me. His eyes drag down my body like he has every right to check me out now that he's done me a favor and pulled me into this room.

He's wearing a cool outfit: black pants and a gray t-shirt with a black jacket layered on top. Add on to that some stylish Nikes, and the overall look is simple but effective. The silver watch on his wrist is a nice touch too.

I hold my breath as I glance back up to his face. There's an air of familiarity about him that I didn't catch on to until now. I narrow my gaze, trying to pinpoint where I could have seen him before tonight.

He kicks his legs out in front of him and crosses his ankles, getting comfortable. "You look like you're really thinking hard...I don't recommend it."

I laugh and shake my head. "You just seem slightly familiar now that I'm getting a good look at you."

"We've never met..." he assures me, and it's as if he wants me to fill in the second part of the sentence for him: *or I would have remembered.*

A feeling of excitement stirs deep in my belly.

"Maybe not."

"What's your name?"

I shake my head.

He cocks his head to the side. "No names? Interesting. Are you a Russian spy or something?"

A laugh bursts out of me.

"Actually..." I arch an eyebrow. "Don't tell anyone, but I have a gun holstered under this dress."

I pat my leg for emphasis, and his eyes heat as he stares at where I'm touching my thigh.

"Show me."

"Nice try."

He grins, not the least bit bothered that I've called him out for trying to get me to lift my dress. We both know there's no gun there...

"No names, huh? Ages?" he asks.

"Twenty-five. You?"

"Twenty-seven," he answers. "Your friends—you think they caught us coming back here?"

"I know they did."

He looks pleased about that, like he's fully accepted his role as my accomplice now. "How long do you think we need?"

"Five minutes? Ten?"

His eyebrows rise. "Damn, you don't have much confidence in me. I could go an hour at least."

"Oh *please*."

His eyes alight with something. "My reputation is on the line here."

"Well lucky for you, I have no idea who you are, so your reputation is safe with me."

His gaze narrows as if he finds this interesting. Am I *supposed* to know him? Is that why he looks slightly familiar?

"Who'd you come here with?" he asks.

"My friends."

"No guy?"

"No."

"What about you?" I asked him if he was single earlier, but I want to be crystal clear on that fact. "Is there a girl? Here or—"

He shakes his head.

The revelation feels dangerous. If he were a lion, he'd be licking his chops.

"Right. Well if you're not giving me your name, I figure you also don't want me asking for your number…"

"No."

The word flies like a missile, said before I've even thought it. I'm working on instinct alone here.

I'm single, yes, and I'd like to find someone I can't live without—sure, sure, that all sounds really nice, but not *him*. Every fiber of my being is telling me this man is not a safe bet for my future.

Some guys would be annoyed by this point. I came on to him, I dragged him into this game, and now *I'm* turning him down. He's not mad though; he merely looks intrigued. I wonder if he's always this easygoing or if he has another side to him. Passion, fire—oh yes, I see them lurking behind his gaze like a heady promise.

"Well your dare is accomplished, I'd say, give or take another few minutes. I guess it's my turn to play."

His eyes gleam with mischief.

He wants me to ask him truth or dare? My depraved mind swirls with possibilities. I could have him down to his boxers in no time. I could have him performing a *Magic Mike* strip-tease while I sit, mouth agape, hand fanning my face.

I grin like a maniacal villain.

"Okay. Truth or dare?"

"Truth."

He doesn't miss my shoulders sagging with disappointment.

"Truth? Okay...fine. Hmm, let me think of something good."

I tap my chin. I'm walking on a minefield here. So many questions I could ask would have answers too specific to his life. I have to keep it general and vague.

"What are you most afraid of?"

His eyebrows shoot up. "Go in for the kill why don't you?"

"It's not too late to swap to dare..."

Take your pants off. No, your shirt. No...pants.

He brings his hand up to rub the side of his jaw, mulling over his answer. Finally, he sighs and shakes his head. "Losing sight of who I am and where I came from."

"*That's* your biggest fear?"

He laughs. "What was I supposed to say?"

"I don't know...falling into a vat of slithering snakes, Voldemort being real, premature balding?"

Now that last one would be a *real* travesty. His hair is so damn nice. There's a slight wave to the black strands. He's probably so vain about it. I would be.

"Snakes don't bother me all that much. Premature balding doesn't run in my family. And Voldemort?" He shrugs. "Well...let's just say my favorite color is green, not gold."

I gasp like he's just admitted to murder.

"Now...truth or dare?" he asks, all business all of a sudden.

"Truth."

"Why won't you give me your number?"

I panic and swap. "*Dare.*"

"Take your dress off."

My jaw drops. "That's not fair."

He shrugs, smooth as ever. "A dare's a dare."

I sigh and reach for the thin strap of my dress. I toy with it on my shoulder as I try to delay the inevitable. He leans forward, utterly enraptured, his breath bated as my strap starts to slip lower. Then I lose the battle with my smile as I put my strap back into place.

"I'm not taking my dress off! Are you insane?!" I lean back against the door. "It's not that I *won't* give you my number. I *can't.*"

"Is this about you being a Russian spy? Because I can help you if you're in trouble."

I love that he's continuing the bit. Why can't more guys be funny? I don't care if a man works out for two hours every day. Your muscles cannot entertain me, sir. I want to laugh. I want to be bowled over by witty banter.

"I'm afraid it's too late for me."

He sighs. "A pity." Then his eyes turn demanding, narrowing slightly. "Now answer the question *truthfully*...or lose the dress."

I nearly gulp at his bossiness. My voice shakes when I speak, knowing I've hit the end of the line in evading his question. "You're not my type."

This surprises him. I have no doubt he's never heard those particular words said in that particular order before. Poor guy. What does your first taste of rejection feel like?

"Then why'd *you* approach *me*? Why'd you kiss me?"

I hold up my hand to explain. "Okay, let me amend that.

You're *too much* my type. Like you tick every box. It's dangerous."

"So you're attracted to me?"

Now, he's grinning.

The truth tumbles out of me like he's worn me down over years, centuries. Why even resist? "As if I conjured you out of a fantasy."

Oh he likes that. His eyes flicker with the power I just gifted him.

"The feeling's mutual."

With that bit of honesty, the tension in the room ratchets up to inhospitable levels. I'm about to have to wipe sweat from my brow.

Then he pushes up and off the workout bench and starts to walk toward me. My breath arrests in my chest as I hold perfectly still, slightly scared, but mostly just hopeful that he'll ignore everything I've said and be done with this fore-play. I want him to shove me up against the door and seal our bodies together. It would be a painful fall afterward, but I'd have the memory of his lips on mine to tide me over for a good long while.

With only a few long strides, he reaches me and it's all so suddenly overwhelming—the intoxicating scent of his after-shave, his sheer size dwarfing me against the door, that burning hot need building inside me—I let my eyes flutter closed as I wait for it to happen.

The final death blow.

I nearly sway forward off balance as my hands fist by my sides.

Long seconds pass...

But it doesn't come.

He doesn't haul me off the ground and pin me to the door. My dress doesn't get shredded to smithereens. My eyes peek open to find he's peering down at me admiringly, *reverently*. There's no hint of playful boy left in him. He's a man possessed as he reaches out to take a piece of my hair between his fingers. He rubs the soft strands for only a moment before he drops it. Then he slowly lifts his hands and weaves his fingers through my long hair. He rubs my scalp, and it feels *heavenly*—like the best part of getting your hair washed at a salon—but instead of continuing on with the massage, he suddenly ruffles my hair, mussing it all up.

I frown. "Wh—what are you doing?"

He tousles my hair once more then drops his hands and assesses his work.

"Do you want this to look real or not? If you walk out of here as put together as you are right now, your friends will know in an instant that this never happened."

"Oh! *Oh.* God. Good point."

Hot *and* smart.

"Now hold still and let me make it look real."

"You're bossy."

His eyes catch mine in battle. It's like he's saying, *And? Your point?*

Sweet Jesus. I look away, not even bothering to deny I like this side of him. Why would I? I'm sure he can read me like an open book.

Once I've officially got "bedhead", he moves on to my dress. One strap is slid off my shoulder while a cascade of goose bumps tingles across my skin. Then he grips the silky material at my waist and takes it in his fist, probably trying to wrinkle it, sure, but he's also exposing so much of my leg it's obvious he's testing the limits of how far he can push this. He stares down at my tan thighs as my dress slides up even more. My panties are *right* there.

Terrified, I cover his hand and squeeze. "Surely that's enough."

He shakes his head, like he's snapping out of a trance. Then he releases my dress, and it's oh-so-perfectly wrinkled.

I smile. "Good work."

He nods.

"Hair, *check*."

As I say this, I take liberties with his hair too, ruffling the thick, soft strands enough that it looks like I've had my wicked way with him too.

"Clothes, *check*."

I reach for his shirt to try to wrinkle it like he did my dress, but it's some luxurious cotton blend that withstands my grasp. *Figures.* My efforts aren't in vain though because I *do* catch a glorious glimpse of his hard abs, and I immediately retract my statements from earlier about funny guys versus buff guys. Jokes, good. Muscles, *gooder*.

He chuckles while my mouth hangs open a little bit.

I'm reduced to three brain cells as I confirm what I already knew: this guy's body is insane. It's less like he lives at the gym and more like he spends his days doing manual labor. Maybe he's not the tech guy. Maybe he's the tech guy's personal *lumberjack*. City folk need firewood too, right?

I glance up at him. "Now what?"

His gaze drops to my lips and my belly swoops.

Oh right.

My makeup is still perfectly intact. I swiped on a dark berry lipstick earlier, and our brief kiss out by the bar didn't smudge it in the least.

Panic spikes my blood. I know what he's planning.

"I could always tell them we didn't kiss…you know…you were against it or something…" My voice lilts up, light and hopeful.

He shakes his head like he doesn't just dislike the idea, he hates it. "I would have kissed you."

The way he says this—with absolute certainty—it's like he's incensed. It's so unbelievably sexy I don't even bother hiding my reaction.

A half laugh, half pant spills out of me. My flush only spreads…

Oh god.

Panic-stricken, I reach up and rub my mouth hard, trying to simultaneously get rid of my lipstick and make my lips bloom with color.

Please, oh please…

His brows furrow, and like a striking boa constrictor, he captures my wrist and then gently peels my hand away from my mouth. My chest rises and falls with unsteady breaths as he takes a step toward me. Slowly, teasingly, our hips meet as he backs me up against the door.

His hold on my wrist isn't tight, but it's assertive enough that I don't attempt to wriggle free. I'm in a steel cage as he tips his head down and studies me. He's weighing his options, toying with his prey. *Will I eat her slowly or tear into her with one big bite?*

His eyes never stray from my lips, swollen now that I've almost rubbed them raw. I feel faint as he repeats my words from earlier: "I'm going to kiss you. I hope that's okay."

It's nothing but a formality. He doesn't wait for my reply. Already he bends, lower, *lower* until our mouths are perfectly aligned. My eyes flutter closed as I inhale his minty breath. I drown in a brief moment of shock that this is really about to happen. Then the thought gets eviscerated with all the others as his lips take possession of mine and he kisses me like he's waited a lifetime to do it.

Falling.

The sensation is so strong I cling to his shirt with my free hand.

Who are you?

Why is it like this?

How can it be like this?

The questions drift to my periphery as he kisses me tenderly, almost tentatively. There's so much sweetness in those first few seconds. It's like he's easing me into the deep end, ensuring I'm there right along with him, but then my hand fists into his shirt and I *pull*. It's a veritable green light, and suddenly, our kiss turns hot and desperate.

There's a clash of teeth, a bite of pain. Then he has me pinned to the door, his hard body flush with mine as our heads slant in sync. He shrouds me in shadows, but I don't fear it; I revel in it. My lips part in invitation and our tongues explore each other. My toes curl as he relinquishes my wrist so he can cup my face with both of his hands. He wants me arching up—at his mercy—and he's not shy about tilting my chin up right where he wants it, proving how bossy I suspected him to be. I feel his kiss in every part of my body. There's a heady thrum deep between my legs.

His hands slip from my face and he pulls back as if to catch his breath, but I chase him, kissing him again, moaning into his mouth. He meets my passion, then surpasses it. It's as if he's almost angry at his reaction to me as he nips and bites his way down my neck. His teeth scrape against my skin and he leaves marks. More evidence for the others, that's all.

His lips sweep over my collarbone and I shake with need, incensed by it as he gathers me closer to him, bending so he can grip my waist so tight my feet start to lift off the floor. I know he's still slightly holding himself back. I see it in his corded muscles, the way he breaks our kiss and inhales an unsteady breath, looking me over like he's fighting to regain his sense.

He doesn't retreat though. His hands gather the soft material of my dress as he roams over my waist and ribs, skimming the underside of my breasts. He stalls there, watching me as his hands shift over my body. Maybe he's seeking permission or maybe he's feeding off my eagerness. I don't miss the wicked appreciation in his eyes as his hand boldly covers my breast, palming it through the thin material of my dress, feeling its weight, teasing me. I ache for more as I gasp and squeeze my eyes closed. He'd only have to peel the thin dress down to my waist and then his hands would be hot on my skin.

This is uncharted territory. My sex life has been...good, fine, even great at times, but not this. *Never this.*

With that harrowing realization, my eyes snap open and I push him, not hard, but enough that he steps back and we break apart. Cool air rushes in to replace his warmth.

We're both panting. I don't even need to look down to see proof of how much he wants me; it's written all over his face. Those tense eyebrows, that tight jaw, those red, *red* lips. I have no doubt my own desire is reflected right back at him.

I feel vulnerable and brittle under his intense scrutiny, a flower made of glass he holds in the palm of his hand. So easy to shatter.

Quickly, I offer a short laugh—it's tight, off—but it succeeds in deflecting the seriousness of the moment.

"That should do it, don't you think?"

He frowns like he's stricken by the comment. Have I gone too far?

What other option is left for me? To proceed? Absolutely not.

Those warning bells from earlier haven't gone silent. On the contrary, they're blaring louder than ever.

Leave.

Go.

Now.

I grip the door handle, turning it even as I look back at him and offer a small, sad smile. Maybe there's an apology there if only he looks hard enough.

Before I can linger over any doubts, I leave, rushing down the hall, back into the party, straight back to the safety of life as I know it.

FOUR

GRANT

MY FIRST NIGHT in New York City was interesting to say the least. A crowded party. Polite conversation. A triple dog dare that led me down a rabbit hole…

The next morning, I'm lying in my bed, staring out at my view of the Manhattan skyline. It's a lot to take in: the towering skyscrapers, the early morning fog, the sprawling concrete jungle stretching out as far as the eye can see. *Toto, we're not in Kansas anymore.* Well technically, I was never in Kansas. I was in Arizona, then Kentucky, then Miami. Now here. And there is no Toto. There's just me in a lonely, sprawling penthouse.

I've lived in this apartment for less than twenty-four hours and the place is a wreck. There are unopened boxes stacked up in the living room and kitchen and *both* guest bedrooms. Some of it is my stuff I had shipped from Miami; the rest was sent over by someone in the Pinstripes' front office. They're aware I've had a tight turnaround, what with signing to the team so close to the start of spring training. They want to be sure I settle in as quickly as possible considering opening day is tomorrow. Can't have me distracted or off my game for any reason.

I peered into a few of the boxes last night when I got home from the party to find they've thought of everything: a set of unopened dinner plates, a knife block, towels, throw pillows, blankets, you name it. It's like they assumed I was eking out an existence in Miami with plastic forks and threadbare hand towels. I'm a bachelor, but I'm not helpless.

Losing my mom when I was young forced me to get my shit together. I've never had someone to do my laundry or pick up after me. My dad worked a lot, and when he wasn't working, he was carting me around to baseball games. I learned at the ripe age of six that if I left a dirty dish in the sink, it was going to damn well sit there until I got off my ass and cleaned it.

Today, my mission is to unpack this place and get every-thing set up. I like to keep a tidy house, and getting every damn moving box out of here is the second most important thing on my to-do list.

First? I'd like to figure out who the hell I kissed last night.

With a heavy groan, I sit up and dig the heels of my hands into my eyes until I feel like I'm ready to join the land of the living. Then I reach for my phone. I scroll down my recent calls list until I see Josh's name.

My old friend answers just before the call's about to switch over to voicemail.

"Are you kidding me?"

His words have no real heat behind them.

"Morning, bud."

"Why? *Why* are you up so early?"

"Some of us have stuff to do today, Schultz."

He curses like he's in physical pain. "Don't you have other friends you can bother?"

Sure, but Josh is one of my oldest friends. We grew up together, competing on the same tournament teams before we continued playing for the same SEC school, but it's been years since we've lived in the same city, and we've never been on the same major league roster. He nearly pissed his pants when I told him I'd signed the contract with the Pinstripes.

"Who is it?" a woman asks on his end of the line, presumably his girlfriend, Sophia. I know he's been dating someone serious for a while. *I love her, man,* he told me when he first mentioned her. I was supposed to meet her when she came to visit him during spring training, but the two of them never left his hotel room. Last night, too, Josh was excited for me to get to know her, but I didn't get the chance. I was wrapped up in various conversations right up until the mystery brunette tapped me on the shoulder and planted her lips on mine.

Needless to say, my night got a bit derailed after that. I didn't stay at the party once she left. I couldn't. It had to be, what, a twenty-minute encounter? Thirty tops? And yet I felt like she was ripping my heart out when she walked out that door.

Absurd.

I'm homesick. Feeling weird. I don't know, maybe there's a full moon or some shit.

"It's Grant," Josh tells Sophia. "Go back to sleep. I'll be back in a second."

I listen to shuffling on his end of the line, and I assume he's taking the phone out of his bedroom so Sophia can go back to sleeping in peace.

A door closes and then he shoots off. "I left a perfectly good bed with a perfectly fine woman, you realize that?"

He won't get any sympathy from me.

"I need your help with something."

"This couldn't have waited until the sun came up?"

I don't even feel bad. So what if it's barely past 6 AM?

"How many people did you know at that party last night?"

"Not many."

"Any girls?"

"Sophia, her friends. That's it. Why?" he asks, curious now.

"Did you see the brunette I was talking to by the bar? The one I disappeared with?"

He curses under his breath. "Listen, I'm happy in my relationship. Almost engaged, in fact, but it must be some life you lead with a face like that. You just walk around getting ass or what? No, I didn't see you disappear with a brunette, but if I know you, she was fucking gorgeous."

"She was."

"She there with you at your place now? Are you calling to rub it in, because there's no need—I prefer the redhead in my bed."

"No, you idiot. I said I need your help, remember? I have no idea who she was and I have to figure it out."

"You didn't get her name?"

"It's complicated."

He laughs like this is comedy gold.

"What'd she look like?"

"Well she was brunette, like I said, but her hair wasn't that dark. Medium brown, chestnut. A little past her shoulders. Her eyes were lighter than her hair, hazel I think, with these long lashes. She was petite. Did I already say she had freckles? Just a few dotting her nose and cheeks, but they were cute as hell."

"Did this girl have dimples?" he asks, sounding wary.

"A matching set. They were really pronounced when she smiled."

He sucks in a sharp breath.

"What was she wearing, Navarro?"

He sounds deadly serious, and now I'm frowning.

"A black dress."

"Oh god. Oh, *fuck me*," he mutters, then when he speaks again, his voice is loud and clear. "Listen to me. Hey, are you listening? Put that girl out of your mind. Erase her from your memory."

"Why? What's going on? You know who I'm talking about?"

My pea brain chooses to ignore the dread circling our conversation and focus instead on the positive. Josh *definitely* knows her. My mystery brunette is a mystery no more.

"Who is she?"

"You think I'm kidding, but I'm not. Forget whatever happened last night and move on. End of story."

"Who is she?" I bite out with a slow, threatening tone. I'm seconds from racing over to his place and shaking the answer out of him. I'm not above it.

"*Tate Allen.*" He laughs pitifully. "Name ring a bell? Yeah, you're fucked. That's Luke Allen's little sister. You better pray you didn't lay a hand on her or there's going to be hell to pay."

My phone slips away from my ear as my hand drops. Meanwhile, Josh keeps talking. Whatever he has to say, I don't care.

Tate Allen.

Luke Allen's little sister.

Luke is the most veteran player on the Pinstripes roster. He's also a walking legend. Not that it matters—he could be the greenest rookie we have and I would still respect him enough to keep my hands off his sister. You don't mess around with family. The girl from last night is officially off limits.

"*Fuuuuuck!*"

My curse rumbles out of my chest so loudly I'm surprised I don't wake the whole building.

FIVE

TATE

THE MORNING AFTER THE PARTY, I'm lying in my bed, too chicken to get up and face my roommates. Too chicken to face myself, even. I have to pee, but there's a mirror in the bathroom I'd like to avoid. I don't need my reflection taunting me about last night's mistakes.

How's that plan working out for you now, huh, Tate?

I feel like I've done something wrong, like I behaved very, *very* badly. Only I'm not totally sorry for it. I almost...*almost* wish I'd stuck around to find out what would have happened if I hadn't pushed away my mystery man last night. We could have made full use of that gym. Exercise ball? *Bounce bounce, baby.* Yoga mat? *Unroll that sucker.* Full-length mirrors stretching the length of an entire wall? *I wouldn't have survived.*

My bedroom door whips open. No knock. No gentle introduction.

Daphne leaps onto my bed, nearly inverting my knee on her way to cuddling beside me. She steals half my blanket and half my pillow.

"Is Sophia still with Josh?" I ask.

"Here!" Sophia says, hurrying in to join us, tucking herself in on my other side. At least she had the decency to bring a spare pillow.

"I thought you went home with Josh last night?" I ask her.

"I did, but then he got a call at the crack of dawn and had to rush out to help his friend with something. So here I am…"

She lets her sentence dwindle, and then they both stare at me expectantly.

I play dumb. "What?"

"We want details," Sophia says. "And be quick about it. I have work in a bit."

"Yeah. Give 'em up, Tate," Daphne adds, no nonsense.

"I would love to, but unfortunately, I'm still trying to sleep here." I squeeze my eyes closed for emphasis.

Doesn't matter. Daphne pries them open. "Are you being serious? You're going to hold out on us?"

I bat her hands away. "Ease up, you were like a millimeter away from my cornea."

"We want to know everything, from the length of his—"

"*DAPH.*"

"To the way he—"

I retrieve the decorative pillow from the foot of my bed and try to smother her with it.

"So no details?" she asks mildly once she's regained control of the situation and smacked the pillow down to the floor.

I huff out a heavy breath. "There's nothing to tell. You guys already know what happened."

I've been intentionally vague on purpose. For starters, I didn't actually hook up with the guy, and if they find out, they'll realize I never completed the dare. Also, more importantly, it feels dangerous to give life to these complicated feelings. My plan was to leave last night in the past, and I can't do that if we sit around all morning waxing poetic about this guy's abdominal muscles.

Fortunately, I'm saved by a knock on our front door.

"Who's that? Josh?" Daphne asks.

"No idea."

It's embarrassing, silly, totally not possible, but a part of me hopes it's the guy from the party. Or if not him, maybe a bouquet of flowers delivered on his behalf. Which is…insane considering he doesn't know my name, much less my address.

Still, because I'm shameless, I straighten my pajamas and finger-comb my hair *just a little* on my way to answer the door.

There's a heavy *knock knock knock*. Then my little niece's voice sounds on the other side.

"Do you want to build a snowman!?" she sings just before I fling the door open with a laugh.

I'm not the least bit sad to see my family standing there instead of my mystery man. Not at all. Nope.

My niece is the cutest little kid in the entire world. We share our hair color and eye color, and she has the same spray of freckles across the bridge of her nose and the apples of her cheeks. Today, she's even cuter than usual because in her hands she has a box of pastries, and these aren't your bodega's moldy leftovers from yesterday. My brother's fiancée, Chloe, is a pastry chef. An amazing one, at that.

She's smiling behind Harper, tucked against my brother's side. They make quite a pair.

Luke took after our dad. He's tall and burly and lovable. Handsome, yes. My big brother is so handsome I could just pinch his little cheeks. Chloe's gorgeous too, Italian, sun kissed, and vivacious. She found my brother during a time in his life when he was absolutely *not* looking for love. Chloe swooped in and made him fall head over heels, first with her cooking—she was his private chef!—and then with her. Now we all love her.

Me most of all because she brought me homemade pastries!

"Surprise! We brought you breakfast!" Harper says, bouncing with excitement.

"Gimme those," I say, yanking the box out of her hands.

She erupts with laughter. "They're for everyone!"

"Yeah well, I'd like to see an eight-year-old wrestle a chocolate croissant out of my hand. Don't you have school today?"

It's Wednesday morning and she's in her private school uniform.

"Doesn't start for another hour, silly. Dad said we could stop on our way there since it's close."

"Ah, you couldn't resist paying a visit to your favorite aunt. I see."

"*Only* aunt."

"Eh, we both know it still counts." I carry the box into the kitchen and call out to Sophia and Daphne. "Chloe brought—"

There's no need to finish the second half of the sentence. My roommates come peeling into the kitchen like two bats out of hell, and we descend on the pastry box like vultures. Sophia thinks she's going to take the most delicious-looking cinnamon roll in the box, but she has another think coming.

"I swear I brought enough for everyone." Chloe laughs, likely worried we're about to come to blows over her baked goods. We won't if only Sophia would do what's good for her and slowly step away from the cinnamon roll.

Daphne, with her mouth completely full of pastry, looks over at my future sister-in-law with hearts in her eyes. "Chloe, I love you. Marry me instead of Luke."

Luke laughs and plants a big kiss on Chloe's head, then he tugs her close, wrapping his arm around her waist like he's actually scared Daphne might steal her from him. I can't help but grin. He's a total goner. Chloe has him wrapped around her little finger. I visited them at their Hamptons house over the holidays, and she had him out in the garden with her. He wasn't even tending it! He was just standing beside her, holding a dainty little basket as she picked vegetables and handed them up to him. I should have snapped a picture. His teammates would have a field day.

Once Sophia and I agree that the cinnamon roll shall be cut in half, I start making coffee for everyone. Luke, Chloe, and Sophia all take a seat at the table. Meanwhile, Harper sidles up to Daphne by the pastry box, curious about her. I get it. Of the two sisters, Daphne just has this air about her. Also, it probably hasn't escaped Harper's notice that Daphne looks like a Disney princess with her long red hair and big blue eyes.

"I like your hair," Harper tells her.

Daphne nods, not even noticing that Harper's staring up at her in awe. "Thanks, kid."

"I'm not a kid."

"Okay." Daphne's tone couldn't have less inflection. It's like she's talking to a fellow twenty-five-year-old.

Harper scoots closer. "I get to be the flower girl in my dad's wedding to Chloe, but it's not for a while. Not until next year, they said, because of baseball season."

"That's nice."

Harper tilts her head, studying Daphne, likely perplexed by my friend.

"Do you have a boyfriend?" my niece asks her.

I barely fight back a snort. Sophia openly laughs.

Daphne finally looks at her. "Nah. Do you?"

Harper laughs. "I can't have a boyfriend! I'm eight!"

Daphne shrugs. "I had a boyfriend when I—"

Luke takes this opportunity to clear his throat very loudly and very pointedly from the kitchen table.

Daphne winks down at Harper, who smiles up at her with delight. As the delicious scent of coffee starts to fill the kitchen, I watch Harper study Daphne, standing like she stands, affecting the same slight lean against the counter, trying to be just like her.

Daphne doesn't even notice, which probably makes Harper want to impress her all the more.

I carry filled coffee mugs and creamer over to the table. Since I didn't get the chance to greet her properly on her way in, I wrap my arm around Chloe's shoulders and squeeze her into a hug.

"Hi."

My brother gets no hug. Instead, we exchange a cool bro nod, the equivalent of saying, *Sup?*

"Thanks for the sustenance," I tell them as I take the last open seat at the table. "We needed it."

"Late night?" Chloe asks, reaching for one of the coffee mugs. "I'm surprised you haven't gone for a run yet this morning."

She's well acquainted with my type-A personality. *Everyone* is. If there were a documentary about my life, the people interviewed would share things like:

"Tate? Yeah, she's kind of intense. Like she's nice, but I mean... she can be a lot."

"What's the opposite of flexible? Rigid? Yeah, Tate's rigid."

"She likes to go, go, go. I'm not even sure that girl knows how to relax."

Then they'd cut to me, smiling, perfectly fine with these assessments. Other people can be chill; I don't claim that crown. My brain simply will not tolerate being idle.

"No run yet..." I tell her.

"And yes, we had a late night," Daphne supplies on my behalf.

I'm annoyed that a comment as innocuous as *that* still makes me blush a little. I definitely made the right choice with that guy.

"Were you with Josh and the guys?" Luke asks.

Luke is slightly older than most of the other players on the

Pinstripes roster. Josh, Dustin, Nick—they all look up to Luke like he's their big brother too. Luke's well aware of how much time I spend with them, strictly as friends, and he doesn't seem to mind all that much, but in moments like this, I'm aware that he would rather I steer clear of his teammates altogether. I've assured him multiple times that I have no intentions of dating anyone on the team, *ever*, which seems to take the edge off his incessant worrying. I don't think it'll ever go away altogether though. Our parents are a gazillion miles away, down in Texas. I know Luke feels like he has to step in for them a bit and watch out for me in the big bad city.

If only he knew what I did last night, the danger I could have put myself in following a stranger down a hallway into a deserted room…

I nearly shiver at the thought. He'd be livid. *Beyond.*

"Yup. The usual suspects."

"Josh still treating you well?" Luke asks Sophia.

Sophia laughs. "No need to worry."

Luke nods, appreciating this. I know he'd take it upon himself to correct that situation if she said otherwise. He's a fierce protector, this one. I pity the poor soul Harper tries to bring home on a date in high school. Hopefully I'm there to catch the drama.

"I can't believe opening day is tomorrow," Chloe says with a little shimmy. Clearly, she's as excited as we all are. I love opening day at Pinstripe Stadium. The energy is electric.

"I brought some tickets in the family section," Luke tells us. "There's plenty for all of you, though I'm sure Josh has already given you some, Sophia."

"Yeah, I'm in that section too so that works out well."

I force down another sip of coffee and keep my gaze on the table as I speak up, trying not to wince as I admit, "I actually won't be able to attend."

"What?"

Everyone in the room has the same shocked expression. I

don't miss opening day. I just don't. It was one thing to skip traveling down to Florida for spring training, but this is different. Can I even call myself a diehard fan anymore?!

"Why the hell not?" Luke demands.

Harper's wholly unfazed by his mild curse. Growing up with a single dad until she was six means she has quite the colorful vocabulary herself.

"Yeah? Why the hell not?!" she echoes.

"Harper!" Luke and Chloe chide in unison.

Harper looks up to Daphne for approval, and Daphne shoots her a conspiratorial wink. Oh god, just what I need: Harper using Daphne as her role model.

"I have to work." I hold up my hand as protests start to fly. "And before anyone says anything, I've already tried to get out of it, but we're seriously short-staffed right now while Kara is away on maternity leave."

"Who cares?! Quit!" Daphne says like this is a perfectly reasonable thing to do.

I don't even deign to respond to her suggestion.

"This is opening day! *Opening day!"* Sophia adds with despair.

I cradle my head in my hands. *"I know.* Guys, don't make me feel worse than I already do. You think I want to be working at the hospital while y'all are basking in the sun, cracking peanuts, and cheering the guys on? I want to be there! I *will* be, just not at this one game."

"You're going to miss the new guy!" Harper adds, as if it's not bad enough already.

I frown and turn back to look at her. "What?"

"The new guy. Navarro." She tilts her head to the sky with a faraway look, like she's in the midst of a daydream. "He's soooo cute! Like a real prince! Ask Chloe!"

All heads spin to Chloe.

She blushes deeply, clearing her throat and fumbling over her words. "I-I merely said that he's *attractive*, Harper."

"Oh really?" Luke taunts, enjoying this way too much.

"I mean, *come on*." She jostles Luke. "Just because I'm wholeheartedly, blissfully in love with you doesn't mean I don't have eyes, okay!"

Daphne finishes off her pastry and swipes the crumbs off her hands. "All right, all right. What does this guy look like? I need to know what we're dealing with if I'm supposed to sweep him off his feet and convince him to fall madly in love with me."

"Yeah, is he really that cute?" Sophia asks. "I didn't get a good look at him when I was down in Florida. Someone pull up a picture before I have to rush off and get ready for work."

Chloe takes her phone out of her purse, and I assume she's Googling him. My suspicions are confirmed when Harper runs around the table so she can peer over her shoulder.

"That picture," Harper says, pointing down at Chloe's phone. "Show them that one. Oh he's *so* dreamy."

Luke groans in agony over this conversation.

Then Chloe turns her phone to show us the photo that's blown up on her screen. It's a close-up image of a guy in a baseball uniform and hat, looking to the left so that he's slightly in profile. Behind him, the field is out of focus. He's smiling at something out of frame, and there's a deep-set dimple curved along his supple lips. The severity to his chin and sharp jawline is softened by the humor evident in his brown eyes. Not much of his hair peeks out from beneath his hat, but I know what color it is.

Midnight black.

Inky dark and luxuriously thick.

I just about lose the contents of my stomach as I stare at it. Surely, this is a mistake. She's Googled the wrong person.

"Who is that?" I slowly and meticulously stress every word so I can be sure she hears me correctly.

She frowns. "Grant Navarro. Haven't you been listening?

He just got traded to the Pinstripes. He's amazing. He's going to be the reason we win the World Series this year, you wait and see."

"*Hello*, some of us are also very good at baseball," Luke says, waving his hand.

Chloe pats his shoulder. "Sure, sweetie. You're very good too."

They haven't noticed yet.

The silence.

Daphne, Sophia, me…we're all too dumbstruck to speak. I can't look at my roommates; I'm scared their expressions will be too telling. Mine surely is. I'm slack-jawed and wide-eyed as I internally freak out.

Mystery man is Grant Navarro. Grant Navarro is Mr. Tall Dark and Handsome. I kissed Grant Navarro last night! He's a professional baseball player! On the same team as my brother, no less!

Oh, this is bad.

This is very bad.

"That—"

Daphne gets only that one word out before I cut her off. "No! *Ha ha!* Don't know him!"

Chloe's eyebrows scrunch together in scrutiny as she takes in my weird response. "I know you don't know him. You just said that. I was showing you his picture so you could see what a hunk he is."

Luke shakes his head. "It doesn't matter. Tate doesn't date baseball guys. Also…I'd break his arm off if he tried anything with her." There's no venom in his voice. It's like he's just stating facts. Breaking people's arms off is perfectly fine table talk to him. He even sips his coffee after like it's no big thing.

"Would you really?!" Harper's eyes light up with the promise of gore and mayhem. "Cool!"

Chloe levels Luke with a reproachful glare. "*No.* Your

father would never, *could* never break anyone's arm off. Luke, you need to chill."

"I am chill. But you also need to realize these guys aren't cute and cuddly. They've spent their entire lives in locker rooms. They have a girl in every city, waiting and willing to warm their beds."

"Warm their beds? How? With fire?" Harper asks. Her little face is scrunched up in confusion.

By this point, Sophia's laughing. Meanwhile, Daphne keeps repeating, "Oh my god. Oh my god. Oh my god," under her breath like she's well and truly lost it, and I'm staying perfectly quiet, sipping my coffee, focusing on one movement at a time.

First, loop your hand around the mug. Good, just like that. Then gently lift the mug and bring it to your face. *Too fast, Allen!*

Some of the coffee dribbles down my chin onto my pajama shirt.

Luke's oblivious, but Chloe's not. She's scrutinizing me from across the table like she's trying to read between the lines. She's too smart.

Good going, Luke! You couldn't have fallen in love with a dumb-dumb?

I stand and my chair screeches as I push it back. "You have to go!"

Luke frowns. "What?"

I try to sound slightly less enthusiastic about kicking them to the curb as I continue, "I mean…surely Harper needs to be getting to school, and Sophia, don't you need to head to work? Daphne too."

Luke and Harper eye me strangely.

Chloe though…she just smiles a knowing little smile.

Damn her.

I avert my gaze. "Yeah, so anyway, y'all should probably go."

Since no one seems to want to listen to me, I take it upon myself to help them on their way out, scooting chairs back and yanking mugs out of hands. Piping hot coffee gets poured right down the drain.

"I was still drinking that," my brother protests.

I tip him out of his seat and prod him and his family over to the door. "Listen, there's a great little coffee shop down the street. The barista loves me. Tell her Tate sent you. Okay, *bye*!"

And then I slam the door in their shocked faces.

Once I've given them enough time to have made it far, far away from my apartment, I turn around to reluctantly face my roommates. They're silently standing there, looking at me for direction. I'm shocked Daphne can contain herself, but maybe even she realizes how serious this is.

"Here's how this is going to go," I start, speaking like a drill sergeant. I need a baton I can whack against my open palm. "Nothing happened last night. *Nothing.* Do you two understand?"

They nod quickly, in sync.

"I went to that party, sure, but I never talked to Grant, and we definitely *didn't* disappear into that room together. Okay?"

"Okay."

Still, no one moves. Sophia looks to Daphne. Daphne looks to Sophia. They both look at me. Then finally, a slow smile spreads across Daphne's lips and she whispers, "*Oh my god. You hooked up with Grant Navarro!*"

A wash of anxiety threatens to take me out at the knees.

What I did last night was the craziest thing I've done in... well, ever. I simply do not act impulsively. Allow me to explain. If I'm going to change what brand of granola I top my yogurt with, it's a week of research, minimum. If I'm going to buy new running shoes, I'm testing those babies out on grass, gravel, concrete, dirt, mud, sand, turf...you get it. You ever wonder who reads through the thousands upon thousands of product reviews on Amazon? I'm the problem, it's me. And guess what? I like how I do things. I mean look what happened when I threw caution to the wind—I accidentally kissed my brother's teammate! That was not in my love plan.

I pinch my eyes closed, knowing one thing with absolute certainty.

I am *so* screwed.

SIX

TATE

I'M ACTUALLY RELIEVED to be at the hospital instead of sitting in the stands at Pinstripe Stadium for opening day. I need a break from my social life. After my brother and his family left, I spent hours breaking down the situation with Grant from every angle, only to realize there's no real solution. There's no good that can come out of this. Luke would never come around to the two of us dating and more importantly, *I don't date baseball guys!* Even if he's the hottest baseball player ever, it doesn't matter. I've convinced myself I have self-control. I'm not going to lose my head and jump his bones. I won't *accidentally* stumble right into his waiting arms. I'm going to snuff out my little crush—bury it under dirt and concrete and more dirt and more concrete until it has no light, no water, nothing to help it grow. I'm confident it's possible, especially if I keep myself distracted at work.

I love my job as a nurse in the pediatric cardiac ICU at Manhattan Children's Hospital. I've been here since I graduated from college and followed Luke up to New York City.

My job is fast-paced and never boring, and I get to help the cutest kids. On top of that, I get along with my coworkers. Sure, there are a few attendings I avoid like the plague and one specific cardiologist who doesn't understand the concept of personal space after he enjoys his garlic-heavy lunches, but even he's not that much trouble. I just breathe through my mouth when he's around.

That said, my job isn't a total cake walk. My patients are often babies, some only a few weeks old. They're as fragile as they come. Days like today make it all worth it though. I have good news to report to a family. Well, good *and* bad.

One of the tiniest patients on our floor, Cece, gets to go home today. She's recovered well from her Norwood operation and is ready to be discharged. However, she'll need around-the-clock care at home. As if her poor mom wasn't overwhelmed enough with her very fresh newborn, now she also has to manage Cece's medications, ensure her sutures stay clean and well-bandaged, and replace her feeding bags in the middle of the night. There are a million things that could go wrong.

Cece's mom is young, only twenty, and Cece's dad works nights in a factory an hour away from the city. I want to give her a hug and tell her the truth: the next few weeks are going to feel impossible, but you can do this. I know you can.

Instead, I wrap up my discharge instructions and stay on topic.

"Remember, we need you to log vital signs daily, including oxygen levels."

Cece's mom looks like she's about to cry.

"I don't think I can do all this. What if I forget?"

I take her hand and squeeze.

"You can do it. I promise you can, and you have my phone number in case you need to call me. Let's start at the top, and I'm going to walk you through the steps again. If there's a part that seems confusing or overwhelming, stop me and we'll clear it up. Okay?"

She nods timidly, and I flip back to the front page of the packet I have in my hands so we can start from square one.

I don't take on her stress. I used to, when I first started here. I'd absorb every mother's worry, every father's fear and make them my own. When they'd cry, I'd cry. We'd be a blubbering mess together. Then I had an attending, Dr. Liota, pull me aside one day. Dr. Liota is an older female cardiologist who is quite frankly superwoman as far as I'm concerned. My dealings with her over my first few months on the job proved to me that she is always level-headed and kind, even to the frazzled medical students who rotate through our ICU, even to me, a green nurse with perpetual tears in her eyes during every shift.

Her advice to me that day was simple: "These patients are not your children. These people are not your family. While you're in the confines of this hospital, do your job to the very best of your ability, facilitate care, give a hundred and ten percent. But the moment your shift ends, leave. Live your life outside of this place. These babies don't need you crying over them. They need you well-rested and logical, confident in your abilities as a nurse. There are social workers and care teams surrounding patients who help fill in the gaps. You are not the last line of defense for them. Do you understand?"

I nodded in thanks and then hugged her.

Which, in hindsight, is pretty funny because Dr. Liota is *not* a hugger or even a toucher for that matter. Once, I saw a medical student try to go in for a fist bump, and Dr. Liota just stared at him and said, "No."

By the time Cece is discharged, I'm starving. I had planned to eat dinner an hour ago, but it's no problem. I can log my notes while I scarf down my food at the nurses' station.

"Game's on," Bianca tells me as I sit down with my dinner.

Bianca is our oldest nurse on staff, and I love working shifts with her. She's shrewd, cutting, loving. She'll look you square in the eye and tell you to "mind your business" or

"That was a really dumb question" or "You have toilet paper hangin' off your shoe, dumbass."

Her phone's propped up between our two computers. She's found a telecast of the Pinstripes game. It's the bottom of the third, and our boys are at bat.

"Two outs. McDowell's on third," she says, not bothering to look away from her computer or stop typing. A lot of the nurses on this floor are dedicated to the Pinstripes, especially because they've met Luke a time or two when he comes up here for a surprise visit with the kids. The younger ones don't know who he is, but I once saw a ten-year-old patient bawl his eyes out when Luke casually strolled into his room holding a brand-new signed Pinstripes jersey. Needless to say, he's a fan favorite around here.

"Who's next in the lineup?"

Normally, I'd know this sort of thing already, but I've purposely kept my head in the clouds with this game. Better that way.

"Navarro."

His name makes me feel butterflies.

I don't say a word about that. Instead, I focus down on my dinner.

Daphne, the kind soul that she is, makes me food before every one of my shifts. *It's the least I can do for the children!* she likes to tell me.

Tonight, she's layered blackened chicken over a bed of whole grain rice with a side of sautéed zucchini and yellow squash drizzled in some kind of amazing garlic sauce. For dessert, she's tucked in one of Chloe's leftover pastries from yesterday.

Bianca has the volume turned down low on her phone so people passing by won't take note of it, but it's still loud enough that I can listen to the game while I eat.

"Good patience from Navarro there on the first pitch," the announcer says.

I'm dying to look at her phone. I know they'll have to zoom in on Grant if he's at bat. I haven't seen him since I left him in that room after our kiss.

I wonder if he's thought about me...

"We saw this during spring training," the announcer continues. "The Pinstripes are extremely good at getting runners in scoring positions. Especially useful now when you consider they have a powerhouse like Navarro."

His voice dies down, and without glancing at the screen, I know the pitcher's about to fire off his second throw. I hold my breath right along with the crowd, then there's the telltale crack of Grant's bat hitting the ball. The announcer's voice builds with excitement.

"Grant Navarro hits it deep in the air toward left center-field...Gardener watches this one sail out of the ballpark...*wow*. That drives in the first three Pinstripes runs for the day. Three to nothing. New York on top."

"Damn." Bianca's attention is now squarely on her phone as she watches Grant run the bases. I can't help myself; I indulge too. What does it matter? No one will ever know.

Grant's finger is raised toward the sky as he rounds second on his way to claim his run. He smiles out at the fans as he shakes his head. Then he looks down for a moment, clearly overwhelmed after having hit his first homer with the Pinstripes during a regular season game. He must be elated.

The camera zooms in on him as he reaches home plate, and he slides off his helmet on his way back to the dugout. His black hair is messy, sweaty, hot. His brown eyes shine with happiness. Just before he heads down the steps to join his team, he stops and looks up into the stands. The crowd's going wild for him, shouting and waving signs, giving him all the love he deserves for bringing in those three runs for us. The camera doesn't pan away. Those cameramen know what they're doing, let me tell you. He's absolutely *devastatingly* handsome. God, it's agony to look at him. The ladies at the stadium must be fanning themselves.

Bianca shakes her head. "That boy is easy on the eyes. And don't bother reminding me that he's young enough to be my son. Let a lady live a little."

I chuckle. "You didn't hear me say anything."

Her gaze slides to me. "Have you met him yet? With your brother?"

"No," I lie. Because what else can I do?

"Well if you ever get the chance, please lord, take me with you."

Luke takes the pitcher's mound at the top of the fourth, and while it might seem like a blessing to get to eat and take notes while I watch him play, it's not really a pleasant experience. I hold my breath the entire time. My hands grip my chair. My stomach churns with nerves and I end up pushing aside the last half of my dinner.

The opposing team doesn't score on him, though, and we go into the bottom of the fourth with our three-run lead.

Bianca looks down the hall and hums *mm mm mmm* like something's absolutely delicious. "Speaking of sexy men..."

I look up to see Michael making his way toward the nurses' station in his navy scrubs. Michael is one of the physical therapists who works on our team. He's a year younger than me with a broad-shouldered frame, sandy brown hair, and these electric blue eyes. He's the hospital's resident hottie. He knows it, of course, mostly because women like Bianca—people with no skin in the game—have no problem skirting hospital HR rules so they can compliment him on his "fine-ass" physique. He takes it in stride, and I don't think it truly bothers him that everyone fawns over him.

He strolls right up to the desk—just on the other side of my computer monitor—and drums his fingers on the counter.

"You're *still* here?" he says in surprise, laying those blue eyes on me.

Usually, I work three 12s a week. With Kara gone on maternity leave, we've all had to shift our schedules a bit. I prefer to not tally up my current weekly workload; it'll only be depressing.

"I'm on from 3 to 11 today. The night is young, I'm afraid." He gives me a sympathetic smile as I continue, "What about you? Usually you're gone by now."

"Lot of patients today."

Bianca leans toward me and cuts in, addressing Michael, "Ms. Matthews was looking for you earlier."

"Yeah, I just came from PT with Jamie."

Bianca nods then stands to head off. "Want me to leave that?" she asks, motioning to her phone.

I take it and pass it to her. "No need. I can keep track of the highlights online. Thanks though."

"All right. Let me know if our boy hits any more home runs."

Michael looks to me with a faint smile. "Our boy?"

I know she's referring to Grant Navarro, but I shrug. "No idea."

I like Michael a lot. Not only is he handsome and nice, he's also a hockey fan. He grew up playing in Canada. Baseball holds no appeal to him, which is slightly intriguing to me considering it's such a big part of my life.

Michael glances down at my half-finished dinner, and I get the sense he feels like he's bothering me. He's not, so I speak up, leaning forward on my elbows as I look up at him.

"So? How were the babies today?" I ask, trying to encourage more conversation. "Did they give you any trouble?"

Michael and I get along really well, but it's always been strictly business with us. He had a pretty serious girlfriend up until a few months ago. I don't know the terms of their breakup or anything—I've never asked—but I do know he's single now. At least that's the word on the street.

"Babies were great. We've almost got Jamie rolling over by himself."

I smile, proud to hear it. Michael's job can vary drastically depending on a patient's age. With the little ones, he works on tummy time, head control, grip strength. With older patients, his focus shifts to big picture: standing, walking, in-bed exercises for strength and conditioning. I've seen him in action, and he's so good with the kids. He makes his physical therapy sessions fun, like a game with goals and prizes. Our patients love him.

It's sweet. *He's* sweet.

"Did you hear Cece got discharged?"

His eyebrows shoot up with delight. "Really? That's great."

Cece will be back, of course. Most of the children that pass through our ICU were born with congenital heart conditions that mean they're in for the long haul: multiple procedures, hospital stays, cardiology appointments. But we were able to send Cece home for now, and a win is a win.

He leans forward, dropping his elbows on the counter. "We should celebrate."

"Totally agree." I lower my voice. "Think you can sneak a bottle of champagne in here? I won't tell if you don't."

I add a conspiratorial wink so he knows I'm kidding.

He pats the pocket on his scrub top. "No can do. There's nowhere to hide it."

I laugh. "Ah, well, there goes that plan. Tell you what...I'll let you pick out a cookie down in the cafeteria *on me*. You know if you go first thing in the morning, they're still warm. Straight from the oven, in fact." I nearly drool thinking about it.

He scrunches his nose. "Not a big cookie guy."

My jaw drops. "That's...not possible."

He shakes his head. "I think we should stick to drinks, maybe dinner too? On me, that is."

"Oh." My dumb ass did not see this coming.

He's amused by my reaction. "Was that rusty? Sorry. I'm not great at this." He stands back up to his full height and rubs the back of his neck, glancing briefly down the hall before peering at me again. There's a little blush building on his cheeks. "I haven't asked a girl out in like four years."

My eyes widen.

"I was dating Liz and we broke up a few months ago."

So the rumors are true then.

"You haven't been on a date with anyone else since her?"

"No." He smiles sheepishly. "I've actually had a little crush on you for a while. I've been working up the courage to ask you out—almost did it last week. Remember when I ran into you in the break room and I talked your ear off about coffee for like ten minutes? I think I went on and on about how they produce and ship it? Yeah…that was me trying to work up the nerve to ask you out. I don't really care about coffee all that much. Half of that was total bullshit."

He grimaces like this is a little painful for him to admit, but I'm charmed by his honesty. It hasn't escaped my notice that Michael fits the bill for what I'm looking for (i.e. he checks off most everything on my exhaustive list of boyfriend requirements), *and* he works in healthcare! He understands the ins and outs of my job! That wasn't even on my list. He gets bonus points!

"You shouldn't have told me that. I was really impressed. I thought you were like a secret coffee genius."

"Really?" He grins. "Okay, forget everything I just said."

The phone at the nurses' station rings and I have to take it.

Michael rocks back on his heels, taking his exit. "Just think about it, yeah?"

I'm already reaching for the phone when I reply, "Yes! I will. Promise."

SEVEN

GRANT

WE'VE PLAYED six days in a row. Our three-game series against the Giants rolled into another three-game series against the Phillies, and we've come away from both undefeated. There's a lot of buzz surrounding how we've started our season. Everyone has something to say, fans, critics—opinions are a dime a dozen, but I know this team has what it takes to go all the way if we keep grinding.

Today's an off day, but we met in the morning to review game footage and get in some batting practice. Tomorrow we head to Baltimore to take on the Orioles. It'll be my first time traveling with the team, but it's the same across most big franchises. Baseball teams travel by charter plane. We're expected to be at the airport by 7 AM. We'll touch down in Baltimore about an hour later, get settled in the hotel, then take a bus over to the stadium to prepare for our game.

Tonight though, I'm with the guys, and we're heading to Sophia's apartment. Josh told me it's the group's unofficial clubhouse, their home away from home. If they aren't on the road or at the stadium, everyone hangs out at Sophia's. I think he tried to temper my expectations by letting me know it's not as big or as nice compared to where some of the guys live, but even still, it's the best place to hang out. It's central to everyone and, according to Josh, "It just feels like home. I don't know, you'll see."

I understand what he means as soon as Sophia opens the door for us. Over her shoulder, I see all the feminine touches my own apartment lacks: good lighting, curtains, throw blankets, a candle burning on the kitchen counter, not to mention the smell of dinner baking in the oven.

"I hope you guys like lasagna," Sophia says as she waves us through the door. "I got this recipe from Chloe."

The guys respond enthusiastically to this, but I'm left in the dark.

Sophia takes pity on me. "Chloe is Luke's fiancée. She's Italian and the best chef I've ever met. Also, *hi!*" She goes in for a hug then steps back with a big, welcoming smile. "I can't believe I'm finally meeting you! I've heard so many stories over the years!"

Oh god. Stories? From Josh? There's no telling what she's heard. "All good, I hope?"

She tips her hand back and forth like a seesaw. "Oh... about half and half," she teases. "Anyway, come in, come in! This is my sister, Daphne."

Another redhead, slightly younger than Sophia, pops her head around the corner. Thanks to Josh, I'm not surprised that I recognize them as Tate's friends from the party. The ones who issued her that dare...

Daphne plays it like she has no idea who I am. "Grant, you said? Pleasure to meet you!"

Then she turns to the other guys, giving each of them a winning smile and a hug right up until she gets to Dustin. Once in front of him, her smile goes slack and her arms cross in front of her chest.

He was the first one in the apartment. He was rushing us

along in the elevator, seemingly eager to get up here. Now, he stares at Daphne with a shrewd expression.

"*You*," Daphne says. "What do you want?"

"Dinner," he says with a sharp, dismissive tone. He sounds like a total asshole, not like the Dustin I know.

She rolls her eyes. "Fine… I guess you can have the paltry leftovers."

She turns on her heels and I stare at Dustin with wide eyes, expecting him to be seething after that interaction, but he's smiling. Happy, it seems.

"What the hell was that?" I ask Nick, leaning in so I'm not overheard.

He waves it off. "Oh, yeah, Daphne and Dustin hate each other. They fight like cats and dogs most of the time."

Right. Good to know.

The guys take off their shoes in the foyer—well aware of the rules of the apartment, it seems—so I do the same. Sophia and Daphne have done the most they can with the small living room, cramming in a couch and two chairs. None of the furniture matches, but that somehow makes it all more endearing. The furniture looks to be thrifted and well loved, right along with the large patterned rug. There are tons of books and board games stacked precariously on a thin table beneath the mounted TV, a basket full of soft blankets, and an old black trunk they've converted into a coffee table. There's an empty mason jar sitting on top of it that Josh grabs. I watch as he takes cash out of his wallet to shove inside before wordlessly handing it to Nick, who does the same. He notices my confusion.

"The girls cook for us a lot, and we usually raid their pantry. At this point they're nice enough—"

"That's right, and don't you forget it!" Daphne cuts in.

Nick laughs. "…to keep our favorite snacks and beer on hand. In return, we're on clean-up duty, and we make sure they don't have to foot the bill."

Sounds like a pretty nice setup to me. I make sure to be generous with my contribution, especially since I'm the new guy.

"Speaking of," Sophia says, "what do you like to snack on, Grant?"

"Oh, whatever you have here is fine, I'm sure."

The guys shake their heads, aware of how this is going to go down. "You might as well just tell her," Nick says. "She'll get it out of you eventually."

Sophia nods. "It's true. Favorite chips?"

"Barbecue," I say, playing along.

"Nice, same here," Nick says, giving me a high five.

"Candy?"

"Reese's."

"I swear that's every guy's favorite candy." Daphne laughs.

"I prefer sour Skittles," Dustin says.

"Nobody asked. Anyway, Grant, there's a huge bag of Reese's in the pantry, help yourself. Just don't ruin your appetite before dinner."

The mason jar makes its way around the room and then Daphne takes it, carrying it back to Dustin.

"It'll be extra for you," she says, jiggling the jar in front of him.

He looks offended. "I already put in a hundred bucks."

"*And?* Sour Skittles are expensive."

He holds her gaze as he reaches into his back pocket and withdraws his wallet again. He slides out another crisp Benjamin and stuffs it into the jar without so much as a blink.

She harrumphs and walks away, making a show of taking the hundred-dollar bill out of the jar and keeping it for herself.

Their situation feels like it might combust at any moment, but no one seems to think it's anything out of the ordinary so it must just be the way they operate, strange as it may seem.

Josh goes to the fridge to grab a few beers. Sophia sets out two bowls of chips—barbecue included—and some cheese and nuts.

"The lasagna only needs another half hour or so. We'll wait for Tate to get back before we eat. Her shift should be ending soon."

Tate.

Her name seems to shift something in the air. Time pauses. I'm aware of my pulse, feeling it in my gut as I wait and listen for someone else to ask the questions I'm wondering: does Tate usually join this group when they hang out? Does she live here too?

Josh failed to fill me in on that aspect, and I don't get any answers now. Everyone's already moved on from Sophia's announcement. Nick grabs a fistful of chips while Dustin takes the TV remote so he can turn on ESPN. Josh asks Nick to pass him the plate with cheese and nuts and the conversation rolls on, but I'm in my own little world. At any innocuous sound, my gaze flies to the apartment door. I will the doorknob to turn. I'm impatient on the couch, jostling my knee as I force down quick sips of my beer.

Someone says my name. It's Nick, asking me something about the game yesterday. I'm about to ask him to repeat his question when the front door opens and Tate strolls in wearing light blue scrubs. Her brown hair is tugged up into a high ponytail, and she's sporting way less makeup than she was at the party. Still, she's stunning. More so, somehow. She's carrying a heavy bag on her shoulder filled with stuff she must need for work. A fleece jacket and an oversized water bottle poke out of the top.

"Tate!" everyone exclaims, happy to see her.

She smiles as she slips off her sneakers. "Hey, guys."

So she was expecting us to be here. I wonder if she was expecting me.

No.

That's made perfectly clear once she looks up and her gaze locks with mine. Surprise is evident in her sharp intake of breath and her parted lips. The others probably don't notice though, it's so subtle.

I can't look away from her. I can't even blink.

"Tate, this is Grant, the new Pinstripes player we were talking about the other night."

It's Nick doing the introduction, Nick who thinks Tate and I don't already know each other intimately. I've kissed her. I'm thinking about that kiss now as my gaze slips down to her mouth. She rolls her lips together and nods.

"Right." She looks away even as she addresses me. "It's… very nice to meet you, Grant. Seems you're part of the group now."

Josh clears his throat but otherwise stays quiet. Sophia and Daphne act completely oblivious.

So what happens next, exactly? Tate and I are going to pretend the other night never happened?

No. I won't accept that.

Instead of playing coy on the couch, I push to stand so I can make my way over to her. I don't miss the way her eyes go round with worry, the way her pulse jumps in her neck. The effect I have on her hasn't worn off in the days we've been apart. If anything, it's strengthened. *Good…*

Her eyes stay pinned on me as I approach. The foyer is too small for the both of us. I tower over her as I reach for her bag.

"Here, let me get this," I say, already sliding it off her arm.

She winces and rolls out her shoulder, glad to let me take it.

"This is too heavy," I chide, looking down at it. "You need all this for work?"

"Unfortunately…"

I try to think of some solution. She's small. This bag easily weighs twenty pounds. How far does she have to walk with it?

"Maybe you could get one of those rolling cart things instead?"

She gifts me a tentative smile. "Like grannies use for their groceries?"

"Hey, don't knock it," Nick chimes in with a mouth full of chips. "Those things rock. I have one."

Tate glances over my shoulder at him, and the change is immediate. Her expression softens and the storm lurking behind her gaze begins to settle, but then she peers back at me and her brows tug together. The spark between us feels as obvious as a match strike.

"Yeah, maybe I'll get one of those," she says, looking up at me, studying my face. What's she looking for?

"Tate, if you want to shower before dinner, you better do it now," Sophia calls out. "I'm taking the lasagna out and it needs to rest for about ten minutes before I serve it."

"Okay, I'll be fast!"

She moves like she's going to take her bag back, but I shake my head. "Where's your room?"

If she's going to shower here, she must live here too. *Thanks for the heads-up, Josh.*

"This one," she says, curving around me, careful not to brush up against me as she leads the way to a door off the living room, just to the left of the TV.

I could follow her inside and shut the door behind us, but I stop on the threshold and set her bag down on a narrow dresser that's within reach. Her room is a tiny space, just big enough to house a queen bed, a side table, and her dresser. There's a cluster of prints hanging above her bed, a lot of framed photos. I see one that includes Luke, and I ignore the tight dread in the pit of my stomach.

"Thanks," she says, nodding toward the bag. She's already

removing her hospital I.D. badge and untucking her scrub top from her pants.

I should leave. She needs to shower, but I'm rooted to my spot. I stand there staring at her in disbelief.

When she left that party, it felt like I'd never see her again. We shared that moment—however brief and weird and fun and sexy it was—and I thought that was all we'd get. Now here she is, standing before me like a dream I get to experience for a second time. I'm scared to walk away.

"Where do you work?"

"Manhattan Children's. I'm an ICU nurse."

My eyebrows shoot up. "Damn."

"Not quite as impressive as an MLB superstar," she teases.

She opens her dresser to retrieve clothes she can change into after her shower. A soft white t-shirt, a pair of blue lounge pants. Dainty blue panties...*fuck.*

I look away.

"You can get to know her later, man!" Nick groans. "Let her shower so we can eat. I'm starving!"

Right. I almost forgot about the audience in earshot of our conversation.

Tate fights back a private smile as she keeps her focus down on her clothes. I wish I had a penny for her thoughts. Is she feeling what I'm feeling? Is her heart racing too?

"Leave her alone! I'm hungry!" Nick continues.

I have no choice but to step back so she can close her door. I expect all eyes to be on me when I turn around, but Josh is the only one looking my way. He shakes his head in warning, but I ignore it. I know the score; he doesn't need to remind me.

The water turns on in Tate's bathroom as I take a seat and retrieve my beer. The walls in this place are so paper thin I can hear her every move. Shampoo bottles jostle around. It feels indecent, like we shouldn't be listening.

But actually, I'm the only one bothered. The guys are

talking and watching ESPN. Sophia and Daphne are finishing up in the kitchen. No one else is thinking about—scratch that —no one else is *imagining in vivid detail* what Tate is doing on the other side of that wall but me.

Daphne and Sophia start passing around plates loaded up with salad, lasagna, and garlic bread just as Tate walks out of her room. I look up because I'm a sucker. She's fresh-faced and gorgeous. Her dark hair is still damp since she didn't have time to dry it. It's long and wild, a few wavy strands hanging over her shoulder. Her cheeks are flushed with color. She's wearing the t-shirt and lounge pants and her feet are bare. Red polish covers her cute toes.

My heart presses up against my rib cage with every hard beat as I retrace my steps back up to her face. She's not looking at me. She's smiling at Nick, who's walked over to give her a side hug.

I force myself to look away.

We eat dinner in the living room, everyone crowding around the couch and the small breakfast table tucked into one corner. It's just enough space for each person to have a spot if Tate sits on the floor. Once I realize that's her intention, I stand.

"Here. Sit," I tell her, lifting my plate as I scoot around people.

"No, it's okay. I actually like sitting on the floor."

I shoot her a pointed stare. "Tate."

She laughs, dimples and all. "I'm fine! Sit. You're the one whose body needs to be in tip-top shape."

"Nurses have hard jobs too," I point out. "You just got off a long shift. You're probably exhausted."

"She always sits on the floor," Josh says with a shrug.

I don't know what to do. I want to press the issue. I could go over and scoop her up off the ground and carry her to my spot on the couch, no problem. But I don't want to make a scene.

I scowl, and she shakes her head, wearing that little smile again. "It's all good, I promise."

If she won't stand up, then I have no choice.

I go over to where she's sitting with her back propped against the wall and her legs stretched out on the floor in front of her, and I do the same. I mimic her down to her crossed ankles, only my legs stretch out a good foot longer than hers do.

She laughs. "You're crazy. Go sit."

"I *am* sitting."

Her eyes narrow playfully, but I pretend there's nothing out of the ordinary, like I splay my 6'2" frame out on the floor to eat dinner all the damn time.

"Lasagna's good. Have you tried it?"

I nudge her arm so she'll pick up her fork and stop staring at me. I'm not moving no matter what she says. We're in this together now.

She shakes her head and scoops up a bite. I watch her eat it like it's new to me. *Huh. So that's how it works…*

Her supple mouth closing around her fork. A little dab of red sauce left behind on her bottom lip. I can smell her shampoo, her body wash, *everything*.

Her eyes glisten as she releases a groan of pleasure. As soon as she's swallowed the bite, she wags her fork at Daphne.

"Daph, you are *the* best. This lasagna is insane."

Daphne pretends to bow forward in thanks.

"My lunch was good too," she adds.

"I aim to please," Daphne responds in a cheesy accent.

"Oh really?" Dustin cuts in, eyeing Daphne like he'd like to eat her up. "Tell me more."

She just ignores him.

I open my mouth to ask Tate something like *How was work? So you like Italian food? I saw a lot of books in your room, you a big reader?* when what I really want to ask is *Why did you leave that party without giving me your number? Did you already know who I am? Did it matter to you?*—but Sophia speaks up first.

"So have you bumped into Michael at work, Tate?" she asks. "Since he asked you out last week?"

EIGHT
TATE

I GO ABSOLUTELY RIGID.

Why, Sophia?! *Why?*

I don't want to dissect my love life with these guys, especially not Grant. But when I look up at her—to telepathically tell her off—there's a knowing gleam in her eyes, a cheekiness that unsettles me. Why bring it up? Is she trying to be helpful? She knows I can't (i.e. *won't allow myself to*) have feelings for Grant, so maybe this is her way of helping us *all* understand that.

I focus down on my plate. "Yes, we talked today actually."

"*And?*" she presses. "Did he mention anything about the date?"

"Wait, wait, wait." Nick flails his arms out like he's a referee. "Some dude asked Tate out at work? Who?"

Oh god, here we go…

"Yes. *Michael.*" Sophia stresses the word like she's annoyed he can't keep up. "He's a physical therapist, right?"

I nod.

"And he's nice and cute *and* he helps babies learn to roll over for a living. I'm sorry, that's just the *sweetest* thing I've ever heard," Daphne adds.

I clear my throat, aware of Grant's intense gaze on me. My cheeks feel hot under all the attention.

I push my salad away from my lasagna so everything is perfectly demarcated on my plate. "I mean...that's not his whole job. He does a lot more than that."

"Okay fine, but did I get everything else correct? He is cute, right?"

Why am I blushing?! I know it's not because of Michael.

"He's...sure. Yes."

It feels wrong to admit it aloud, like I should be lying or downplaying it to help safeguard Grant's feelings, but why? This is what I want; it's all part of my plan.

I can't look at Grant even though I'm dying to know what he thinks about all of this.

"Does Luke know about this guy?" Dustin laughs.

I roll my eyes. "Luke won't care."

The guys snort like they know something I don't.

"Oh really?" Dustin continues. "I think he threatened the last guy you dated with his life."

My head jerks up at this news. "*James?*"

"Was he the blond guy? Kind of skinny?"

"Yes..."

Dustin nods. "Yeah, him."

What?! James and I dated for three short weeks back in November. I thought it was going well. He enjoyed running, he had a good job as an accountant, and he wasn't interested in Luke or his career. Sometimes guys are only interested in me for the perks. Getting to know Luke and the Pinstripes is just too tempting.

You're Luke Allen's little sister?! Are you kidding me? You think I could get his autograph? I mean...after we finish making out, that is.

An average accountant with an average personality who always showed up on time for our dates and wasn't shy about letting me know he was looking for something serious seemed too good to be true. Then one day, poof, he ghosted me. I assumed it was something I'd done. Now I know Luke is to blame.

"The guy was a total dud anyway," Dustin confirms with an apathetic shrug.

"How would *you* know?!" I ask, suddenly defensive of a man I didn't even like all that much in the first place.

"I was there with Luke when he went to the guy's office."

They confronted him at work?!

"Oh my god. You guys need a hobby."

Dustin unfurls a confident smirk. "We have one—*baseball*."

Grant laughs under his breath, and for the first time since the start of this conversation, I look over at him. He's clearly amused. He's wearing a cheeky smile, just big enough to make his dimple pop. God, he's handsome. Lethal, even. He should come with a warning label.

I could fall under the spell of that smile, *those eyes*, no problem.

"What's so funny?"

One cocky eyebrow rises to the challenge. "Nothing." But his daring gaze says the exact opposite.

"Michael's different though," Daphne chimes in. "Luke would approve."

Grant holds my gaze. He's waiting for me to confirm what Daphne's said. *Is* Michael different?

With everyone's eyes on me and on the heels of Dustin's declaration about Luke meddling with James, I feel like I have no choice but to nod and reclaim a slice of my dignity. "Yes, *he's perfect.*"

Take that, assholes.

Upon hearing my assessment of Michael, there's an infinitesimal change in Grant's expression. A layer of ice hardens over all that warm honey. Regret churns inside me. I almost reach out to touch him, to clamp my hand on his forearm and force him to listen to me. I could come clean with the truth and rewrite the last few minutes so we don't find ourselves worse off than we were before.

But isn't that the point? Isn't that why Sophia brought up Michael in the first place? This is what has to happen. Keeping Grant at arm's length is the only safe option.

We don't say anything else after that, not while dinner wraps up and I continue pushing food around on my plate, forcing down a few bites only so I don't go to bed hungry later.

I'm relieved when conversation shifts and Daphne claims control of the remote—an eternal struggle within our friend group—and changes it from ESPN to HGTV. The guys always moan when we put on our "girly shows", but it's merely a front. Without fail, they end up more invested in them than we do. We had them watching *The Bachelor* last season, and when Nick's favorite girl got sent home without a rose, he actually cried. CRIED. We have video of it somewhere.

As is tradition, the guys throw their hands up in protest over the house flipping show Daphne chooses, but then Nick starts critiquing the design choices.

"That blue is going to clash with the green. And marble countertops? *Big* mistake. Those are going to be a bitch to clean."

"Pipe down," Josh argues. "I can't hear what they're saying about the backsplash."

While everyone settles into the show, I sneak off to the kitchen to figure out dessert. I can't make anything as fancy as Chloe. She could pull random ingredients out of my cupboards—cardamom, baking soda, and chia seeds—and produce the most jaw-dropping delicacy you've ever tasted. Me? Yeah...I settle for foolproof break-apart chocolate chip cookies.

I've just turned on the oven to preheat when Grant strolls into the kitchen, presumably to refill his water glass.

I'm not buying it.

"Thirsty?"

He ignores my question, fills his glass, and takes a sip. He could leave now and rejoin the others in the living room, but instead he lifts his chin toward me. "What are you making?"

I open the fridge and retrieve a package of cookies to show him. "Only the *finest*, *fanciest* food for you all. Homemade, *from scratch*," I tease, crinkling the package for full effect.

He pats his stomach like he doesn't care one bit where the cookies come from as long as his mouth is their final destination. "Please say you have more than one package. I can polish off a dozen of those by myself."

I reach back into the fridge to pull out two more packages. I'm well aware these guys have appetites that could rival hungry lions. Three dozen cookies should do it though.

I set them on the counter then bend to get our baking sheets from the drawer under the oven. It's a tight squeeze in our little kitchen. The way our apartment is set up, you can only access it from a doorway that juts off from the living room. The tight galley design pushes the oven-stove combo and fridge onto one side, leaving a sink and some minuscule counter space on the other side. Daphne, Sophia, and I have gotten into some nearly-friendship-ending fights because of the size of this kitchen. So help me god, if one person is trying to use the stove and another person wants to wash a dish... well, nice try. It's not happening.

But tonight, for some reason, I'm more than willing to share the confined space with Grant. In fact, it's my pleasure.

Though it flies in the face of everything I'm trying to accomplish concerning my crush on him, it's still interesting to test the limits of my attraction. I've never been so wholly aware of another person's presence; his every breath seems worthy of attention.

Grant steps back so I have room to pull the drawer open.

When I go to take out the cookie sheets, he leans down and drops his hand on my back. "Here, let me help."

His touch makes me freeze. It's astounding that he can cover so much of my back with his large hand, shocking how a simple touch can make me feel cherished and safe.

Oh god…

I hop back up to my feet, cookie sheets in hand. "It's nothing. I just have to spread the cookies out on the baking sheet."

He shakes his head, fighting back a smile. "It's really a two-person job. What if you don't get the spacing right?"

I shake my head, playing along. "You're right. It'd be a travesty." I set the baking sheets on the counter then gesture behind him. "Can you get those scissors?"

Over the next few minutes, we work together laying out the cookies. It's a tight fit to squeeze three dozen onto only two baking sheets, but we figure it out. With him in the kitchen, there's no space left. If he turns sideways, he'll all but cover the entire width of the room, and he proves my theory once the cookies are ready to go and we're waiting on the oven to finish preheating.

Our task is done. He could leave, but instead, he turns and blocks the living room from view. I'm stuck between him and the wall. A rock and a hard place.

"So you're Luke Allen's little sister…"

His voice is low enough that it won't carry, especially not while everyone out there is arguing about paint samples.

"Who wants a pink bathroom?!" Dustin exclaims.

I cross my arms and tip my chin up. "And you play for the Pinstripes…"

"Interesting turn of events if you ask me."

"Is it?"

He shrugs. "You're effectively off limits to me now."

The dark look in his eyes coils my stomach into a tight ball of tension.

"If it helps…you were *always* off limits to me. I don't date baseball guys, so it would have never worked out between us."

He edges closer, not enough to draw attention from the others, but enough that I feel slightly off-kilter as I inch backward.

"Is that the truth? Is that the real reason why you didn't want to give me your number the other night?"

I have to force a swallow.

"No. I didn't know you played baseball then. I told you the truth at the party...I didn't give you my number because I didn't think it was a good idea for...other reasons."

And I'm glad I trusted my intuition. Maybe I didn't realize how tightly our worlds overlapped then, but deep down, instinctively, I knew he wasn't right for me.

"Tell me."

I laugh like the suggestion is preposterous. *"No.* It's just—"

"What?" he goads like he knows the answer more than I do, like he's privy to my innermost thoughts.

"There are too many reasons to even count," I say, exasperated.

His eyebrows skyrocket though his amusement doesn't fade.

"Too many to even count?" He shakes his head. "Sounds like a tricky situation. Silly me, I thought it was just Luke standing in our way..."

"It's that and more, so just accept defeat and walk away."

He hums like he considers the idea for a moment and then decides to cast it aside. There's a wickedness to his expression now, a tantalizing appeal that sets my nerves on edge.

"I'm a pretty competitive guy..."

Another step closer, and I feel like I should cower. I almost lift my hands as if to block him from getting any closer, but thankfully, I resist the urge. How silly to be scared of a man like Grant, to worry about what he might do to me...

"There's no winning here," I assure him, though for some reason it sounds like I'm laying down a challenge at his feet. Is my tone not firm enough? Are my flushed cheeks divulging my true feelings?

"So you want me to wave a white flag," he notes, sounding as though the idea bores him.

I gulp. "Yes."

Please.

"Sophia told me you and Josh go way back, which means you'll clearly be around a lot, so we should try to make it so we don't have to feel weird around each other. I'm going to accept that date with Michael."

"Great."

I lift my chin again, hating how acidic my next words taste. "And you can date whomever you'd like too."

He gives a short laugh, like dating someone else is the absolute last thing on his mind.

Still, he nods and tacks on a little salute. "Got it. Roger that."

"This could work out. Think of it this way: what if we could rewrite history? What if you'd been at the apartment when I got home and we'd met just like that? Simple."

"I'd still want to kiss you."

"Grant!" I shove his arm playfully. "You can't say things like that!"

There's no contrition on his face, no mercy in his tone. "Why?"

Because it makes me feel like I might combust. Because it's too appealing, too tempting, too dangerous.

I don't give him those answers though. I settle for something far less revealing.

"Because friends don't kiss."

BEEP!

The oven's preheated.

Grant takes a step back and shrugs as if to say, *Eh, we'll see about that.* Then he leaves me in the kitchen, damn near close to bending over and clutching the counter for support while I suck in huge swaths of air.

What was that?! Did we agree to keep things platonic or not?!

Why does it feel like we just took one step forward and three steps back?

Dammit, dammit, dammit.

I don't like this. I don't do well with feeling out of control. I like to keep a tight rein on all aspects of my life. Most decent men would take a woman's rejection in stride, so why isn't Grant doing that? And why am I secretly glad he's pushing this, pushing *me* in ways that make my blood boil?

"Tate? How much longer on the cookies?" Daphne shouts from the living room, and I jump a mile in the air.

Right. Cookies. I don't have time to worry about any of this! I have to tend to the cookies, after all. They can't bake if I'm not staring through the oven door, fogging up the glass. It's wimpy, I know, to hide out in here while I try to calm down. I'm just not well versed in situations like this. It's been a long time since I've been this nervous around a guy.

I can recall exactly when it last happened: eighth grade. Brett Lawson came to sit by me during lunch and I could barely contain myself. *The* Brett Lawson was gracing me with his presence! Turned out he had a crush on my friend who was sitting across from me, but whatever, those are minor details. The point is, I know how rare it is to feel that zing of electricity when your crush walks into a room, that overwhelming innate attraction that's either there or not, it can't be forced. Grant is the only person in my adult life who has made me feel that way.

I'm still worrying about all of this when I bring the cookies out into the living room. Daphne scoots over on the couch so I can nestle in beside her, and as everyone talks and laughs, I can barely repress the urge to sneak glances at Grant.

I fail miserably the entire night. I'm watching him out of the corner of my eye like I've been tasked with keeping tabs on him and reporting back on everything he does. He eats three cookies then licks some melted chocolate off the pad of his thumb, and I feel the innocent action deep in my loins. Is he trying to drive me crazy on purpose? *No.* I don't even think he's paying attention to me anymore. He laughs at something Dustin says and he's so overwhelmingly sexy it makes my heart beat uncomfortably fast.

"You don't want a cookie?" Daphne asks, holding one out for me to take.

I shake my head then fist my trembling hands on my lap. I can't eat. My stomach is in knots.

"What did you and Grant talk about in the kitchen?" she whispers.

"*Nothing,*" I reply swiftly, wanting to snuff out any hope she has of something happening between us.

"So then it's full steam ahead with Michael?"

Yes.

"I'm going to talk to him tomorrow."

It's done. Decided. Michael is the man I belong with. Despite everything I feel for Grant, I'm going to follow my carefully laid-out plan and accept that date with Michael, and not to drop a huge spoiler, but the pieces are going to fall perfectly into place. Sophia and I might just have a joint wedding!

Dum dum dee dum…

NINE
GRANT

I PUSH open my hotel room door and toss my keycard and bag onto the entry table. The luxury suite is empty and quiet and clean. A maid has come and done turndown service, leaving a little square of chocolate on my pillow. I don't want it, still full from our postgame dinner in the Guardians' clubhouse. Our manager has gone all out this week, treating us first to all the other good food Baltimore is known for—Maryland blue crab and pit beef—and then switching it up once we got to Cleveland with pierogies and extravagant spreads the guys and I have devoured. It almost makes all the travel worth it.

I slide my shoes off as I reach for my cell phone to call my dad. It's a ritual I perform after every game.

He knows to expect my call and answers after the first ring.

"Hey, Dad."

"Boy, tonight was *not* your night."

I groan and sit down on the edge of the bed, rolling out my neck.

"I got a hit," I argue, albeit it was only a single.

"Sure, sure. And that catch in the bottom of the fifth was

damn good. If you'd let that ball slip past you, Alvarez would have made it to second."

"Yeah. I have the bruised ribs to show for it though," I protest.

He chuckles. "I'm not surprised."

"You getting to bed soon?"

It's 10:30 PM in Phoenix and I know he'll have to be up early to get to the garage. My dad has worked at the same auto shop for over thirty years. It's not his; he never did break away and start out on his own like he wanted. He said it'd take too much of his time, and when I was young, he wanted to be able to focus on my baseball, not some fledgling business. His pay isn't great, but he's always managed to eke out a living just fine. He's still in a small apartment, the same one where I grew up sleeping on the couch in the living room. I send money back, but he won't let me do much else. I tried to buy him a car, back in my first year in the majors. I wanted to surprise him with it, but it didn't go quite as I'd planned. When he saw the truck in his driveway with a big red bow, he threw his hands up and started cussing me out in Spanish, made me return it to the dealership that same day. *"You think I want you wasting money on me? I have a car and it works just fine. You be smart about all that money you're earning. You better be socking it away, you hear me? Don't be a fool."*

"I'll go to bed in a bit. I'm watching the game highlights." I can imagine him sitting there in his favorite old leather recliner with his TV tray set up in front of him, the remnants of a microwave dinner beside a mostly empty can of Coke. "They take care of you after the game?"

"Yeah, I saw the trainer after. He made me take an ice bath."

He hisses then clucks his tongue. "For how long?"

"Just a few minutes. It wasn't too bad."

"Tomorrow it'll be better, yeah?"

"Yeah. I'll call you after the game."

"Get some rest."

After we hang up, I toss my phone onto the other side of the bed and fall back onto my pillow, exhausted. Six days on the road has me eager to get home soon. We've been going nonstop since we left for Baltimore. One day stretches into another. Tonight, our game against the Guardians went late. Afterward, I hung back and showered, ate dinner, watched *SportsCenter* with the guys in the clubhouse for a bit and then headed back here to the hotel. A lot of them are still going and won't crash until 2 AM or later. It's part of life on the road.

In New York, it's easier to justify going home to your family, or at the very least, going back to your apartment with all your stuff versus going back to another lonely hotel room.

Two nights ago, I went out with Nick and Dustin to a little bar near our hotel. We shot the shit for a while and then Nick disappeared with a girl he met on Raya, the app some of the guys use for hook-ups and dates. I tried it last year and found it's not really my thing, but I understand the appeal. During the season, there's so little time for a personal life. It's not like most of us are going to meet women in the grocery store or at the gym. I don't even know anymore—is that where people meet? I haven't dated the traditional way since college. The second I donned my first MLB jersey, any sense of normalcy in my social life went up in smoke. People I hadn't talked to in years suddenly wanted to be buddy-buddy with me. Girls I knew from middle school were sliding into my DMs, asking if I wanted to reconnect, and if it wasn't old friends, it was total strangers reaching out with clear, explicit "requests".

Hey, if you're ever in LA…

Saw you play last night. You're sexy as hell. Here's my number if you want a good time…

And sometimes there are no words at all. Just pictures.

I stopped looking at my Instagram messages a long time ago. I only have a public profile on the app because it's a requirement. I don't even take the photos; we have a team photographer who works with the social media and PR teams to capture images of us during the games. They email out batches of them once a week so we can select our favorites and post them to help drum up interest for the franchise. Not that they really need any help with that...

I haven't posted a picture in a month. My last photo was from spring training, which means I'm probably on the social media team's shit list. I'll post one tomorrow. For now, I go to Tate's profile. It's private, but I have access to it now. The night I went to her apartment for lasagna and cookies, she started following me. I requested to follow her back, and she accepted. Now, at least once a day, I give in to the urge to check her profile, though she doesn't post as much as I wish she would. Some of these bloggers post every second of their day like I give two shits. With Tate, I would. I'd watch her fold laundry.

When I look at her profile, I'm careful. I don't like her pictures or leave any comments on her feed. As wild as it sounds, fans track that stuff. It's bad enough that we're following each other, but that can be written off. Tate follows most of the guys on the team; there's not much to read into with that. Now if someone were tracking the amount of time I spend scrolling her feed...*that* would be pretty incriminating. I've gone all the way back; I almost accidentally liked a photo she posted years ago, from when she was still in nursing school. *Can you even imagine?* I would have thrown my phone over my hotel balcony. Feigned amnesia. Told her someone hacked into my account. I would have said anything but the truth, which is something along the lines of *I can't help it. I'm insanely intrigued by you and it makes me feel slightly less lonely to look at your Instagram feed.*

Maybe I should put a stop to it. Right now, it's late, and I could fall asleep in an instant if I just put my phone down and closed my eyes. That would be the smarter choice, but

Tate posted a few things to her stories today and I have to watch them.

In the first clip, she shared a picture zooming in on her Apple Watch screen with a blurry Manhattan street in the background. *"Best feeling ever!"* she says while showing off an impressive 8-mile run. I know from scrolling her feed that she's an avid runner. She's posted a few photos of her at the finish line of various half-marathons, beaming at the camera, looking winded and beautiful while proudly holding up her race medals. Luke and his daughter, Harper, were with her in the most recent one. Harper held up a neon pink sign that read: *"My aunt runs faster than your aunt! Love you, Aunt Tate!"*

In her second story post from today, she has two dresses laid out on her bed, one white, one blue. *"I can't decide! Which one??"* the caption reads. Beneath that, she added a poll where friends can vote.

I don't vote.

The dresses are short and sexy. They're not something she's going to wear to lounge around in her apartment. They're dresses for a night out with friends, or maybe a date night with Michael.

The story is a few hours old. By now, she likely already made her decision, wore one of the dresses out on the town, and now she's back home. *Hopefully.*

My thumb hovers over the "Send message" prompt down at the bottom of the screen. I shouldn't. I haven't done it yet. If she doesn't want me to have her phone number, she probably doesn't want me messaging her on Instagram either. I've managed to resist the urge up until now, but tonight, I can't find the willpower.

Grant: Which one did you pick?

I send the message fast, before I can talk myself out of it.

A shot of adrenaline pumps through me and I sit up in

bed, staring down at my screen. Cleveland and New York share the same time zone, but it doesn't matter. It's nearly 1 AM; she should be asleep.

Tate: White.

She replies quickly. Then, she sends a picture of her in the silky white dress, standing next to Sophia and Daphne.

Tate: We went out. Daphne is a bad influence. Let me tell you...

In the picture, Tate has one leg wrapped around Sophia and one arm flung up into the air, holding a drink while she laughs.

Grant: You sure about that? That picture looks pretty damning...

Tate: I swear I was good.

I look at the picture again. Tate's dress is riding up, nearly to the top of her thigh, her long, toned legs on display in her four-inch heels. Her back is arched, her hair tumbling down around her shoulders. Jesus. She's insanely sexy.

Grant: I bet the guys were all over you.

Tate: If they were, I wasn't paying attention. There was a game on the TV behind the bar I was too interested in.

Tate: You should have seen it—the entire bar went crazy when you dove and got that catch in the fifth inning. They kept replaying it in slow motion. Some guy bought a round of shots for everyone to celebrate.

I love the fact that she was watching our game, watching me.

Grant: It hurt like hell. You probably saw me clutch my ribs afterward.

I took two Advil back at the clubhouse, but still, my body aches a little.

Tate: I'm sorry. Want me to kiss it and make it feel better?

Fuck me.

I'm about to fire off a quick reply, but then I slow down. Tate was drinking tonight. There's no telling her state of mind right now. Even if she's totally sober, she could just be teasing. I hate that I can't hear her tone, can't see if she's biting her lip or wearing a goofy grin.

Then a second later, another message pops up.

Tate: Off to bed! Didn't realize how late it is. Good luck against the Twins tomorrow!

Her green active status goes dark. She's gone, and though it feels like a gut punch, I tell myself it's for the best. She's setting boundaries, and I should heed them. I'm aware.

I toss my phone across the bed, hoping that will save me from continuing to endlessly scroll through her photos.

It's been two weeks since we talked in her apartment, two weeks since I crowded her in that tiny kitchen and fought the urge to kiss her. Two weeks is *plenty* of time to get over a tiny crush. A crush, mind you, who has made it perfectly clear she won't entertain the idea of us under any circumstances. But that's where it gets tricky because I know deep in my fucking bones that Tate isn't pushing me away because she doesn't want me, she's pushing me away because of everything else working against us.

She's my teammate's little sister—that's enough right there. It's a huge red flag, bedazzled and lit up like the Fourth of July. I should be deleting her from memory for that alone.

There are other factors too. I'm not dying to be in a relationship right now. In fact, presented with anyone else other than Tate, I'd put up a roadblock. I *just* moved to a new city and signed on with a new team. I'm still getting my bearings with everything. The last thing I need is someone clouding my focus, pulling my attention off the field. I can hear my dad warning me to keep my wits about me, and before Tate, I could have done that in an instant, no problem. I'm damn good at doing my job.

Only now, in this dark hotel room, I feel like this thing is growing out of my control. It coincides with an anxious, gnawing feeling I can't so easily set aside.

So just block her on Instagram, common sense tells me.

Impossible. I'd delete the whole app before I did that.

I want to know if she's gone on a date with Michael. I've wondered about it a dozen times a day since I first heard about the guy. What does she even see in him? I mean, come *on*, he's a physical therapist for babies? Big whoop! I hit baseballs real hard, real far, and I get paid a lot to do it, okay? So who's the real hero here?

God, this is stupid.

Worse than stupid.

Hopeless.

TEN

TATE

IF PHONE BOOKS were still a thing, I'd find one and scroll through it until I landed on W, for witches. I need to hire someone to work a little magic and erase the last twelve hours because what kind of idiot am I messaging Grant that teasing comment?

WANT ME TO KISS IT?!

I want to shrivel up and die.

Against my better judgment, I tell Daphne and Sophia about it the next morning, and they both gasp in horror.

"I should take your phone right now," Sophia says.

"Yes," Daphne agrees. "You're in phone jail for the next twenty-four hours. No checking Instagram! No messaging Grant!"

"It's not my fault! I was still kind of tipsy from those drinks."

"That's no excuse! Everyone knows..." Daphne looks to Sophia, who chimes in so they say in unison, *"No texting while drunk."*

It's a tried-and-true rule we've all learned the hard way. Nothing good comes from drunk texting.

"So I messed up. *It happens!*"

I was being honest with Grant last night about watching his game. At the bar, I stared at that TV screen like the final score hinged solely on my viewership. Sophia was right there with me. Meanwhile, Daphne chatted up a guy who'd been gutsy enough to approach her, and even though nothing took ("It just didn't click with him"), at least she was putting herself out there, which is much more than I can say. I was crushing on the guy on screen in the Pinstripes jersey, the forbidden athlete I should be forgetting about.

To be frank, between you and me, I don't even feel guilty about staring at him during his game. I'm no different than all the other women in America drooling over him. There are thousands upon *thousands* of TikTok videos of Grant that range from the innocuous (slow-motion footage of him walking into the stadium accompanied by killer music) to cheeky (him stretching before the games in a way that shows off his butt) to the downright dirty (grown women poring over footage, analyzing *every* angle, trying to determine what kind of *ahem* heat he's packing in his baseball pants). The comments on these videos are feral. Fan girls *galore*. It makes me wonder if Grant ever reads through them. He must know he's in the heart of every female baseball fan across America.

Still, admiring the view is very different than sending that flirty message and actively trying to sabotage my plan.

That was dumb. I've made up my mind: there is no Grant and Tate. The very idea of the two of us is bad news. I'm pursuing love elsewhere. With Michael.

Just as soon as I accept that date.

I've been dragging my feet, but today, I'm going to take the plunge.

I'll leave early for my 3 PM shift and hunt him down first thing. He's been patient with me, but how long is he willing to wait for me to figure my life out? He's going to think I'm uninterested, and that's not the case...not really. I'm just sort of apathetic. However, I think with a little nudge in the right direction, we could get somewhere. Beyond the fact that he meets my minimum boyfriend requirements, there's a basic attraction. I think he's cute, and I enjoy his company. Relationships have been built on far less than that. How will I know if we have a real connection if I don't at least try?

Daphne and Sophia agree that I should give Michael a fighting chance. After I go for a run (to force myself out of this hangover fog) and shower, they make me apply a little makeup, something I don't usually bother with for work considering three-week-old babies don't tend to notice whether I've applied bronzer or not.

"Now, are those the sexiest scrubs you own?" Daphne asks as I'm on my way out.

I pause and look down. I'm wearing Figs, a stylish scrub brand. They're cute and fitted versus the oversized hospital-issued kind some of the doctors and nurses wear.

"*Yes?*" The word lilts because I have no clue where she's going with this.

My answer disappoints her. "You don't have anything that's a little more low-cut?"

I level her with a glare like, *You can't be serious.*

She tosses her hands up. "*What?* I just think maybe you should sex it up a bit more. Wear your hair down."

"No."

"Okay, maybe roll your scrub top up so it's like a crop top?" She's smiling now. I know she's teasing, but even still, she continues. "You know what? I actually have a nurse costume from a few Halloweens ago! I bet that would be fine to wear for your shift."

I ignore this and step through the doorway.

"Don't say I didn't try to help!" she calls out after me, affecting a 1950s housewife drawl as she continues, "*You'll never attract a beau with that snarky attitude!*"

At the hospital, Michael is leaving a patient's room when I find him.

"Michael!" I call out, hustling a bit to catch up in case he's in a rush to get to his next patient. His workload is slightly different than mine. He only has to stay for as long as it takes him to get through the patients on his schedule for the day, so I'd hate to stall him for too long. If he's anything like me, efficiency matters.

His face lights up when he turns and sees me. "Hey, Tate. You just starting your shift? Should be a relatively light one with Dr. Liota and Dr. Zhao both out at that conference."

I huff out a breath. "Let's hope so. How was your day?"

"Not bad." He checks his watch. "I should be out of here before 6, easy."

"That's great."

There's a natural lull here. He's waiting for me to explain why I've hunted him down, and I'm trying to work up the courage to accept his offer of a date, but it's been so long since he originally issued said offer that now it feels like *I'm* the one doing the asking.

"So…about that date," I say, rocking back on my heels. "Is it still on the table?"

He blinks as it takes him a moment to realize what I've just said. He's stunned.

"*Date?* Y-yeah." He stammers for a moment before continuing more vehemently, "I mean, yes. *For sure.*"

I smile with relief. "Okay. Great! I'm off tomorrow?"

"That works. I'll probably be out of here before dinner. I could pick you up around 6:30?"

Wow, this is actually working! It almost feels too easy.

"Okay, and since I sort of sprung this on you, I'm happy to help plan things. I could make a reservation for us somewhere?"

He plays like he's completely affronted by this suggestion. "Don't worry about it." He winks. "I got this. Just text me your address. You have my number, right?"

We've shared numbers for work purposes. There are times

we need to coordinate procedures and exams with the PT and OT teams.

"Yep. Okay so, *tomorrow*?" I ask, sounding hopeful.

"Tomorrow."

I feel…a lot of things as I walk down that hallway away from Michael. It's not every day that you accept a date with a coworker. It could be the biggest mistake of my life trying to mix romance with work—something I've never done before—but there's no real way around it. Michael's the first guy I've met in a long time who doesn't make me feel like too much or too little, which I know sounds bad…but maybe it's a good thing to feel like Goldilocks in a relationship? There's nothing worse than feeling like the scales aren't balanced in your favor, as if you're chasing after a guy. This way, I have the slight upper hand, and that's for the best.

It means I can start work without any distractions. I'm not losing my head over it like I would be, say, if I'd just agreed to go on a date with Grant tomorrow. I could puke just thinking about that scenario. If I had a date with Grant instead of Michael, I'd be locking myself in a supply closet somewhere and huffing into a brown paper bag. I'd be walking around here with my head in the clouds the entire day.

Without a doubt, this is better for me *and* for my patients. In fact, I'm so focused through my entire shift I forget to update Daphne and Sophia about the Michael news until I get home.

They're perched on the couch with their feet up on the coffee table, watching the tail end of the Pinstripes away game with individual pints of ice cream.

"You just missed Grant bat," Sophia says, licking some chocolate off her spoon.

I ignore that, drop my hospital bag by the door, and launch into my news instead. "Michael and I are going out on a date tomorrow!"

Sophia's jaw drops. "What?! Really?!"

Daphne squeals.

Their enthusiasm rubs off on me. This is a good thing, for sure.

"You don't work tomorrow, do you?" Daphne asks.

"No. I'm off."

I grab a spoon from the kitchen before I take the seat beside Daphne so I can steal some of her blanket and some of her mint chip.

Her eyes grow wide with possibilities. "Okay, here's the plan! We wake up and go on a run. Shower, get ready. You branch off, get waxed, like *really* waxed, you catch my vibe? Then we can shop around for an outfit."

I laugh. "It's not *that* big of a deal."

She reaches over to jostle my shoulder. "This could be your *last* first date ever, Tate!"

Oh wow. When she puts it like that, I almost feel sick.

"Okay, whatever. Let's do it."

Agreeing to her plan feels like the easiest way forward. I love a good plan. Step-by-step instructions I have to follow? Be still my heart. It takes all the thinking out of it. Emotions be gone.

I believe this is all exactly what I want—or at least I pretend to—right up until I tuck myself in my bed that night and check my phone to see a message from Grant waiting for me on Instagram.

Oh Jesus, where's a brown paper bag when you need it?

Don't check it!

Check it!

Don't.

DO IT.

I set my phone down and pick it back up a dozen times until impulse wins out and I hold my breath and open the message.

Grant: Turns out your luck worked tonight...we won.

He only sent it a few minutes ago, which means I can do one of two things: ignore it and go to sleep...zzzz...*or* reply and open up a can of worms.

Before Grant, I would have had no issue choosing the wiser option. My fingers hover over my phone's keyboard, and then, as it turns out, I simply can't do what's best for me in this situation, which is odd considering how much restraint and self-control I exhibit in all other areas of my life. I am extremely by the book in every other respect.

So why do my fingers *tip-tap-type* a response to Grant? *Why* can't I keep myself from walking into the fire when I know I'm going to get burned? Nay, *scorched*.

Tate: Oh yeah? I could only catch the last inning because of work. Did you play well?

Good. Play it cool. Pretend you weren't just glued to your television screen hoping for a glimpse of him on the field.

His response pops up and it makes my heart flutter.

Grant: Yeah, you'll have to catch the highlights on ESPN.

Tate: Too bad I'm already in bed...

I immediately regret the ellipsis. "I'm already in bed *period*" says: Bummer, maybe tomorrow. "I'm already in bed *dot dot dot*" is an invitation, plain and simple.

Tate: I'll look in the morning.

I add the second message quickly to help keep us on track. What track, you ask? Who knows. We're playing at friendship, I think.

Grant: How was work?

Tate: Same ol' same ol'. Lots of bandages and wound checks. I did get to help celebrate a birthday for one of our patients, though, which was fun. She's four and she loves princesses. Her mom begged me to dress up.

Grant: Costume and everything?

Tate: Oh yes.

Grant: I'd love to see a picture of that.

Tate: I don't have one, but I'm sure you can imagine it well enough. Amazon-issued Ariel costume, stuffed Flounder, synthetic red wig...

Grant: Damn. Slow down. Trying to seduce me here, Tate?

I burst out laughing and then immediately cover my mouth, hoping Daphne and Sophia didn't hear me.

Tate: I assure you, it was very tame.

Grant: That was sweet of you to do that for her.

Tate: It was no big deal. How are your ribs?

Grant: Eh, they're okay. I took another ice bath after the game and that seemed to help. I guess that offer of a kiss is off the table?

My jaw drops. Oh my god. I have to put my phone face down on my chest and squeeze my eyes closed for a second, because I'm *that* excited.

After a few seconds and some calming breaths, I reach for my phone again.

Tate: Grant! In my defense, I was drunk last night when I said that.

Grant: Were you?

Tate: A little…

Grant: So then I should be a gentleman and forget about it?

Tate: Yes. Exactly. Please!

I'm relieved. *I am.*

But it takes him far too long to respond here. Seconds stretch for years.

Grant: And if I pushed my luck and persisted? If I still wanted that kiss…what would happen then?

Holy.
Shit.

My breaths come quick and shallow as a swarm of butterflies take flight in my stomach. I can't help but imagine him on the other end of this conversation, alone in a dark hotel room, stretched out on his bed with one arm bent behind his head and his phone propped up on his hard abs as he waits for my reply.

The mental image isn't good enough. I want to know exactly what he looks like right now. What he's thinking. How he feels.

This conversation is dangerous. Already, my resolve is starting to splinter and crack. I need Grant to make this easier on me. Pushing him away is no easy feat. I've somehow managed up until now, but there's something about this back and forth that makes it feel like the consequences don't count.

There's a clandestine cloak to messaging that doesn't exist when you speak to someone face to face.

Tate: Grant.

That's all I manage, just his name.

There's a lull here where he doesn't respond as fast as he has been. For a second, I think he might have given up on me, but then another message pops up and my heart soars.

Grant: Dustin just came by my room and asked why I was smiling like a fool…

I blush, glad no one can see.

Tate: What'd you say?

Grant: I told him I was talking to you.

All of my big complex emotions whittle down to a pinprick of understanding right then.

I need to wrap this up. What might have started innocent enough has all the potential to devolve into something we can't come back from.

Without responding, I exit Instagram, put my phone on my charger, and lie awake, wondering why my life feels like it's slowly starting to unspool all because of Grant Navarro.

ELEVEN

TATE

THE NEXT DAY, Michael arrives outside my apartment for our date at the exact minute he told me he'd be there, which means he gets brownie points for being dependable and punctual. He's also holding a bouquet of roses and a big plastic bag.

"Flowers?!" I smile as I take them from him.

I lower my head and inhale deeply, because it feels like that's what you're supposed to do when you receive flowers, but they don't smell like anything. Still, I beam. They're the most saturated pink roses I've ever seen. I'll take them up to my apartment before we leave. I don't want to have to carry them around all night.

"And for you," he says. "Sorry I didn't have time to wrap it, I had to grab it on my way over."

I'm intrigued as I peer down into the bag.

It's a folded jersey.

A Pinstripes jersey.

"We're going to the game." He smiles shyly. "I figured it'd be fun. You can teach me all about baseball. Considering how much you love it, I should probably know more about it."

I almost laugh. I mean, this is funny, right? Not like ha-ha funny, more like cry yourself to sleep funny.

I don't have the heart to tell Michael this is the absolute last place I want to go on a date. I'm actively trying my hardest to put Grant out of my mind, and now we're off to watch him play in person?

I peer up to see Michael chewing on his bottom lip. He's clearly put a lot of effort into this, and he probably wasn't sure how it would land. He holds his hands out and explains, "The tickets aren't great, but you've probably sat in the best seats in the house over the years. Maybe it'd be fun to live like the rest of us peasants?"

"I assure you, no seat is a bad seat. Let me see the tickets."

He retrieves them from his back pocket and holds them out for me.

I inspect them then slap them against my hand excitedly. "Yes, see, this section—section 326—has my favorite hot dogs."

He frowns, confused. "Don't they serve the same hot dogs everywhere in the stadium?"

"Yes, *technically*—but Russell works in section 326 and he's the hot dog *king*. I've seen people wait in line for an entire inning to get one of his hot dogs."

Michael is absolutely delighted by this turn of events. Never mind that I've totally made it up. *Russell?* There is no Russell, but Michael was probably feeling insecure about the seats. Yeah, they're not like right behind home plate or anything, but they're fine. This could be fun, I tell myself, trying for the sake of this date to not let my real reaction show on my face—something akin to a foreboding wide-eyed grimace—which proves extremely hard once we're in the back of an Uber, heading toward the stadium, and I finally pull my new jersey out of the bag to look at it.

"That's Grant Navarro's jersey. He's the new guy." He

fidgets on his seat before pointing to the garment. "Not sure why I'm explaining that as if you don't already know who he is. Anyway, I figured you probably had enough jerseys with your brother's number on them…"

The color drains from my face as I hold it up. The laugh I held in when Michael first told me where we were going bursts out of me now because what are the odds? Truly, what are the odds?! But Michael takes it as a laugh of delight, like I'm so pleased to be receiving a jersey with Grant's name and number on it I can barely contain myself.

Want me to kiss it and make it feel better?

And if I pushed my luck and persisted? If I still wanted that kiss…what would happen then?

The tremor in my pulse is for the wrong man.

I clutch the jersey in my lap and try very hard to seem appreciative as I lean over and give Michael a chaste kiss on the cheek.

"This is all really great—the flowers, the tickets, the jersey. You didn't have to go to all this trouble. We could have just had a quick bite to eat somewhere."

His smile fades slightly. "Like I said, I haven't been on the dating scene in a while. I wasn't sure what girls expect these days."

"Oh yeah, I forgot. Here, I'll get you up to speed. Diamonds are an absolute *must* on the first date. You have those, right?"

I make a show of looking around his seat, like I'm trying to find the Tiffany's box he's hiding from me.

He pats his shorts and sighs with disappointment. "Dang. I forgot them at home."

My eyebrows shoot up and I shake my head. My tone is disapproving when I reply, "I guess I'll let it slide *this* time…"

He laughs and nudges his shoulder against mine.

"You're already doing great," I assure him. "Even just showing up on time is pretty rare."

He rolls his eyes. "Tell me that's an exaggeration."

The rest of the way to the stadium, I regale him with all of my recent dating woes, and we laugh. It's easy conversation and nice company. It feels less like I'm spending the evening with a date and more like I'm spending it with a new friend, which is fine. The romance will come later.

We're a little late getting to the stadium because traffic is horrendous. By the time I change into my jersey and we make it up to our seats on the terrace, we've missed all the pre-game announcements, the national anthem, and the line-up presentation. Roberto Romero is pitching for the Pinstripes and the Twins already have a runner on first. Luke pitched last night, so he won't take the mound again for another three or four games. Besides Luke, Roberto is the best starter the Pinstripes have.

I try to explain this to Michael, bragging about Roberto's strikeout percentages.

"His ERA—"

Michael cuts me off. "ERA?"

"Earned run average. The lower it is, the better the pitcher."

He nods along then asks, "Okay, and just to clarify, we're the ones in the white jerseys?"

I look at him, absolutely aghast. There is no hiding my despair that he would know so little about this sport I love so much.

But he breaks character with a silly grin and grabs my shoulders to shake me gently. "I'm *kidding*. Come on, I know a little bit about baseball. I'm not a total moron."

This is debatable considering he stands to get us hot dogs and beer in the bottom of the fourth, right when things are getting interesting. He asks if I want to go too, but Nick's next at bat and the bases are loaded. Grant's on third, anxious to make his final dash to home plate. He's already posed to run, rolling out his shoulders, keeping his eyes pinned on the action. He shifts his weight between his front and back leg, staying light on his feet.

"Tate?"

"What?" I snap, somewhat impatiently.

I immediately cringe as I realize the poor guy is just trying to ask if I want any condiments on my hot dog.

"Sorry...I get really into the games." I say this while not taking my eyes off the field. Nick's walking up to the plate while the crowd chants his name. "Come on, Nick," I whisper under my breath, channeling every ounce of magic I have in me. I cross my fingers and chew on the inside of my cheek and try not to feel sick as he gets in position.

Meanwhile, Michael still leaves to go get food. During this moment?! *This one?!* A meteor could be hurtling through the sky heading straight for me, spitting fire and debris, and it would be the second most pressing matter. First is Nick clearing these bases.

The Twins pitcher wipes sweat from his brow, checks second, then third. He digs his front toe into the dirt, twirls the ball in his hand. It's all just a ritual, a pattern rooted in superstition, no doubt.

Nick sways a little forward and back, keeping his body loose, his eye on the ball. The pitcher winds up and then hurls a fastball toward home plate. It cracks against Nick's bat, shoots out directly between the shortstop and the second baseman. They both dive for the ball and narrowly miss it. It's not out of the park, but it doesn't matter. It sends two runners home, Grant and Dustin, who immediately turn and grab ahold of each other to celebrate. The stadium goes wild. I'm jumping up and down and screaming my head off. I turn left and right, giving high fives and hugs to the strangers sitting beside me.

"Did you see that?!" some random old guy asks me.

"YES!" I shout back.

"They're unstoppable!"

Michael returns a few minutes later, carrying a tray with beers and hot dogs and nachos. I hurry to help him unload everything so nothing spills.

"Did I miss anything good?" he asks, so genuine and sweet.

Uh…yeah dude, you missed everything.

I don't have the heart to tell him. "Just two runs. Pretty cool. Anyway, I appreciate you getting us food. Let me Venmo you."

"No, it's all good. It's a date, remember?"

Is it though? Am I a little rusty? Are dates meant to be like this?

"I just feel bad," I persist. "Ballpark food costs more than most fancy restaurants."

He laughs. "Well these are Russell's world-famous hot dogs, right? Worth the cost, I'm sure."

Oh god. Right. The acclaimed hot dogs.

He takes a bite and closes his eyes, savoring it as he groans.

I try mine and it is, in fact, amazing. Maybe I wasn't wrong about this section.

We lock eyes and smile, appreciating the moment.

This is going fine, I reprimand myself. Michael has been nothing but nice. I'm the one taking the baseball game way too seriously. So what if this sport isn't his passion? Isn't that what I want? Someone who doesn't care about the game or my relationship to it? Someone who can balance out my obsession?

I know Luke would approve of this guy, not that I was planning to find out tonight. My plan was to scurry out of this stadium as fast as my feet could take me as soon as the game ends. Unfortunately, Michael turns to me at the top of the ninth—when it's obvious we're about to finish this game well ahead of the Twins—and asks if it'd be possible to meet the team.

"The team?" I ask like the word confuses me. What team do you speak of, sir?

"I just thought it could be cool." Already, he's backpedaling. He shrugs like it's no big deal. "I mean that's your brother. How wild! Do you get to talk to him after the games?"

"Yeah…sure, we go down onto the field and stuff, but—" I'm scrambling here trying to come up with an excuse for why that would be a bad idea tonight. "Meeting the family on the first date is kind of a lot, right?"

He rubs his palm on his jeans like he's started to sweat a little. "Sure, yeah, it's too soon. Not to mention it would probably be a little intimidating to be face to face with athletes like these guys."

Right, sometimes it's hard to remember the celebrity effect the players have on other people. To me, they're just my friends. I mean, I helped Nick buzz his hair last year, and to be silly, we paused at every phase along the way: bowl, mohawk, mullet, etc. We were laughing so hard by the time we got to Terry Bradshaw (aka bald crater up top) I peed my pants. One time Josh and I found an antique trunk sitting on a curb and he made me help him haul it five whole city blocks before someone chased us down, screaming at us about stealing their stuff. Dustin was once so drunk on our couch that he wouldn't stop singing sea shanties. They never stopped coming. One would roll right into another, and short of being impressed that he had so many different ones memorized—like was he a pirate in a past life??—we all just wanted him to stop freaking singing. Daphne threatened to suffocate him with a pillow. I bet she regrets not taking the opportunity while she had it…

Michael looks away like he's slightly embarrassed. "Forget I said anything."

My poor pathetic heart can't take it. I reach out and touch his shoulder. "Sure. Yes, let's do it! We can go down there. My niece and my future sister-in-law are probably here. You can meet everyone. Just…don't say I didn't warn you."

TWELVE

TATE

SINCE IT'S a Saturday evening game, I know Chloe and Harper are both here to support Luke and the team. Sophia and Daphne would normally be here too, but they're at an old friend's birthday dinner. *Thank god.*

I purposely didn't tell Chloe and Harper I was at the game because, well, I'm on a date. I was trying to preserve the moment and give this fledgling relationship time to breathe, but now we're heading toward the dugout where all the Pinstripes families, friends, and special VIP guests are waiting to go down onto the field, and I regret not giving them a heads-up. There's no telling how this is about to go. Harper, especially, has no filter.

Security guards create a blockade around the group of guests, and most of the time you'd have to present I.D. and some kind of proof that you're allowed down past this point. I've seen players occasionally have to come up into the stands and personally retrieve people themselves when issues arise, but I nod to Mitch and Dan—two men who've worked security at the stadium for longer than I've been alive—and keep right on walking.

Michael chuckles behind me, sounding thoroughly awed. "This is the coolest thing ever."

I smile over my shoulder. "Just wait until you step foot on the field."

There's nothing like it.

Among the crowd, Harper and Chloe are standing beside the low concrete wall near the dugout, chatting with two more burly security guards positioned near the locked gate temporarily holding us off the field.

"Tate!" Harper screams when she spots me, breaking free of Chloe to run up to get to me. She wraps her spindly arms so tightly around my waist I nearly tip forward, taking us both on a tumble down the stairs. Fortunately, Michael reaches out to hold me steady.

"I didn't know you were here!" Harper steps back only far enough so she can look up at me with her big hazel eyes. She's beaming from ear to ear. "How come you didn't sit with us?"

"I was watching the game with my friend. Michael, this is my niece, Harper. Harper, this is my friend, Michael. We were sitting up there," I explain.

Her nose scrunches as she follows the direction of my finger. "Why up *there*? You can't see anything."

Michael clears his throat, and I nearly die of mortification. "Be-*cause* sometimes it's fun to see the games from a different vantage point. I liked it! Anyway, come on. Chloe's waving us down. They're about to let us onto the field. We can talk more down there."

After every home game, security runs through the same protocols. They hold us off the field for fifteen to twenty minutes so there's time for the opposing team to clear out after postgame interviews. Sometimes, if it was an especially intense game, it takes longer. In the meantime, friends and family are allowed to gather here. Once security deems it safe, we're allowed in for a few minutes to hang out with the players and take pictures. Harper usually runs the bases with the other Pinstripes kiddos. It's such a special thing not many people get to experience, and I'm happy Michael suggested coming down here. His eyes are wide with wonder as I continue to lead him down through the throng.

I recognize most everyone: girlfriends, wives, friends, family. We've all done this song and dance a hundred times before. There are a few new faces, though, like Michael, and they *ooh* and *ahh* the moment our feet touch that turf.

"*Wow*," Michael whispers under his breath as he turns in a slow circle.

Harper realizes how awestruck he is, and it makes her laugh. "Cool, huh? Want to meet my dad?"

Before he can even comprehend her question, Harper has him by the hand and she's tugging him over toward Luke. Since he didn't pitch tonight, my brother has already wrapped up his interviews. When he sees his daughter and fiancée, he wastes no time getting to them. Chloe reaches him first, and she gets scooped up off the ground so he can lay a big kiss on her. He's doing it because he loves her, plain and simple, but the photographers on the field eat it up. Their flashes go off like fireworks even after he sets her back down, laughing. She shakes her head, no doubt admonishing him playfully.

Then Harper reaches them and pushes Michael out in front of her.

Oh the awkwardness. I cringe.

I should be over there helping to smooth over the moment. To my credit, I do take a step in that direction, but that's as far as I make it because then I spot Grant only a few yards away, talking to a reporter.

I freeze.

He's unbelievable.

I've seen him in street clothes and he's *beyond* sexy, but in his baseball jersey, he takes my breath away. He hijacks my thoughts and my good sense. It's why I'm standing here with one foot positioned in front of the other, midstride, staring at him with my jaw scraping the dirt. He looks up and finds me like that, which is just great.

If he thinks my reaction is weird, he doesn't let on. His eyes flit over me, down across my jersey and jean shorts and sneakers, then his attention shifts right back to the reporter without giving anything away. He's talking to Sandra Neal, one of my favorite female sportscasters. She knows her stuff and is well-respected. She's also not some cutesy twenty-one-year-old. She's well into her forties—beautiful, *yes*, but damn good at her job. I admire her, usually. Right now, I'm wondering what the hell she could be saying that's so funny. Grant gifts her a dimpled smile and the cameraman zooms in 10x, probably. I'm sure every audience member at home hits pause so they can swoon, men, women, children included.

It's not fair to compare Michael and Grant, and yet my brain just can't help itself. They're both handsome men. That's irrefutable, but they're polar opposites. Michael's brown hair is a lot lighter, almost blond next to Grant's. His skin is fairer, his cheeks are a little rounder, and his eyes are softer, almost sweet. Michael is cute, but there's nothing intimidating about him. He gives off golden retriever energy, which isn't a bad thing, I remind myself. It's what I'm looking for!

Meanwhile Grant is pure mischief. His dark sweaty hair peeks out from beneath his backward baseball hat. His piercing brown eyes—so light compared to his dark brows—make me feel slightly off-kilter when he chances another quick glance over at me.

I try, I *really* try to snap out of it and keep walking, but then he nods at Sandra, gives her one last smile, and curves around her with the intention of reaching me.

There's no pretense, no other reason he'd be walking in this direction. How do I know? I check. I look behind me to make sure there's not some buxom blonde in a bikini rushing toward him. No offense to buxom blondes, that is. But there's no one, just security.

His stride is long and confident. It's like the world is his for the taking, especially in that damn uniform. I find I'm a little starstruck, which is totally insane because I've been around professional baseball players for my entire adult life. I don't care about them! Not at all!

So tell me why I can barely swallow, why my hands start to tingle and my heart beats so fast it's like it's tripping over itself trying to keep up...

He comes to stop just in front of me—too close—and I can tell he's fighting back a smile. He studies me, tilts his head to the side, and then rubs his chin.

"I like your jersey."

His eyes are on my chest. More specifically, on the Pinstripes logo stretched across it.

OH GOD.

"I didn't buy it." I rush to clarify that fact. I'm wearing his jersey! He thinks I bought it and wore it to his game on purpose! This is so mortifying I can barely work up the courage to continue standing here.

"Oh yeah?"

"M-Michael surprised me with it. Just like he surprised me with tickets to this game..."

His mouth loses the battle with a cocky smile. "Did he now? Turn around, let me see how my number looks on you."

My stomach squeezes tight as I sweep my hair over my shoulder and spin so he can see his name stitched across my shoulders. He reaches out and traces the 2 and 5 that fall across my mid-back. He accidentally brushes his finger against my spine, and I shiver. He feels it. He has to. I twist back around quickly, hoping the stadium lights aren't showcasing my burning cheeks, but who are we kidding, they definitely are.

Grant's eyes are the lightest shade of brown I've ever seen in person, like pale amber. Right now, they're narrowed teasingly at the corners like he's trying to bore past the bullshit and get to the real grit inside, the fleshy truths.

He takes a step toward me. It's the most mundane thing, a mere step, but it feels as good as a promised threat. I have to fight to keep from stepping back.

"I scored three runs tonight. That's more than any other game this season."

He doesn't need to tell me this. I watched him like a hawk the whole time. I probably know more about what happened in the last nine innings than *he* does.

He nods his head to where he was just standing for his interview. "That reporter was asking me what was different tonight, if I'd warmed up more, maybe changed my pregame stretches. I laughed it off, and then she asked if *maybe* I had a good luck charm here with me tonight. That's when I looked up and saw you over her shoulder, wearing *my* jersey…"

I don't want to indulge him in this. I should cut past him and hurry over to Michael, apologize for the delay, and do my best to introduce my date around to everyone. But I'm as useless as a puppet on strings.

"My jersey had nothing to do with your performance tonight."

"Prove it."

If I were still wearing my original shirt underneath, I'd strip his jersey off right here and now. He knows that. It's like he's imagining the exact same scenario. It's why there's heat building in his gaze.

He so clearly has the upper hand even if he's not gloating about it—*yet*.

I look away for a moment, failing to regain my composure before I look back. I force a swallow and try to sound confident when I speak but end up failing miserably. My voice wobbles. "I probably need to get over to Luke and them. Do...do you want to meet Michael?"

His eyes darken like a threat. "Not even a little bit."

"He's nice, I promise."

He tilts his head, studying me. "Are you two on a date right now?"

I almost feel bad as I reply with a small nod. "Our first."

"And he put you in my jersey?"

His smile damn near twists me up inside.

"He brought you to *my* game?" he continues, sounding almost cruel.

Oh god, I'm losing my head here.

"Does he know about us?" he asks.

The question sends a torrent of anguish through me.

"There is no *us*, Grant."

There can't be.

His jaw tightens then flexes. I watch the muscle there and damn near shiver at how intimidating he looks right now. I'm not even the one on the receiving end of his annoyance, not really. For a moment, I think he's going to continue the argument.

Instead he nods. "Fine, lead the way..."

He falls in step right beside me. Too close. He towers over me stride for stride until we reach Michael and my family.

They seem to have started off on the right foot. They're talking and smiling. I don't even think Michael's noticed that I haven't been by his side the last few minutes. It's easy to get distracted down here, though. I mean, look at me.

"Michael?" I say, catching his attention. "Thought you'd maybe want to meet the man whose jersey you bought."

Michael turns, notices Grant, and then just starts gaping, unable to control his reaction. He blinks and shakes his head, glancing back and forth between Grant and Luke like he can't quite believe they're both standing here with him.

"This is unreal."

We laugh.

Well, I take that back—everyone laughs except Grant. His mouth is a tense flat line.

"Good to meet you, man," Grant says, stepping forward to take Michael's hand. "Michael?"

"Yes. God. It's so cool to meet you. Awesome game you played today."

Grant blows right past the compliment and furrows his brows. "You work with Tate at the hospital, right?"

Michael grins proudly. "Yeah, we work in the same department, though I'm a PT, not a nurse."

"*Riiight,*" Grant says, keeping hold of Michael's hand. I stare down and wonder if I'm imagining how tightly he squeezes it, how easily it seems Grant could hurt him if he wanted to. "You two have worked together for a while and this is the first time you've had the courage to ask her out?" He laughs good-naturedly (only I know it's not). "What took you so long?"

Michael chuckles, but it's short and strained. "Oh, well...I was actually in a pretty serious relationship up until a few months ago."

Grant's eyebrows shoot up as he takes this in before concluding, "So now you're looking for a rebound."

What?

I aim a sharp warning glare at him, but he ignores it.

Michael is no longer laughing or smiling, but he's still trying to keep things as light as possible as he shrugs. "No, no way. Nothing like that."

My brother has been watching this exchange right along with Harper and Chloe, and I've watched his friendly expression slowly melt away. As far as he knows, I haven't had much interaction with Grant—I'm not even sure I've told him we've met—and now here's Grant, giving my date the fifth degree. It probably seems more than a little odd.

"*Grant*," I hiss quietly under my breath, hoping he's the only one who hears it.

"Sorry," he says, not sounding the *least* bit apologetic. "Just trying to play catch-up here."

"No, no worries. It's clear that Tate has a lot of people looking out for her. I'm glad." Michael shoots me a warm smile, and I can feel Grant stiffen beside me as he finally lets go of Michael's hand.

This was a huge mistake. I should have never brought Michael down onto the field. I didn't realize Grant was like this. Territorial, jealous—*over me?!* It's hard to believe it's possible.

I step forward, putting myself slightly between Grant and Michael. "Anyway, I'm sure Grant has more postgame press to get to…just wanted you to get to meet him really quick."

I feel Grant's gaze boring into the back of my head, but I can't turn around, not while everyone is looking at me curiously, wondering what's going on. If I want to keep the peace and avoid an awkward conversation with Luke *and* Michael, it's crucial I play my part to a T, which means facing forward, plastering on a smile, and waiting with bated breath.

With Grant behind me, it's like having a lion at my back. Every instinct is telling me to turn around, to assess the danger. I know objectively I'm doing everything right, and yet it feels so wrong to leave Grant hanging like this, to be choosing Michael right in front of him. I hate it.

"See ya around" is as warm a farewell as Michael gets before Grant skirts around us.

Luke pats Grant's shoulder as he passes by. "Good game, man."

I hold my breath, but that's it. No questions asked. No barbs thrown from either camp. I almost delude myself into thinking the last few minutes weren't that strange.

Only then I look at Chloe and she widens her eyes.

"*What was that?!*" she mouths.

Panic seizes me. I give a tiny shake of my head and turn away.

"Anyway…Michael, you want to see what it feels like to stand on first base in Pinstripe Stadium?"

––––––

LATER, Michael and I take the subway home since there's no chance we'll manage to get an Uber now that the streets outside the stadium are packed with celebrating fans. On the way, he picks my brain more about the game and repeats for the *one-hundredth* time how cool it was that he got to meet the guys on the field. Just before he drops me off, he kisses my cheek on the doorstep of my apartment building and tells me he'll have to take me to a hockey game next time.

It feels like a huge relief when he walks away, like I can finally drop the phony act and dissolve into my real feelings as I take the elevator up to my apartment. Sophia and Daphne aren't home, and I'm glad. I don't want to answer a million questions about tonight. After I shower and put on my pajamas, I check Instagram.

I'm not really surprised there's a message from Grant waiting for me. If I'm honest, I was hoping there would be…

My hand shakes so bad I can't even read it. I set my phone down, walk away, and brush my teeth in the bathroom. Then I try again, this time with both hands holding my phone.

Grant: Don't pull that shit again.

WHAT?
Immediately, my blood boils.
That's not the message I was expecting.

Tate: Are you kidding me?

I send my response before I even think of taking a second to cool off. Is it the best decision of my life? Probably not, but it's too late now. And anyway, it doesn't matter. He's already replying. I wonder if he was just sitting there, stewing, waiting for me to get back to him.

Grant: Imagine you were in my shoes. What if I showed up at your work on a date and shoved the woman right in your face? What did you think was going to happen back there?

No.
NO.
Already my anger is starting to give way, regret seeping in. He's right, of course. Had I considered that beforehand, I would have handled things differently.

Tate: I didn't mean for it to play out that way. Like I said, I didn't even know we were going to the game until he picked me up.

Grant: You didn't have to bring him down onto the field. You didn't have to introduce me to him.

Tate: I agree. That wasn't my best moment. Even so, you didn't have to intimidate him like that. I mean you're not exactly innocent here!

Grant doesn't say anything to this, and his silence starts eating away at me.

Tate: We agreed this was a bad idea. I thought we were on the same page.

No response.
I groan in annoyance and drop my phone onto my night-stand, wishing I could just throw it right out the window. I'm

not doing a great job of defusing this situation, but I can't help it! Introducing Grant to Michael obviously backfired, but that's not all on me. I didn't realize Grant would come out guns blazing—I didn't think I mattered all that much to him!

However, in the long run, it could be a good thing Grant met Michael tonight. Maybe now it'll start to sink in for *both* of us that we aren't meant to be together.

I look at my phone again, but there's no response from Grant.

I check incessantly for the next hour, and then finally, when I'm annoyed and ashamed by how lovesick I feel, I plug my phone into a charger across the room, out of reach, crawl into bed, and turn off my light.

The next morning, I go out on a run before the sun has fully risen. I didn't sleep well and there's no better way to tire out my whirring mind than by getting some miles in. On the second leg, when I'm nearing Luke's house, I slow my pace and start my cooldown. There's a coffee shop nearby that I love so I stop in to pick up my usual order: to-go lattes for Luke, Chloe, and me and a hot chocolate topped with whipped cream for Harper.

My family isn't surprised to find me on their doorstep. I'm usually over here on Sunday mornings. Sometimes I bring bagels, sometimes breakfast tacos. One thing's for sure, I never come empty-handed.

"Tate's here!" Harper calls, bounding into the foyer to see what I've brought. I find Chloe in the living room watching a morning show. Harper's Barbies are set up on the coffee table in front of her.

"Hot chocolate," I say, holding the cup up out of Harper's reach for a second. "Be careful, I think it still needs to cool off a bit."

"I'll take Dad his coffee," she volunteers. "He's still sleeping."

"Really?"

It's nearly 9 AM.

I look over at Chloe and she shrugs, though I think I detect a faint blush on her cheeks. "Late night, I guess…"

I nearly gag. "Say no more. Here, vanilla latte."

She greedily accepts the cup before she retreats back to her comfy spot on the couch. "You're the best. I was about to drag myself into the kitchen to make myself coffee, but I couldn't muster up the energy."

Harper dashes off to deliver Luke's latte, and when she returns, she's laughing. "He growled at me to leave him alone! He must be so tired! Did you and Dad stay up and watch a movie last night, Chloe?"

Chloe clears her throat. "Yes. Yes, exactly. A late-night movie."

I'm about to stick my fingers in my ears to block out the rest of this conversation, and Chloe realizes. She shifts topics. "I can't believe you already got your run in. Do you have a shift at the hospital later today or something?"

I shake my head. "I'm off until tomorrow. Then I work three days in a row."

Today, I'll go to the grocery store, clean the apartment from top to bottom (including the inside of our refrigerator), get through some laundry, drop off dry cleaning, make dinner for Daphne and Sophia, maybe catch a yoga class. Y'know just a casual Sunday…

Harper comes to stand in front of me with a pouty lower lip and her hands laced together in a plea. "*Now* can I drink my hot cocoa?"

I check and it's still piping hot.

"Here, go put some ice cubes in it, they'll help cool it off faster."

She dashes off, and the moment she's out of earshot, Chloe leans closer to me. "What was going on last night with Grant and Michael? Just so you know, your brother isn't *that* obtuse. That was so weird! I didn't even realize you *knew* Grant."

"Just barely," I say, focusing on the lid of my drink.

"So the two of you aren't…"

"*No.*"

"There's *nothing* going on?"

"Absolutely nothing."

This isn't even a lie. After the messages last night, we might not even have a friendship anymore.

She nods. "Okay, if Luke brings it up, I'll tell him that." Then she pauses for a second and lowers her voice even more. "Though if there *were* something going on with you two…I mean…between you and me…" She fans her face dramatically like she's trying to cool herself off. "The man is insanely gorgeous."

I lean closer to her too, smiling. "I know."

"Like 10 out of 10," she stresses emphatically.

"*I know,*" I respond with a little wistful sigh.

Then, remembering, she adds more mildly, "Michael was cute too!" She's trying to save my feelings, so she tacks on, "And nice."

"*So* nice."

There's a healthy pause as we look away, then back toward each other. "But Grant…"

We both start laughing.

Then Harper runs back into the room with a whipped cream mustache across her upper lip and wide sugar-filled eyes. "Aunt Tate, you're the BEST!"

THIRTEEN

GRANT

I'M NOT in the mood to be at this club right now. I want to be on the field or in the weight room, or better yet, in a boxing ring, unloading my anger and annoyance on my opponent. Maybe someone who happens to look a little like Michael.

Jesus, it's crazy in here.

Dustin's managed to find the loudest club in Manhattan. I can't even hear my own thoughts, let alone what anyone is saying around me. People shout and I'm just nodding like, *Whatever you say, man. Sounds good.*

It wasn't my idea to come out tonight, in case that wasn't already very obvious. It was Dustin's plan to leave from the stadium after our game and head straight here with the guys. There was no getting out of it. I think if I'd tried to break away, they would have wrangled me into the back seat of the Uber anyway.

They know I'm in a bad mood. I have been since last night. Getting into a fight with Tate on Instagram was dumb as hell. Typing out ten more replies to her last message and never actually having the guts to send them? Yeah, I don't really recognize myself these days.

I don't know what came over me when she introduced me to Michael on the field. I should have shaken his hand, signed a baseball for him, and been on my way. Instead, I turned into a seething asshole. I mean I swear I almost cracked bones in the dude's hand when I was shaking it back and forth like a menace.

Ask me how many girls I've felt this possessive over. Zero. The answer is zero. I'm not marching around the streets beating my chest and marking my territory. Well, I wasn't before I met Tate. Who knows what the future has in store for me. Maybe this is who I am now. Annoying as hell.

Anyway, tonight, Dustin's arranged for some girls to meet us at the club, but they aren't our girls. The fact that I even think of Sophia, Daphne, and Tate as "our" girls is part of the problem.

"I want to set you up with someone tonight," he told me in the back of the Uber as we were heading over here. "She's great. Real chill."

I was staring out the window and didn't bother looking over at him. "I'm not interested."

"You will be when you see her."

"Why don't *you* go after her?" I suggested, thinking that sounded like a brilliant plan.

He pulled a face. "I've messed around with her sister. Just seems wrong."

Now, I lean on the high-backed bench in our booth, scanning the club. It's awkward how many gazes I catch. Everyone's staring up here, squinting, gossiping, trying to figure out who we are. Most of them realize right away. I can read their lips enough to know they're saying our names.

We just had our last game against the Twins tonight, and we blew it out of the park. This city is in love with us, the girl to my right is evidence of that. Lizzy is the woman Dustin wanted me to meet. She's really nice, and yes, beautiful. Her hair is dark brown, almost black, and her eyes are a vivid green. She works at a daycare. All day she wrangles toddlers. I can't even imagine.

She leans closer to me and asks something, but I can't for the life of me hear anything over this music. I think I've gone deaf.

"Sorry?"

She shakes her head, as exasperated as I am.

"Where are you from?!" she shouts into my ear.

Goddamn, Dustin. I'm going to send him the bill for my hearing aids after tonight.

"Phoenix. You?"

"Tulsa."

I want to nod and turn away, but then I'll be right where I've been all evening, pissed off about a situation that can't be helped. I might as well make some kind of effort here, if for no other reason than so I don't make this girl inadvertently hate me.

"Your parents still there?"

She smiles and nods. "Yeah. And my siblings. I miss it."

"Do you make it back often?"

She shrugs. "Airfare is expensive. I try to go around the holidays and they usually come up to visit during the summer at least once."

She scoots a little closer to me, nothing too obvious or anything. It's not like she's rubbing her hand up and down my leg, but it's a signal all the same. She's interested. I'm...distracted.

I reach for my drink and take a small sip. I'm trying to go slow tonight. Meanwhile Nick is up at the DJ booth surrounded by ladies feeding him Jell-O shots. He just stole the mic and shouted, "I LOVE NEW YORK CITY!" The crowd went wild. He's going to hurt in the morning, but something tells me he doesn't care.

I catch Josh suddenly scoot around the table and stand, eagerly watching the entrance of the VIP section. My stomach tightens as I follow his line of sight. Sophia's here. Behind her, Daphne and…

Fuck.

I hiss the curse under my breath, and Lizzy asks, "What? Sorry, I can barely hear in here."

I shake my head to let her know she didn't miss anything, just my impending doom walking toward this table in a pair of sky-high heels. Tate has the sexiest legs, long and lean from all her running. The dainty clasp of her silver heels wraps around her slender ankles. I want to replace it with my hand, grip her there and then slowly draw my hand up her calf. I can imagine how much she'd love it. In another life, I'd get the chance to find out.

She's poured herself into a short red dress, and her hair is twisted up off her neck. I don't take my eyes off her as she approaches. I wonder if she knows to expect me or if my presence here will be a surprise.

She hasn't looked my way yet. As she walks, she scopes out the VIP section like she's trying to take it all in. I'm sure people take note of her as well. In a room full of beautiful women, she's still one of a kind.

Finally, her attention shifts toward our table as Daphne leans in to whisper something in her ear. Tate's gaze slowly circles the booth. She sees me, notices the way Lizzy's nestled against me, and then…nothing. She moves on as if I'm made of air. There's no hint of emotion to decipher on her face, no sign of recognition at all.

When their group gets close, Josh scoops Sophia up and wraps a possessive arm around her waist. He draws her down onto the bench beside him, and the two of them are instantly off in their own world.

Across from them, Dustin stands.

"Scoot! Scoot!" he says, and everyone shifts around the table so that Lizzy is pretty much on my lap at this point.

Dustin wants Daphne to sit by him, but she pushes Tate

into the booth first. Then she takes the outside seat. Dustin laughs, and I wish I could hear what he's telling them. They're too far away and I'm sandwiched right in the middle of everyone now. Fuck knows what I'll do if I need the bathroom.

Before Daphne, Sophia, and Tate arrived, Dustin was chatting with Lizzy's friends, the two girls on my left, but now he has his back to them. Lucky me, now *I'm* the target of their attention. Thanks, Dustin. I drain a beer and order another when the waiter comes around. He asks Daphne and Tate if they want a drink. Daphne orders a cocktail, but Tate shakes her head. She has her purse clutched on her lap like she's ready to bolt at any moment. Maybe she doesn't plan on staying long.

Look at me.

But she doesn't.

I still don't exist.

Lizzy's friends ask me about baseball, but I've lost the ability to carry on pointless conversation. I did it long enough with Lizzy. I'm tired. It's been a long day and I'd be just as happy sitting here in silence, stealing glances at Tate.

Our moods seem to match. She's not talking much either. Daphne and Dustin are doing most of the heavy lifting, leaned forward so they can talk over Tate. When the waiter comes back around with the drinks, Daphne takes hers then turns to ask Tate something. She shakes her head, and Daphne leaves the table.

Dustin watches her go, his jaw clenched as she cuts across the dance floor.

The song changes, and the volume drops a noticeable amount. Someone must have complained about it. I want to kiss that person on the lips.

Dustin turns back to Lizzy and her friends. "Should we go dance?"

The girls squeal with delight, no doubt happy to have

Dustin's attention again, especially considering I've made it clear they aren't getting anywhere with me unless they enjoy sitting in strained silence.

Tate stands to let them all out of the booth, and then once they're gone, she stands there, staring back and forth between our table and the VIP exit. She's weighing her options.

She doesn't look at me once.

I hide my smile and wait.

Then finally she sighs and sits back down in the booth, albeit as far away from me as she can get. We aren't totally alone. Sophia and Josh are still here, just...not paying any attention to us. I don't need to look over at them to confirm they're heavily making out.

Tate fidgets, shifting to turn her back to me so she can people watch out in the club.

How long are we going to sit here avoiding each other? Who knows. I have a beer to drink, so I'm more than content.

It's not even a full minute before Tate flags down a passing waiter and asks for a cocktail of her own.

"I thought you weren't going to drink tonight," I say, biting the bullet.

She swallows and then reluctantly looks over her shoulder at me. Her eyes narrow. "I shouldn't. I have to be at work in..." She pauses to do the mental math. "Less than eight hours."

Fuck. I feel bad. "I can take you home."

"Like hell you will."

If she could, she'd spit on my offer.

I smile. Feisty tonight, I see. I don't mind...

"Where's Michael?"

She raises a taunting eyebrow. "Where's the girl who was grinding on your lap?"

"I don't know. I'm sure I'll find her again later."

It doesn't feel good to say it. If my dad were here, he'd slap me upside the head. We're being immature, the both of us, but I can't seem to dig my way back from this. I'm annoyed. On edge. Looking for a fight.

"If you scooted closer, I'd be able to hear you better. We could talk."

"I'm fine," she says, turning her attention back toward the club.

Her dress cuts low so that most of her back is on display, no bra strap covering any of her beautiful tan skin. It feels wrong to look, too intimate to see all that skin...the slope of her spine begs to be touched. I want to run my hand across the smooth skin, down until I reach the small of her back. Would she shiver for me like she did last night? When I traced the numbers on her jersey? *My* jersey.

"You don't want to go dance with Daphne?"

"I doubt she's dancing. She's probably off somewhere fighting with Dustin."

"What is it with those two?"

The waiter comes back and sets down her cocktail. Tate reaches for her wallet in her purse. "I'll go ahead and pay now if that's okay."

That way she can make an easy exit...

"You can put it on my tab," I tell the waiter.

He nods without confirming this with Tate then walks away to take care of another table.

Tate doesn't thank me for the drink. Of course not. If anything, she's about to pour it out onto the floor slowly to teach me a lesson.

I'm smiling, imagining it as she peers back at me. "What's your problem?"

I raise a brow but otherwise stay quiet.

Sophia and Josh stand to leave the booth, and I don't even look at them go. Tate doesn't either. She's too busy scooting closer to me. She's finally within arm's reach.

I keep my hands firmly on my beer just in case I can't resist the urge to touch her. Her slender neck on full display.

Her tantalizing cleavage in that low-cut dress. Her cinched waist in that short dress…

"What's changed?" she demands haughtily. "Is this about Michael? Because I already apologized for that and you have no right to be jealous."

My gaze clashes with hers on that final word.

Jealous.

"Why can't you just accept that he's good for me?" She says this while staring directly at my mouth. I'm not even sure she realizes she's doing it.

"Is he?"

She swallows and looks away. "He fits the mold I'm looking for."

"Mold?" I press. What the hell is she talking about?

"I have certain things I'm looking for. Standards, you could call them, for what I want in a boyfriend."

Her voice is so wobbly it's like she doesn't even buy this crock of shit herself. It's why she can't look at me.

"You mean it's easy to feel nothing for him? To be completely bored at the thought of him? Is that right?"

"Yes."

My short laugh his caustic and angry. "What are you so afraid of?"

She looks down briefly. "Luke—"

Oh god, she can't be serious.

"This isn't about Luke," I snap.

She lifts her sharp gaze.

"He's part of it," she argues, her eyes challenging me to tell her otherwise.

I want to call bullshit, but instead, I skirt around it.

"What else?"

"I don't date baseball guys."

"*What. Else.*"

God, does she really buy these excuses?

"Can't you just get it through your thick skull?" She

comes even closer on the bench. It'd be so easy to lean in and kiss her. She'd taste like that margarita she ordered. "I don't want you. You scare me. You make me feel everything. Every damn emotion, and not just the good ones. *The worst ones*—jealousy and rage. God, you bring it all out."

"*Good.*"

Those emotions? That's passion. That's something deep down inside—within our cells—recognizing what this is.

"Not good, Grant!" she argues, clenching her jaw. "I don't want that. I enjoy being in control. Ask my friends, they'll tell you. In school, I studied hard for my exams and earned straight As. With my running, I always, *always* keep to my schedule and my route. I never deviate from my training plans and there's a box filled with clinking half-marathon medals in my closet to show for it. I go to work where I complete the same tasks, check, check, check, done and done. There's no drama, no high highs, no low lows, and I *like* it that way."

"What a life." My tone drips with sarcasm, and her eyes narrow on me.

She leans in, seething. "How dare you judge me? You know what? You should have felt what I did walking in here and seeing that girl on your lap." She raises her chin, like her mind is already made up on this entire topic. "It told me everything I needed to know. I don't *ever* want to date someone like you. I don't want to constantly have to worry about how many women are lusting after my boyfriend, who he has sitting on his lap in clubs when he's out on the road week after week. *No thank you.*"

I know she's spinning this web, convincing herself of anything she can so she doesn't have to feel this thing growing between us, but she doesn't realize her words cut as sharp as knives.

I drain the last of my beer and then drop it on the table with a hard, finite *bang*. "Well damn, you have it all figured out, don't you? You've certainly made a lot of assumptions about me, and quite frankly...I'm glad you at least had the courage to voice them."

Her brows tug together with regret as she shakes her head. "You asked—"

"And you answered. Truthfully, for once. So now I get it. You're right. This thing"—I point between us—"it won't work. Understood."

A beat passes. She takes her bottom lip between her teeth, worrying. Then she peers over at me.

"We could be friends, you know," she says, her voice softening just a bit. "It doesn't have to be like this. So...explosive."

She's right. We're bickering like an old married couple. No, not even—more like two hormonal teenagers.

I want to stomp on her offer of friendship. If she can't figure out why we can't be friends just by looking at me, she's delusional. Surely she sees it. I'm not even trying to hide how I feel about her.

Maybe she feels like she can choose to put me up on a shelf in a nice tidy box labeled Friend. But to me, stowing away my feelings for her would be like fighting against gravity. Some things are just meant to be.

I grab my wallet and take out enough cash to cover everyone's drinks and then some. I drop it down on the center of the table and scoot around to leave the booth without making Tate get up.

"Grant..."

I don't turn around. We've said it all, haven't we?

It's settled. *Done.*

FOURTEEN

TATE

I CAN'T PRETEND Grant doesn't exist. I tried that, and I lasted all of three minutes before I thought of him again and my perfectly constructed *No Grant* world imploded on itself. So, my only option is to trudge forward and proceed with life as if everything is fine. For the next few days, I go through the motions, getting through each mundane task to the best of my abilities. I run my normal route, drink my standard coffee, work long shifts. I go out with Daphne and Sophia, and when we can't make it to the stadium, we watch the Pinstripes play from the comfort of our apartment. I accept a second and third date with Michael, and I feel totally in control of my life, good even—until I come face to face with Grant and my forward momentum comes to a screeching halt. It's only happened twice since the night in the club.

Once, after a game, I was about to go down onto the field with Harper and Chloe to see Luke, like usual. Grant was walking up the steps that lead from the dugout to the field, and for a split second, we were close enough I could have reached out and grabbed his hand. There was a physical ache when he turned and locked eyes with me. My lips parted as I racked my brain for something to say, some kind of magic word that could set us to rights, but then someone called his name. He stalled, giving me a chance to speak up, and when I didn't—*couldn't*—he walked away.

I bumped into him a second time a few days later. I was off work and eating lunch out with Sophia. Josh wanted to come say bye to her before he had to catch a flight with the team, and Grant happened to be with him. I certainly wasn't expecting to see him, or I would have changed out of my running clothes, given myself a blowout, maybe had a quick call with my therapist (aka Harper).

I saw Grant first through the glass windows and my heart soared, then quickly plummeted. It straight-up sank right down through my chest and stomach until I was sure I had a real ailment, a diagnosable malady.

I stared on—wonderstruck—as he strode in the door behind Josh, carrying the sunshine into the restaurant with him. His hands were tucked into the pockets of his jeans and his gaze was focused straight ahead. His expression was closed off and stoic. He was clearly in a bad mood that only worsened when he saw me. His step faltered, his expression tightened. Frustration took hold of every feature.

They came right up to our table and Sophia leapt up to greet them, kissing Josh and hugging Grant.

I rose shakily to my feet, assuming I too needed to act like a decent human being, but I shouldn't have bothered. Josh, of course, gave me a side hug and a warm smile, but Grant played it like I wasn't even there. He was going to look straight through me. No hi, no nothing. I was beginning to wonder if maybe we'd jumped into different dimensions. Like hello, you *can* see me, right?

His attitude got to me that day. I couldn't help myself.

"Hi, Grant," I said, convincing myself I was being the bigger person when in reality, I was trying to needle him a little bit. *I'm not perfect, okay?*

Grant *still* said nothing, just looked at Josh and shrugged as if to say, *What do you want from me, man?*

It got to be so awkward that Josh made a joke. "Grant, you remember Tate? The girl you won't shut up about?"

Oh god.

If he was trying to help the situation, he was going about it the exact wrong way. That was as helpful as dousing us both in kerosene and striking a match.

Grant's intimidating gaze finally fell on me, and my knees nearly gave out from underneath me.

"Tate. *Riiiight*," he said, rocking back on his heels. He had the audacity to narrow his eyes as if he was having a hard time placing me.

My hackles immediately went up. I wanted to wrap my hands around his neck and squeeze. I wanted to scrape my fingers down his chest. I wanted to pound my fists against him and and and…realization dawned then.

This is what I've been trying to avoid all along, this overwhelming response he draws out of me for better or worse. I've never met anyone in my entire life who had such possession of my good sense. Passion is all well and good, but it's scary too. I'm not trying to get hauled down to the police station on a random weekday afternoon just because I can't keep my hands to myself. *Can you imagine?*

So instead of engaging, I looked beyond him, over at Josh, and smiled my most winning smile—we're talking no-holds-barred, dimples and all—as I wished him good luck on the road.

"I hope you have a great time in Tampa." Then my gaze flicked to his *friend*. "Grant, you can go to hell."

Okay, so maybe I engaged a *little*.

And with that, I dutifully retook my seat, picked up my sandwich, and resumed eating as if I wasn't a hair's breadth away from crying.

That was last week. At this point, everyone in our group

has been thoroughly filled in on the situation. Sophia and Daphne know not to bring up Grant with me, which is good because everyone's coming over to the apartment tonight to hang out for the first time in a while. We're cooking dinner and doing the usual thing, only now, Michael's invited. I'm so excited I spent two hours wallowing on my bed this afternoon, near tears. Woo! *Yay!* That's normal, right?

It's actually so very annoying that Grant has the ability to make me feel like this without actually existing in my day-to-day life. It's not like I'm stalking him on Instagram (much) or purposefully seeking him out during the Pinstripes games (mostly), but he's still there in the periphery, *just* foreboding enough to make my life feel like a poorly constructed house of cards.

I mask all this worry with a killer outfit and some makeup. There is nothing a good lipstick shade can't fix. As Jay-Z would say, *Boy problems? I feel bad for you, son. I got 99 problems but a good Maybelline shade ain't one.*

I know Grant is coming tonight because I've talked about it with Sophia and Daphne. Sure he's newer to our friend group, but he's concretely become "one of the guys" now. And while it would be gentlemanly and kind and arguably the right thing to do, he isn't going to avoid coming around just to save me the trouble of having to see him.

Daphne doesn't even feel sorry for me.

"*Hello*, have you forgotten you're not the only one in this predicament? I have to be around Dustin all the time for the sake of the group. Suck it up, buttercup."

She has a point there…

Daphne and Dustin have existed in this friend group together since its inception, so maybe there's hope for me yet.

Tonight's menu consists of steak fajitas and all the toppings: queso, guacamole, pico de gallo. I'm leading the charge for once because growing up in Texas, I ate Mexican food once a week, *minimum*. I've had the meat marinating in the fridge since last night, and Chloe brought me some home-made tortillas earlier today because she's an actual angel.

I think I have a handle on most of dinner by the time the guys arrive. I don't leave my hideout in the kitchen as Daphne and Sophia play dutiful hosts. I listen though, trying to pick apart voices until I hear Grant speak up and greet them.

Goose bumps bloom *everywhere*.

I shake my shoulders and give myself a mini pep talk. So he's here. That's fine. I don't have time to care. I have a lot I still need to prep for dinner.

After I can avoid no longer, I walk out of the kitchen to say hi to everyone. They're all in the living room.

"Tate, it smells amazing in here," Dustin says, patting his stomach. "But should we be worried?" He looks to Daphne. "You're usually the cook. You're so good at it…"

Daphne doesn't fail to spin his compliment into an insult on my behalf. "Tate is more than capable of cooking."

"What are you making?" Josh asks.

"Fajitas with all the fixings."

"*Damn*, trying to impress Grant?" Nick asks.

There's an awkward moment of silence followed by a few forced laughs. I finally muster the courage to look at Grant where he stands near Josh. Never mind the way he looks in those jeans and that simple black t-shirt, the freaking injustice of him having bone structure *that* defined, eyes *that* sensual… I try to look at him like I do the rest of the guys, as a friend, and I'm glad to see he's not scowling at me today. He's chosen a neutral glower, and hey, I'll take it.

"Do you like fajitas or something?" I ask, my brows tugged together in confusion.

His expression eases, like he's almost about to smile, but he doesn't. "I'm half-Mexican so…*yeah*."

Sophia laughs. "Well perfect! Would you mind giving Tate a hand in the kitchen then?"

Every head in the room whips in her direction. She might as well have asked him to throw me over the balcony railing with the way we're all looking at her, horrified.

What the hell, Sophia?!

I shoot daggers at her then hurry back into the kitchen, knowing it's in my best interest not to hear all the reasons Grant will come up with to avoid being in my presence. Even if it's mundane, it'll still hurt.

I go back to adding lime juice to the guacamole, focusing extremely hard on my task, then Grant walks into the kitchen.

Air? *Poof.* Gone.

My nerves? Shot.

I clear my throat and force a swallow. "I'm not sure there's much for you to do..."

"What's this for?" he asks, ignoring me as he points to the vegetables still sitting in the colander in the sink. "Pico de gallo?"

I nod. "I haven't gotten to it yet."

"Is there cilantro?"

"In the fridge."

"Cutting board?"

So we're really going to do this? Confine ourselves to this small space?

I finally look at him, and I sound bone-weary when I speak up. "You don't have to help. I know you don't want to."

His eyes meet mine and there's a hard edge to the way he's looking at me, like he's in as much pain as I am.

"I wouldn't be in here if I didn't want to help," he says in a stern tone that sends a shiver of *something* down my spine.

Someone turns music on in the living room as Grant spots the other wooden cutting board resting against the back-splash in front of me. Instead of asking me to get it for him, he gets it himself, walking up behind me and so-very-nearly brushing against me as he does it. I hold stock-still, and he notices.

There's a soft chuckle. "Relax."

I puff out a breath like the suggestion is ludicrous. "Oh, easy for you to say!"

"What's that supposed to mean?"

"Don't act like things are normal between us. You hate me."

He rears back. "I absolutely *do not* hate you."

I release a disbelieving *pfft*. "Could have fooled me. The last two times we've been around each other it felt like we were about to come to blows! I really thought I was going to kill you in that deli."

Something in his expression breaks, like it pains him deeply to hear me say this. "I'm trying, Tate. I'm *fucking* trying as hard as I can here…"

The air whooshes out of my lungs like someone's just stabbed me.

I don't say a word. I can't. I'm rendered mute by his confession.

Tension builds, binding us so tightly we can't even move. Then finally, he blinks and shakes his head. "Let's just cook. Okay?"

I nod, knowing it's in my best interest to accept this temporary ceasefire he's proposing. I think we're both aware that this moment could go up in smoke in an instant if one of us gets provoked. We're like two warring mafiosos trying to break bread together, our armed henchmen hovering behind us with their rifles drawn.

I decide to see if we can't keep the good will going by striking up what I hope will turn out to be a polite conversation.

"I didn't know you were half-Mexican, though now I feel silly for not realizing. There's something about you…"

He arches a brow, encouraging me to continue.

"The tan. The dark hair. The sultry bedroom eyes."

"The *what*?" He laughs, and the sound feels so good. There's nothing better.

I smile. "Come on. Women have to tell you that all the time. We're all very jealous of those long dark eyelashes, by the way."

He shakes his head. "Believe it or not, *no*. I've never heard that before."

Right. Maybe other women aren't paying that much attention to his eyes. There are a lot of other things to admire about him, after all.

I turn back to my task as he takes a knife out of the knife block and starts slicing tomatoes for the pico. I half expect him to look like an amateur while he does it. I'm not sure how much time he's spent in a kitchen, but if anything, he's more adept at it than I am.

"You're from Arizona, right? Did you visit Mexico often while you were growing up?"

He shakes his head. "Never been, actually."

"*Seriously?*"

He seems amused that this would surprise me.

"I come from humble beginnings here in the States, though my dad's family in Mexico was pretty wealthy. He could have stayed and enjoyed that life, but he chose to come here and be with my mom instead. When he did that and left his family, they cut him off. There's a lot of bad blood there."

"Wow, that's…" I shake my head, not even knowing what to say. "How did he meet her? Your mom?"

"She was studying abroad in Mexico City, taking art and architecture courses. She went out to a bar one night with friends. My dad was there." He shrugs. "The rest is history. They fell in love fast and it never faded. Even after my mom passed away, my dad never so much as thought about remarrying. He sees no reason. The love of his life still lives." He taps his fingers over his heart as if to say, *Here*.

God, I hope everyone enjoys their guacamole with a side of tears. I can't imagine. My parents are devoted to each other too, but it's not like either of them had to choose their relationship over their families. That's quite a sacrifice.

"Do you speak any Spanish?"

"Nah, not really. I've learned some only because I've taught myself. My dad prefers if we speak English."

"Really? Why?"

"I'm not totally sure. I've never asked. I assume he just wanted me to fit in and settle here in a way maybe he never really could." He narrows his eyes as if mulling this over. "His name is Javier, and he still has a pretty thick accent. It hasn't always been easy for him. It's probably why he named me Grant, after my American grandfather."

"But your last name is Navarro," I point out with a smile. "So you at least have that. And it's a great last name by the way. I love the way the announcer says it at the stadium."

He laughs. "Yeah? Hopefully my future wife feels the same way about it."

Oof. Why does that hurt?

I pretend all is well as I ask, "How long has it just been you and your dad? You mentioned your mom passed away—"

The door to the apartment opens then and I hear Michael's voice over the hum of music and conversation in the living room.

Michael.

Oh no.

I was expecting him tonight, but well…quite frankly, for the last few minutes I completely forgot all about him.

"Michael, hey!" Sophia and Daphne greet him, but it's crickets from the guys.

"Hey, everyone. What's up? Is, uh…is Tate here?"

Someone must lead him this way, letting him know where

to find me, because he appears in the small doorway of the kitchen holding a bouquet of flowers.

He always comes bearing gifts before our dates: flowers, chocolates, all the stereotypical sweet things. It's thoughtful, but right now I can't smile. Hell, I can barely breathe.

The way the tiny kitchen is laid out, Michael can't get to me, and I can't get to him so long as Grant stands between us. And Grant doesn't get out of the way. In fact, he turns and blocks me so he can look at Michael, no doubt assessing him and his flowers with a highly visible scowl. It's suddenly too hot in here.

Michael leans to the side so he can see me past Grant's shoulders, and he smiles.

"Hey, Tate," he says, cheery and oblivious. Then he reluctantly looks at Grant. "Good to see you." Which I think is big of him considering their last encounter at the stadium was awkward to say the least.

Oh my god. Get me out of here. We're all crammed together in like five square feet of space (thank you, New York City), and though I've never been claustrophobic in my life, I'm currently headed that way.

Michael shakes the flowers and Grant slowly looks back at me as if waiting for something, but I can't decipher what he wants me to do quickly enough and then he's already on the move, setting his knife on the cutting board and sliding past Michael. I swear the air crackles between them as Grant brushes his shoulder with no apology. They're total opposites, a warm front and cold front meeting and wreaking havoc in the sky, with me down below, a peon holding an inverted umbrella whipping in the wind.

"Nice guy," Michael says with a laugh.

I almost, *almost* tell him off. Which is absurd because he's only trying to cut the tension.

Grant *is* a nice guy. Only, not to Michael.

What a mess.

"Got a vase for these?" Michael asks, holding the daisies out for me.

I'm slightly annoyed. The flowers are a nice gesture, they really are, but it's also mildly irritating because we keep the few vases we have in the cabinet over the fridge and to get them I need to retrieve the step ladder from the hall closet and I can't do that because I'm in the middle of cooking dinner for a big group of people, and I don't even really *like* daisies all that much but Michael's never bothered to ask me that so here we are.

I force a smile. "Why don't we just put them in a water glass for now?"

"Really?" he asks, frowning a bit. It's like he's disappointed I'm not tripping over myself to arrange the bouquet this very second.

"Yes. I can't get a vase right now."

"Oh okay."

I know I'm not being fair to Michael. I would absolutely cut him free if I were only using him as a pawn to make Grant jealous, but that's not it at all. I genuinely like him. The more I get to know him, the more I think he and I could have a real chance together. He kissed me the other night. A gentle kiss right in the middle of dinner. It was a little cheesy. I had pizza sauce on my lips and he was trying to tell me where it was so I could wipe it off. We were laughing and being silly and the next thing I knew he was leaning across the table and kissing me. Simple, lighthearted, fun. Every one of our dates leaves me feeling content.

Isn't that all that matters?

I could safeguard our relationship and not bring him around everyone, but that won't work in the long run. I'm not avoiding my friend group just because of Grant. He doesn't get to take a wrecking ball to my life. These are *my* friends too.

So Michael stays, and his flowers go into a water glass. I

finish the pico de gallo *and* the guacamole and I pray the whole time that I'm doing this meal justice now that Grant's going to eat it. I want to finish our conversation. I want to know more about his family, his life.

When dinner is ready, everyone piles their plates with food and I hold my breath, carefully surveying them as they take their first bites.

At the first audible *mmm,* I exhale a relieved sigh. The knot of tension in my stomach eases slightly, but it doesn't go away altogether. I don't think it'll ever go away as long as Grant is in my vicinity.

"It's so good," Sophia says through a mouthful of food.

"The steak especially," Josh adds. "I like the marinade you used."

Nick shoots me two enthusiastic thumbs up, which in this apartment is as good as getting an "Extraordinary" rating in the *New York Times'* Dining section.

I peer over at Grant. He's sitting across the room from me on the floor, the same spot where we sat together the first night he was here. It's not that I want him to wax poetic about the meal (I do), but even some small sign that he deems it edible would be nice. When he catches me watching him as he brings his fajita to his mouth for a second bite, he winks.

It's so subtle and so fast I doubt it happened the moment it's over.

I flush like he just stood up and screamed aloud to everyone, THIS IS THE BEST MEAL I'VE EVER EATEN.

Oh lord.

Get a grip!

Right. Good. I'm glad he likes it and, at the moment, I'm not going to delve into the reasons why his opinion matters more than everyone else's, including Michael's.

"It's great, babe," he says from beside me.

Babe.

That's a new development.

I've never been a "babe" person, but that's okay. I could *become* a babe person. And so what if it makes me think of the "Dinner Party" episode from *The Office* when Jan and Michael use the endearment incessantly. This is different. This is *my* Michael saying it.

"*Babe?*" Daphne mouths to me from the other end of the couch.

I shake my head to let her know to drop it.

The meal goes surprisingly well. There's nothing left by the time everyone has had seconds. We bought ice cream for dessert, but no one has room for it now, so we sit around, nursing our drinks as we talk. Well, everyone else talks. Grant, Michael, and I purposely stay quiet. Michael, because he's brand new to the group and likely just feeling everyone out. Me, because I'm barely following the thread of conversation. And Grant...well, who knows what Grant is thinking. That wink really threw me. Is it a peace offering? A way forward for us?

I so desperately want to get to a good place with him, I really do, right up until I see Dustin lean over to hold up his phone so Grant can read something on the screen.

"Lizzy and her friends just sent that," Dustin says with a proud smile. "They're at a bar not far from here. Should we go?"

How rude! If you have something to share, share it with the whole class, *Dustin*. Maybe we *all* want to go to the bar with Lizzy and her fun friends!

Grant doesn't even hesitate. He nods and pushes to stand, and every single bite of the dinner I just ate turns to stone in my stomach. They're going to go meet them. Grant's going to leave so he can go flirt with Lizzy, beautiful Lizzy, stylish Lizzy. She's probably a genius too. I imagine she's like a civil rights attorney or something equally as impressive because I'm already drowning so why not make it just a *little* bit worse for myself?

Before they leave, Grant and Dustin collect dirty dishes and cart them into the kitchen. The two of them get to work in there cleaning, and I'm nearly fuming. How dare Grant make it less easy to hate him?

Run off to Lizzy, already! Scram.

Once they're done, they stroll back out into the living room, but I can't even look up at them.

"We're heading out," Dustin says. "Kitchen's spotless. Just the way you like it, Daphne."

She hums but ignores him, texting away on her phone like he's not even worth a moment of her time. I wish I could be like that with Grant.

"Where are you going?" Nick asks, offended that he's not included even though up until now, he's been fully splayed out on the floor groaning about how full he is. He has a throw pillow under his head and a second ago, he asked Sophia to toss him his favorite fuzzy blanket. He's full-on cocooning down there.

"To a bar," Dustin supplies.

Nick doesn't move. "Count me out, boys." Then he salutes them on their way to the door. "Don't worry about me! I'm all set here!"

They totally ignore him.

"Really, wouldn't want you guys to stay back on my account!" he calls out. "Tell the girls I'm sorry. I know they'll be asking about me!" Once they leave, he turns toward us. "Well…what should we do now? You guys want to play strip poker?"

FIFTEEN

TATE

I'M NOT REALLY FEELING like myself lately. Something's off. Last night, I was watching TV and a commercial played where a war veteran returned home to be reunited with her golden retriever. When the soldier bent down to pet him, she realized he was surprising her with a Le Vian chocolate diamond necklace, which he was wearing around his neck like a collar. Never mind the logistics of a dog purchasing fine jewelry. I'm tearing up right now just thinking about the moment she wrapped her arms around his furry neck and in return, he rested his paw on her shoulder. So tender! So poetic! Daphne had to wrestle the TV remote out of my hand and hide it from me after that. She's totally fed up, not just with me, but with Sophia too.

Sophia thinks something is going on with Josh. It started a few weeks ago with him starting to distance himself from her a little bit, but she brought it up again last night.

"I feel like he was rushing me off the phone last night."

Daphne didn't see the problem. "So? Big deal."

"*Big deal?* We're in love! We want to spend every second of every day talking to each other!"

"Blech. You need a hobby."

"You're not helping!"

This is when I chimed in from my dramatic supine position on the couch. Half my body hung off, draped onto the floor. I was staring off into space, damn near catatonic. "He's probably going to dump you," I said, completely monotone.

The two sisters looked at me like, *Really? That's your advice right now?*

I followed it up with, "You might as well break up with him before he breaks up with you because love is a sham anyway. Has anyone heard from Dustin about that Lizzy girl? I can't find her on Instagram…"

"Enough about Lizzy!" Daphne groaned. "Stop moping around and go clean something! Cleaning always makes you feel better. And Sophia? Get out of your head. Josh is insanely in love with you. God, what is it with you two?"

What is it with me?

Who knows.

Today, I'm on aunt duty, and it's for the best. I need a little one-on-one time with Harper. It's a Monday, but her school is closed for a random teacher in-service day. Luke's with the team in Toronto, and Chloe's trying to carve out a bit of time to work on a business she's growing: a pop-up bakery in the Hamptons. My future sister-in-law is a badass. She's about to marry Luke, who basically has more money than Mark Zuckerberg. She could be lying on some exotic beach sipping mai tais and role-playing *White Lotus*, but here she is, working her butt off.

I told her this when I picked up Harper earlier.

"I just want to say I'm so proud of you."

She frowned. "Okay…"

"You're such an inspiration."

"You're hurting me."

I *was* hugging her extremely tightly, so I eased up a little bit.

"It's going to be so fun to be sisters."

She pried me off her then, holding me at arm's length and adding a little shake for emphasis. "Are you losing it? What's going on? You're never like this. Did you forget to run this morning?"

"No, I took the exact same route as always, didn't veer off track once."

Harper came barreling into the room with her red heart-shaped sunglasses already in place. "Ready to go, Aunt Tate?!"

Harper and I thrive when we're alone together in the city. We go on a shopping spree at the toy store, and I let her pick out a Barbie because it gives me endless amounts of joy to both let Harper have whatever she wants and to piss my brother off in one fell swoop. *She's spoiled enough as is, Chloe!* Never.

Then we go to a bookstore and a candy shop, stop off at McDonald's for lunch, and while we're on our way to the Central Park Zoo in the afternoon, we pass a hair and makeup boutique. Peering through the window, I see the shop owner—an older woman—drumming her fingers on her desk, waiting for customers, and I feel bad so I ask Harper if she wants to get a makeover.

Now, we sit in front of the snow monkey enclosure sharing a bag of cotton candy in full hair and makeup. I can't describe the way we look except to say JCPenney would be tripping over themselves to book us for one of their early '90s catalogues. There is so much blue eyeshadow caked on my eyelids I'm surprised I still have 20/20 vision. So much industrial-strength hairspray is layered onto my locks I barely have the strength to lift my head.

We scared a small child who walked in front of us a second ago. I worry he thought we were clowns. Harper thinks we look amazing though, like one of her Barbies, so whatever.

"Pass the cotton candy," I say, pointing to the bag she's going to town on.

She hands it over and keeps swinging her legs back and forth beneath the bench, looking at the snow monkeys. They're kind of cute, I guess. Sort of like baboons but with a thick winter coat.

"Why are you sad today?"

Her question takes me aback.

I've got a mouthful of pink sugary goodness. I swallow it down and insist, "I'm not sad."

"Oh, maybe I was wrong."

She shrugs and accepts the cotton candy bag as I hold it out to her again. The fact that she doesn't press the issue means I feel like *I* have to.

"Do I seem sad?"

"Yeah, I mean you've barely said two words all day."

Crap. I thought I was being fun. Have I been quiet?

"I'm just…"

I'm about to feed her total bullshit because why not? She's eight. But then I pivot and just go for it.

"I'm having boy problems."

She furrows her brows. "Like a boy is being mean to you? You should tell Dad. I bet he'd punch him for you."

Noted.

"No, not like that. This is more like love problems."

She nods soberly as if she understands completely. "Love is really hard." She speaks like she's a hardened veteran of the dating and relationship world. "Back in winter, I sorta had a boyfriend."

This absolutely shocks me, but I try not to show it. I don't want to spook her into clamming up, so I just give an ol' nonchalant "Oh yeah?"

"Yes, Eugene. He's really cute and so popular."

"Eugene, huh?"

Woof.

"Yeah, anyway, we were getting pretty serious."

"In what way?"

Dear god, I hold my breath for what she's about to say.

"Like he would walk me to lunch *every* day."

I make a noise of understanding. "I see."

"And he wouldn't let anyone else play with me at recess. It had to be just us two."

Sounds like Eugene needs to back off.

"Anyway, the thing is, the entire time I was with Eugene, I actually had a crush on a boy named Corey." She sighs. "It's complicated. Corey used to be kind of mean to me. To everyone, really. But it's because his parents were going through a divorce."

I'm sorry, is the kid sitting beside me 8 or 48?

"So what happened?"

"Oh, I dumped Eugene and now Corey is my boyfriend. We're in love."

"Does he let you play with your friends at recess?"

"Of course. There's a whole group of us. We play tag or hide and seek almost every day. Corey's the best."

"Do you guys like...hold hands or anything?" I ask, wondering how far adolescent love goes these days.

Harper scrunches up her face, absolutely disgusted by this idea. "*Ew*, no."

Phew, good. I wasn't sure if I was going to have to give some watered-down version of the birds and the bees talk right here in the zoo. *Harper, you see how that male monkey is like really interested in jumping on the back of that female monkey? Well guess what...*

"So anyway," she continues, "I can give pretty good advice. I'm really smart about this stuff."

I don't say anything. Instead, I watch the snow monkeys groom each other.

She bumps her shoulder against mine. "Is it about Michael? Because I don't think you really love him."

My eyes widen in alarm. "What makes you say that?"

"Because...I don't know. Just little stuff I see. Like okay, that one time we went to lunch with you guys, we were standing in line to order at the deli counter and he tried to wrap his arm around you and you moved away before he could."

I don't even remember that.

"I must not have realized he was trying to do that. I was probably having a hard time deciding what sandwich I wanted to order."

This is a lie, of course. I order the same thing every time I go to that deli.

She frowns. "No. You order the same thing every time we're there."

Dammit. She's smart.

"You do that everywhere we go. You like things the same, always. Dad says you're borderline OPD."

I think she means OCD, which like, okay...the shoe fits, but STILL.

She perks up and turns halfway toward me as she remembers something else. "*And* you also didn't laugh at his joke later when we were eating. It was something silly, I can't remember it, but it made me laugh and I looked at you and you weren't even paying attention. You were staring out the window."

God, now I feel bad. Have I really been that checked out lately?

I sigh, feeling sadder. "You done with that?"

She hands me the remnants of the cotton candy and I tip the bag into my mouth, reveling in the last few morsels of sweetness.

"Maybe you're in love with someone else?" Harper says, all innocent and naive.

WHAT. A cotton candy cloud gets lodged in my throat. Once I hack until I think I've dislodged a rib, I crush that plastic bag between my hands like I want it to die a painful death and then I stuff it into a trash can nearby.

"Nope, that's definitely not it." I stand. "You ready to go?"

That night, Sophia and Daphne set up shop to watch the Pinstripes away game in the living room, but I beg off with an excuse about being tired. I slink into my room where I end up watching the game on my laptop in bed. I don't know why I do it. Maybe I just don't want to deal with more prying questions. Maybe I want to sulk in peace. Maybe my head hurts from scrubbing off all that hairspray. Who knows?

Grant plays well—he gets a line-drive triple in the fourth inning and a great double play in the eighth—but even still, the Pinstripes barely come out on top. During postgame press, the reporters ask Grant the usual questions and the camera zooms in on his face. I study him in a way I'm never able to in real life, with unblinking, unflinching interest. The bead of sweat trickling down his cheek must be a paid actor at this point. The stadium lighting shines so beautifully on him. There's stubble on his jaw, which he usually shaves, but I like it. Of course I like it.

Since the live feed I'm watching lets me pause and rewind, when his interview is over, I treat myself to a rewatch, lying back on my pillow, closing my eyes, and listening to the heady cadence of his voice.

In the morning, I wake up, roll over onto my side, and stare out at the street with the full realization that it's time. I need to be honest with Michael about my feelings.

He texted me last night, wanting to hang out, and I blew him off. That's not nice. *I'm* not being nice. However long it took me, I'm at least aware of that now.

Ending this brief relationship is not something I want to do over the phone, and though I'm aware that work is the *last* place to have this conversation, it feels paramount. We need to talk. Now. I can't keep dragging this out. It's not fair to Michael.

In the hospital, I look for him out in the central hallway of the ICU, but he's not there. My phone buzzes in the pocket of my scrub pants with an incoming text, but I ignore it. I can't get sidetracked.

Finally, I find Michael in an office some of the mid-level providers use. Thankfully, he's the only one there now, typing at his computer when I knock on the open door.

He looks up and smiles. "*Hey*, Tate. I was wondering if I'd see you today."

I nod. "Surprised you're here already."

"I had some notes to catch up on and I don't want to have to stay late."

He pushes out a chair nearby him in invitation. After I walk in, I tug the door closed behind me so our voices won't be so easily heard by passersby out in the hall.

"How was your night?" he asks.

His light tone belies a slight annoyance in his expression.

"It was fine. Turned in early. Sorry we didn't end up hanging out."

"No, it's all good. I know it's not always easy, especially the night before you work."

I look down and realize I've been attacking the cuticle on my thumbnail. I force my hands apart and smooth them down my thighs. "Actually, it's kind of more than just that…"

Oh god, here goes.

"Michael…I'm a little confused at the moment."

His forehead wrinkles. "Confused?"

"About how I'm feeling with things, I mean. I like you, I do. I just…I'm kind of in a weird place in my life right now."

"Okay."

He says the word slowly like he's having a hard time keeping up. It's understandable. To him, it probably feels like this is coming out of nowhere.

"I don't want to waste your time." I rush to continue, "I

know we've never said we're exclusive or anything, but still…"

He shakes his head. "No, yeah, I get it."

"I just don't want us to be on different pages here. Maybe it's better if we put things on pause for now?"

I know I'm not using forceful enough language. I know some people would march in here and say, *Hey Michael, yeah, buddy, it's over.* But he's been nothing but kind to me, and I don't relish the idea of trampling all over his feelings.

"I totally get it," Michael says with a wistful smile. "Honestly, I'm kind of there too, myself."

"Yeah?" My tone brims with relief. I haven't noticed him pulling back, but quite frankly, I've been a *little* self-absorbed lately.

Just then, my phone buzzes again in my pocket. Whoever's texting me is being annoyingly persistent. It's probably Daphne and Sophia; they get carried away sometimes. I ignore it and keep my gaze on Michael as he nods.

"This whole dating thing is a little weird for me after coming out of such a serious relationship. I get where you're coming from."

I feel like a huge weight's been lifted off my shoulders. I'm about to tell him I appreciate how nice he's being about all of this, but then the office door opens. Michael and I aren't sitting overly close to each other or even remotely in a compromising position, but still, I lean back slightly to put a little more distance between us as one of Michael's colleagues walks in.

I push to stand, not quite sure how to end this. Michael gives me a thumbs-up because it's not like we can keep the conversation rolling now that we have company. I give him a nod and a last, appreciative smile.

As I leave, I get yet another text, and finally, I tug my phone out of my pocket to find that it's actually Chloe and Luke blowing up my phone this morning.

Chloe: Tate! Any chance you're free tomorrow night? I was supposed to go with Luke to this fundraiser, but I just realized Harper has a dress rehearsal for her spring ballet concert and I have to be there with her! It's mandatory! Also…she'd kill me if I missed it.

Then my brother responded.

Luke: Tate, come on, be my date. I promise I won't stomp on your feet too much on the dance floor. And hey, you can go to Bergdorf's and pick out any dress you want.

Chloe: Say yes, say yes! Please!

Tate: Hmm…what about shoes?

I'm just being silly, but then Luke responds right away.

Luke: Get those too.

I laugh as I shake my head. My brother is absolutely crazy.

Tate: I was kidding! Besides, I don't have time to shop between now and then. I work a twelve-hour shift today and tomorrow.

Chloe: Leave it to me then. I know your sizes. I'll have a few things sent over to your apartment that you can pick from.

What?! *No!*

Tate: Luke, I'm happy to join. It'll be fun. We can snap a picture and send it to Mom and Dad. They'll love to see us all dolled up. Chloe, you're so sweet, but no need to send stuff over, I promise. I have a black dress that should work just fine!

I get home from work close to 7:30 PM that night, and I go to push the front door open only to find it won't go all the way in. There's something blocking it from the other side.

I push harder and squeeze through the small gap just as I call out, "Uhhh...guys? What's—"

There's no need to finish my question about what's blocking the door. It's a huge clothing rack set up in the hallway that leads from our minuscule foyer into our minuscule living room with no less than a dozen dresses hanging in individual garment bags. Shoe boxes are stacked up underneath, enough that they're overflowing everywhere into the apartment. I recognize the designer names—Louboutin, Jimmy Choo, Manolo Blahnik—but I've never owned a pair of any of them. The dependable high heels I have in my closet are all from DSW or Macy's.

Sophia leaps off the couch and calls out, "Daphne! She's here!"

"NO! DO NOT LET HER START WITHOUT ME!" Daphne shouts frantically from her room. A second later, she flings the door open and comes flying out in a towel with soap suds slipping down her hair and face. She's still clutching her razor in her right hand.

I laugh as I slide my hospital bag off my shoulders. "Relax. I just got home. I'm not starting anything."

"What is all this stuff?!" Sophia asks, going over to flip through the garment bags.

"I mean we know *what* it is..." Daphne admits. "We looked through everything already, obviously. But why did some *Devil Wears Prada* fashionista drop this stuff off for you earlier?"

"Yeah, are you like rich now?" Sophia asks like this is a serious inquiry.

Daphne chimes in again, her mouth gaping with shock. "Oh god! It just now occurred to me. I know what this is— you signed a sex contract with a billionaire, didn't you? And now he's going to like take over your life and control how you dress and do weird stuff. I read a book like that once."

Sophia levels Daphne with an unamused glare. "*Once?* Your Kindle is riddled with variations of that same story."

Daphne smiles and shoots her a wink. "What can I say…I enjoy a good billionaire kink fest."

Oh good grief.

"The dresses and shoes are from Luke."

They're both crestfallen at this news.

"Ugh, your brother?" Daphne's shoulders slump. "That's so boring."

I roll my eyes. "I'm doing him a favor and going with him to a fundraiser tomorrow night. He told me to get a dress, but I don't have time to go shopping between now and then, so Chloe had all this stuff sent over so I could pick something to wear."

"God, I wish I had a cool sister like that."

Sophia tosses her hands up. "I'm right *here*."

"Oh sorry. You're great. I just meant hypothetically."

I laugh on my way toward the kitchen, in need of dinner, stat.

"Wait!" Sophia leans off the couch. "Aren't you going to look at the stuff?! We want a fashion show!"

"Yeah, we've already taken inventory and there's a silver dress that would look *amazing* on you. Though we would also accept the strapless blue one."

I look back over my shoulder at them. "Okay, well Daphne, you're currently dripping water on the floor and you still have conditioner in your hair, so why don't I get some food while you finish your shower and then after, we'll decide what I'll wear tomorrow. Deal?"

"*Deal!*"

SIXTEEN
GRANT

I'M ADMITTEDLY NOT a tuxedo guy. I've spent most of my life in baseball uniforms and workout clothes. This tuxedo fits like a glove though, which isn't shocking considering I had it custom-made. Dustin pressured me into it. A month ago, he took me to a tailor in the city.

"He's *my* guy," he said like some hotshot.

I thought I was going to walk out with the tuxedo *that* day.

When I told him this, Dustin looked at me like I'd just hobbled out of a trailer park. "No, you swine. He's taking your measurements today. That's it. Where did you grow up again?"

I shot him my middle finger. "In a one-bedroom apartment with a *mechanic* for a dad. I don't think I'd even *seen* a tuxedo until I was an adult."

"Don't pull that 'woe is me' crap. You've made plenty of money for plenty of years. I know, because so have I. Didn't you need a tuxedo when you were playing down in Miami?"

I shrugged. "I just rented them."

You would have thought I'd just admitted to killing his beloved family pet with the way he looked at me.

"Well *now* you'll never want to rent again. Today, this guy will take your measurements for a custom tuxedo and a few suits. You can tell him what colors you like, but he'll end up choosing the fabric and cut. Just roll with it. He's a magician."

"How much is this going to run me?" I asked right before we pulled open the shop door.

He just laughed. "You don't want to know. Close your eyes when you sign the bill."

At the time, I wanted to deck him for forcing me to shell out so much money for something I'm going to wear once, *maybe* twice a year.

Now, as I walk up the steps of the New York Public Library to attend this gala, I've changed my tune. Not to toot my own horn, but I look sharp as hell, like James Bond but with a Latin flair.

Dustin nods in my direction. "If I were a chick, I'd take you home."

I laugh. "I like your tux too."

I opted for traditional black, which is lucky for me because the tailor wouldn't have it any other way. Something about my complexion. Dustin switched it up with a white tuxedo jacket paired with black pants and a black pocket square.

We get stopped by photographers on the red carpet on our way into the fundraiser. It's new for me. In Miami, I kept my head down and focused on my game. Part of that had to do with being a rookie still finding my footing in the majors, young and truly on my own for the first time. Also though, the limelight isn't really for me.

"You think Lizzy's mad you didn't bring her tonight?"

His question surprises me. "Why would she care?"

"She seemed pretty into you at the bar the other night."

He's talking about the night we left Tate's apartment together. The night I had to watch Tate sit next to Michael and, instead of doing anything about it, just had to eat my dinner like a good little boy. I was dying inside. Leaving with

Dustin was the smartest thing I could have done. The evening wasn't going to end well if I stayed.

"She's nice."

"*And?*"

I smooth down my jacket. "I don't usually bring dates with me to things like this. You know how it gets when you bring someone into the public eye like that."

"Yeah, speaking of…they got pictures of us leaving the bar the other night. My publicist sent them to me."

I saw them too. So did my dad.

I can still hear his annoyance when he brought it up. "*You better keep focused. Don't let New York distract you from your game.*" New York was a euphemism for women, drugs, drinking, partying—his worst fear is that I'll lose sight of what's important.

The pictures were innocent enough, just a group of friends leaving a bar together. I wasn't even standing by Lizzy. Dustin and I were in the middle laughing about something, though Dustin was smart enough to keep his head down. I just looked like a wide-eyed Bambi. No one really ran with the story though, just a few online gossip blogs that cover professional athletes.

We reach the top of the stairs and get swept into the ensuing madness of the event. I might not know many people here, but they certainly know me. Last year, the Pinstripes narrowly missed their opportunity to make it to the World Series. I'm the only new addition to the team, and we've gone uncontested so far this season. The city has definitely taken notice. I've seen some of the headlines about me, but I try not to think about it too much. It can get too overwhelming if I'm not careful.

Eager attendees come up to shake hands with Dustin and me, congratulating us on the start of the season, on my introduction with the Pinstripes, anything to keep the conversation going. A few of them ask for photos, and we oblige.

Eventually, we all gather in the foyer of the library where the overhead lights have been replaced with huge candelabras. A man steps forward on the second-floor landing with a microphone to welcome us to the Hope Gala, an annual fundraiser held in conjunction with the New York Public Library and New York City Public Schools to raise critical funds to support the city's mission to inspire lifelong learning, advance knowledge, and strengthen communities.

Musicians start to play on the periphery of the room, and Tony encourages us to follow the orchestra upstairs to gather in the Rose Main Reading Room for the dinner and program.

"There's Luke," Dustin says, pointing ahead of us. "Oh, cool. I didn't realize Tate would be here too."

Her name is spellbinding. It stiffens my shoulders and stops me dead in my tracks. I look for her in the crowd with the intensity of a dying man searching for water in the desert. There, she's walking ahead of us, alongside her brother and another man. For a second, I suspect it's Michael, but then he turns to address someone else and I'm proven wrong. Thank god.

"Luke!" Dustin calls out to our teammate.

I curse under my breath as he and Tate both turn in our direction. Luke smiles, but she goes completely still. She's shocked to see me here. Nervous too, by the looks of it.

I take her in from head to toe, and quite frankly, I'm surprised Luke let her out of the house in that dress.

Her silver sequined gown is tight from her shoulders down to her hips. Even then, it only flares slightly, just enough that she can walk without having to shuffle one inch at a time. The deep V neckline sits snugly across her chest. Her hair is swept back in a twist, and her shimmering earrings dangle down on either side of her slender neck. I'm left looking back and forth between her red lips—the only pop of color on her—and the slit that peels up her right thigh when she moves to say something to her brother.

Dustin looks over at me and raises his eyebrows. "Guess we won't be friendless losers here after all. C'mon." He hurries to catch up to them, leaving me as the last straggler.

Luke claps his hand on my shoulder when I reach them. "Good to see you, Grant."

"Hey, Luke."

Of all the guys on the team, I know Luke the least. He's slightly older than us, engaged, and a father. He's at a totally different point in his life than I am. When we're playing in the city, he wants to be with his family. When we're on the road, he wants to be focused on the game or back at the hotel, resting up and FaceTiming Chloe and Harper. It doesn't leave a lot of wiggle room for team bonding, which is why I still feel slightly nervous around him. This is the guy I cheered on from my dorm room in college. A legend in the sport. Someone I hope to be in a few years.

Oh, right, *and* I want to sleep with his sister. There's that minor detail to contend with…

"You know Tate, right?" Luke asks. Before either of us can answer, he continues, "Of course. Yeah, I saw you two talking at a game a while back. Remind me, did you meet through Josh and Dustin?"

Am I reading too much into it or is there a sharpness in his voice? I don't know. Maybe I'm only imagining it.

"No. *Actually*, we met at a party," Tate says, lifting a taunting brow.

I'm surprised my jaw doesn't drop. Is she about to…

"Grant came with Josh and the guys, but I didn't realize that." Her hazel eyes scold me playfully as she continues, "He let me think he was just a normal guy the whole night when *really* he was the Pinstripes' newest hotshot."

Dustin laughs. "See, I'm still confused by that. Didn't you recognize him?"

Tate shrugs. "Somehow…no."

Luke smiles as his gaze shifts to the attendees surrounding

us. "We're blocking traffic. C'mon, Tate, let's find our table. You guys should be near us. In fact, I'd be surprised if they didn't seat us all together."

He's right. The event organizers placed us all at a table in the center of the room, right in front of the stage. Everyone claims their seats and I'm left between Tate and Dustin, which seems like a recipe for disaster.

Tate sits down, and that provocative slit rides up her thigh —nearly too high—before I help tuck her chair in.

"Is that good?" I ask, wanting to make sure she's comfortable.

"Perfect."

Luke nods in thanks, likely because he was about to do the same thing himself.

"You have any sisters, Grant?" he asks as I take my seat.

"I wish. I'm an only child," I tell him as I adjust my tuxedo jacket.

"Where's your family?"

"My dad is in Phoenix."

He nods in understanding. "Did he play ball?"

"He played as a kid back in Mexico then some as an adult."

Luke's brows shoot up.

"Not like what you're thinking," I correct with a chuckle. "There are adult rec leagues where I live, guys who get together on Sundays and play. Nothing serious."

"He must be so proud of you," Tate cuts in with a warm smile.

I don't have to wonder. I hear it after every game. I feel it every time I round those bases and claim a run for my team. It's all because of the sacrifices he made for me.

Waiters come around to fill our wine glasses.

Luke teases his sister. "I like the dress you picked. Clearly, you weren't going for subtlety. You almost look like you're back in your pageant days. Mom would be proud."

"Pageant?" I ask, butting in.

It's hard to imagine. Even now, done up to the nines, Tate doesn't seem like the beauty queen type. I don't know why, exactly. She's beautiful enough to participate in that world, sure, but I just can't see her prancing around on a stage like that.

Tate blushes. "Yes, if you can believe it, I competed in pageants for almost a decade. Just little shows around Texas."

Luke grins. "Tate was Miss Teen Texas. Don't let her fool you."

Tate covers her face with her napkin for a moment like she couldn't be more embarrassed if she tried. Then she peers out from behind the cream linen. "It was my mom's passion. I went along with it because I was her only daughter and..." She shrugs as she replaces the napkin on her lap. "I was pretty good at it, but it was never my thing."

"What *was* your thing?"

She frowns, confused by the question.

I smile, letting her know it's not that serious; this isn't a job interview.

"Does getting carted around to my brother's baseball tournaments count as a hobby? I did love watching him play." She looks over at Luke and winks. "Still do, actually."

He laughs. "You were good at everything you tried, Tate. Dance, cheer, baseball. I guess you picked up running in high school too, right?"

She nods. "True, but I've never competed in that, short of a few half-marathons."

"It's probably better that way," I assure her.

"I agree. I can get...*competitive.*"

"Oh really?"

Luke pipes up, looking at his sister. "It's totally obvious to anyone who's ever been around you for half a second that you play to win in everything you do."

She bumps her shoulder into his and narrows her eyes playfully. "*Watch it.*"

An announcer states that the dinner program will be starting soon, and Luke stands and excuses himself to use the restroom. Dustin's enthralled in conversation with the woman on his right, which means Tate and I are left to our own devices.

I don't want to look at her, but I can't help it.

She lifts her wine glass to her lips and sips, smiling as she does it.

"Stop staring at me," she chides teasingly.

I can't.

She's stunning. Every detail is worth memorizing. The little hollow above her collarbones. The thin sparkly straps sliding over her smooth shoulders. Her red lips.

"You look beautiful."

She closes her eyes, briefly reveling in my words, then she sets down her glass.

I like this. I like being able to tell her exactly how I feel. We got off on the wrong foot. All the stuff with Michael...the jealousy...

"Well, I'd be lying if I didn't say the same. You wear a tuxedo impossibly well. It should be criminal." I grin, and she groans. "Don't do that. It's worse with the dimples."

I try to flatten my mouth into a stern line, but I don't succeed.

"Would you believe this is my first tuxedo?"

Her eyebrows shoot up like she finds that hard to believe. "Well it won't be your last. Designers will see photos of you tonight and clamber over themselves to dress you for your next gala. Tom Ford will be beating down your door, you watch."

"Yeah?" I hum, sort of disinterested in the idea. "I don't care about any of that."

She peers over at me thoughtfully, too long even. I almost can't resist the urge to shift in my chair.

Then she says, simply, "Well, even still, you should send a photo to your dad. Make sure he sees how handsome you look. Do you take after him?"

"Some, yes. He's not quite as tall."

"Do you have to look at my mouth while you're talking?"

I force my gaze up to her eyes. "I can't help it. What shade is that?"

She lifts a shoulder. "How should I know? Some delicious shade of red judging by that gleam in your eyes."

"How's Michael?"

She swallows and looks away, and it's as if a partition has gone up between us. "I don't want to talk about Michael."

"*Michael?*" Luke asks, reclaiming his seat at the table.

Tate huffs in annoyance. "No. Forget it. I won't let the two of you gang up on me."

Luke looks at me with a mischievous smile. "I didn't realize Grant and I were on the same team. Does he not like Michael either?"

Tate rolls her eyes and grabs for her wine. "Last I checked, neither one of you should be concerned about my love life."

If Luke only knew…

"Oh look," she continues drolly, "someone's coming on stage. We should pay attention so they don't think we're rude."

She's saved by the presenter. Dinner includes a speech from the chairman of the library's board of trustees and one from New York City's mayor highlighting his own experiences using public libraries as a child growing up in Brooklyn. He then introduces this year's charitable honorees, and they each take to the stage one at a time to discuss how this gala raises critical funds to support New York City neighborhoods through educational programming and vast research collections. Most importantly, support for this event ensures that library resources and services remain freely available for communities who need them the most.

It's a powerful evening, and when they open up donations via an app on our phones, it's apparent everyone's in a giving mood. As money pours in, names flash across the screen onstage.

The Jackson Family - $5,000
Laurie Anderson - $15,000
The Hillstone Group - $200,000

The emcee calls them out, keeping the energy up as everyone exclaims with excitement. My donation is made anonymously. I tuck my phone back into my pocket and Tate glances over at me with wide eyes.

"That was generous of you."

She must have been snooping.

I clear my throat. "My mother was an art teacher at an elementary school in Phoenix before she passed from cancer. I like to think she'd be happy to see me putting my money back toward public schools."

Tate's expression saddens even as she smiles and nods. "Of course she would be."

After dinner wraps up, there's an afterparty in Astor Hall where dessert and cocktails are served alongside dancing and a silent auction. Luke sweeps Tate out onto the dance floor— beneath a huge gold disco ball—and they dance while they talk. He's silly with her, spinning her around and around, making it fun. Dustin takes a picture of them so he can send it to Luke. After he fires it off, he looks to me with a commiser-ating expression.

"You're not being nearly as subtle as you think you are. In fact, I'm not even sure you're trying to hide the fact that you like her."

I shamelessly turn my attention back to Tate. It's rare, after all, that I'm allowed to just watch her like this, without her realizing.

"I've tried to move on," I admit because it feels futile to lie to my friend. "Believe me, I've tried to talk myself out of it."

Dustin huffs out a disappointed sigh. "It's just not smart, man. It could explode a million different ways. With the team, with our friends." He shakes his head. "My advice? Call Lizzy."

Luke dips Tate so low she squeals, scared he's going to drop her.

Lizzy doesn't exist.

No one does. There's only Tate.

I find her a few minutes later, alone near the bar. I don't know where Luke's gone, but at the moment, I can't force myself to care.

I walk up to her and press my hand to her lower back, leaning in. "Come dance with me."

She whirls around and shakes her head, frowning. "*Grant.*"

My name is a warning and a weapon. *Stop this*, her expression commands. *Don't make this harder.*

I'm helpless in this, Tate. Haven't you come to understand that now?

"Dance with me," I say again, starting to walk backward onto the dance floor. I smile and wait as she chews her bottom lip and looks around. For what? An escape route?

She squeezes her eyes shut for a moment, and then she shakes her head before finally starting to walk toward me with a reticent look on her face.

"It's just a dance, Tate," I tell her as I take her small hand and step forward to wrap my arm around her back. The song is slower than the one she danced to earlier with her brother. The orchestra plays something sweeping and sad, a bit foreboding for my taste. It's not what I would have picked for a dance with her, but here we are, moving slowly, not quite chest to chest but close enough that I feel like I'm on fire.

She trembles in my arms. I'm equally as nervous. Can she tell?

I haven't touched her in weeks. Not since that kiss.

"You must have reapplied your lipstick after dinner."

The red is so perfect.

Her hand on my shoulder squeezes tight. She won't look at me. Her eyes scan the room.

I don't remember her feeling so small in my arms before. It brings out a gnawing sort of panic in me, this possessive protectiveness I'm unaccustomed to.

We don't talk. Maybe it's her way of punishing me for dragging her out here, or maybe it's her way of ensuring I don't read too much into this. It's just a dance. Harmless.

Only I'm confident if I pressed my lips to that spot on the side of her neck, just below her chin, her pulse would be racing. Her panic is so obvious.

"Tate?"

Still, she won't look at me.

"My turn!"

Dustin comes barreling onto the dance floor with a laugh, capturing Tate and spinning her away from me.

Laughter bubbles out of her. *"Dustin!"*

"What? I've waited long enough. Don't I get a turn? C'mon. I slipped the musicians a hundo and told them to play something fast. What's with this music? It's like I'm at a funeral."

Tate doesn't look back at me as Dustin whisks her away. For a beat too long, I stay where I am—smack dab in the middle of the dance floor, among the crush of bodies. Then I realize I have to move. Carry on. *Something.*

I could use a drink anyway.

Luke's nearby, talking to a few of the honorees from the evening. When I walk past and our gazes meet, his eyebrows furrow, not exactly in anger...more like simple curiosity.

I only nod my chin toward him, continuing on my way toward the bar.

Luke catches up to me again a little while later, after I've looked over the silent auction items, smiling to myself as I imagine my dad's reaction to everything they have listed. *Why the hell would someone buy a custom cowboy hat from some place in Aspen for $10,000?* "It's for charity" would not be a good enough reason for him.

That's when Luke hurries over to me, grabbing ahold of my arm, panic written all over his face.

"Hey, would you and Dustin mind getting Tate home? Chloe just called me and Harper spiked a fever. Nothing major, but she keeps asking for me and I need to get home."

He's already looking away, searching for the fastest exit.

"Yeah, of course."

"Thanks, man. I owe you."

Once he's hustled out the door, I leave the silent auction room right away and go in search of Tate. She's not on the dance floor, not near the bar, not mingling in the hall. She's waiting in line for the women's bathroom when I finally find her. I touch her arm, just above her elbow, and lower my voice, letting her know quietly, "Luke just had to leave. Harper's sick."

Her eyes widen as she looks up at me in alarm.

I rub my thumb on her arm, instinctively wanting to reassure her. "He didn't seem to think it was anything major, slight fever, but she wanted her dad."

Her bottom lip juts out. "Poor thing."

"Luke asked if Dustin and I could help get you home."

Her worry morphs into an indignant laugh. "I'm perfectly capable of getting home by myself. Besides, Dustin just left a little while ago."

"What?" The jerk didn't even come tell me bye.

"Yeah, did he not tell you? He said he was going to look for you…"

"I was in the silent auction room and then I was out searching everywhere for you. Maybe we just missed each other."

She nods. "Well…" The line moves and she shifts forward, slipping out of my grasp. "Consider your duty complete. I can call an Uber."

"I have a driver."

She rolls her eyes. "Of course you have a driver. That's all well and good, but us normal folk still manage just fine without them. There's a thing called the subway, have you heard of it?"

The elderly woman in front of her laughs and looks back at Tate. "If I were you, dear, I'd take the damn driver. Especially if this fine gentleman comes with it."

Her tone drips with innuendo as she gives me a pointed once-over before she turns and tugs open the restroom door.

Tate's left smiling in disbelief.

"Well…" I prod. "You heard the woman."

Ten minutes later, I lead Tate out into the warmth of the early summer night, down the steps of the library, toward a line of waiting cars.

"Mine is that black Escalade."

"Yes, as opposed to *that* black Escalade," Tate teases.

To be fair, there is an obnoxiously long line of sleek black SUVs.

I lift my hand to press it to the small of her back, then think better of it and tug my hand into a fist to let it fall back at my side. There are still photographers out here and it's better to play it safe.

My driver rushes out to open the door for us, and I help Tate step up and slide into the back seat. Once I've given the driver directions for Tate's apartment, I slide in beside her.

The second the door closes and we're confined to the small space together, the air becomes charged with the electricity we've been ignoring for the last few weeks. It's impossible to ignore that we've put ourselves in a pressure cooker. I know Tate is as aware of it as I am. It's why she's turned toward the window, scooting to the edge of her seat as if she's trying to flatten herself against the door and make herself as small and invisible as possible.

Now that she's sitting, the slit on her dress rides up seductively on her thigh again, only it's no longer hidden under a tablecloth. She catches me staring and I look back toward the front seat. She fidgets and tries to fix her dress, but it's hopeless.

"Apologies about the traffic," the driver says. "I think everyone had the same idea to leave right when you two did."

"It's fine." I say it brusquely only because I'm wound tight.

"Damn dress," Tate whispers under her breath.

I fight back a smile as I peer back over at her again. She's adjusting the top so less of her chest is showing, which only tugs the slit on her thigh up higher. So much tan skin on display...

"Don't look at me like that."

I have to fight back my smile. "Like what?"

"It's not that indecent."

"I never said it was."

"Your eyes say otherwise."

"It's a sexy dress," I say point-blank, leaving off, *on a sexy woman.*

I lean forward, starting to tug off my tuxedo jacket. "Do you want this? For your legs? Or..."

She scowls at me, which is the last reaction I was expecting. I damn near apologize for my offer before she shakes her head.

"Just...yes, I'll take your jacket."

I hand it over and she puts it around her shoulders. It easily covers her once she clamps it tight across her chest.

She inhales against the lapel and sheepishly smiles. "It smells like you." Her eyes catch mine, and with an air of vulnerability, she adds, "I like it."

Fuck it. I almost lean over and kiss her right then. I can imagine her plush lips on mine...

"What are you thinking? Your expression is so dark..."

"Kissing you. I'm thinking about kissing you, Tate."

She rolls her lips between her teeth like she's putting them in timeout. A smile barely peeks through.

I don't expect my honesty to go well. It hasn't worked well in the past. But then she surprises me by asking, "Then what? What would happen after you kiss me?"

"*Tate.*"

My voice is close to a growl.

Doesn't she realize I've been starved for her all night, utterly obsessed? Doesn't she know it felt like a cruel punishment to have to sit by her through that dinner and not touch her, not even once?

"Forget I asked. It was an accident." I can't help but smile as she nods emphatically, trying to prove her point. "It *was*. I can't be held liable for the things I say and do right now. I meant what I said earlier. You...you really shouldn't be allowed to wear a tux."

She angles toward me, and we stare at each other across the seat, playing a game of copycat.

I narrow my eyes; she does the same.

I tilt my head to study her; she tilts hers too.

I reach out to take her hand so I can turn it palm side up on the middle seat between us. It's just a hand, as innocent a body part as any. So then why is she shaking? She watches me with bated breath as I slowly run my pointer finger up the length of her middle finger then across the middle of her palm. I feel her shiver when I capture her wrist in my hand and tug.

She falls against me so easily. My hand reaches up to grip

the back of her neck. It's completely exposed thanks to all that lovely brown hair tucked into her up-do. Someone could just...bite her right there.

"An accident?" I ask again, this time with her lips nearly touching mine.

She's staring at my mouth, wetting her bottom lip as she nods. "Yes."

Her eyes are as wide and innocent as a doe's.

"It's always like that with you. You accidentally goad me, tease me, and then you withdraw like you're scared. It kills me every time you do it."

Her eyebrows shoot up in contest. "I'm not scared."

She's almost smiling now, trying to tip us back toward friends, but I won't allow it. My thumb rubs back and forth along her neck and her eyes flutter closed for a brief second before she realizes what she's done and blinks them open again, tugging to get away from me, but I don't let her.

"I wonder what Michael would think about this."

His name is like a magic word. I utter it and she goes rigid.

She tries harder now to reel back, her hands coming up to push against my chest. Still, I easily hold her steady against me.

"We're here," the driver says.

I look toward the front seat to see his eyes are on the road. I grab cash from my wallet to tip him and then tell him I can get home from here. Who knows how long I'll be. I'm certainly not just letting her get out.

"I'll walk you up," I tell Tate, taking her bicep in hand. It could be gentlemanly, but it's not. It's possessive, borderline rude.

"No need," she says in a rush.

I'm already out the door, tugging her behind me. The doorman for her building lets us in with a wave and a smile, and we make our way to the elevator. She's not cooperating, but I know how to get to her place just fine on my own. I call the elevator, and when the gleaming chrome doors sweep open, I lead us inside.

"This way, Tate."

"You don't have to sound so pissy about it."

"I'll show you pissy."

I press the number for her floor.

She throws up her free hand. "Oh please. *God*, you're so annoying. How dare you ask me about Michael when you're over there with Lizzy flirting all day *every* day, I'm sure. How are you two, by the way? Was she so sad she couldn't be on your arm tonight? You'll have to call her on the way home and tell her how desperately you missed—"

I whirl her around until she's pressed back against the side of the elevator, right up against the rail. Her breath hisses out of her.

"—her."

I lift her so she's precariously propped up on the rail, hiking that slit up until I can easily stand between her legs. I nestle right where I belong as we start to ascend floors.

For once, *finally*, I have her in my hands as my mouth dips down to claim hers.

SEVENTEEN

TATE

GRANT'S KISS IS SOUL-SEARING. He cradles my face like I'm as fragile as a baby bird, which is hilarious considering he was just manhandling me with such arrogant possession a part of me still wants to scream at him to let me go. I shouldn't be here, kissing him back, moaning into his mouth. This damn elevator is too efficient for its own good. We reach my floor just as I'm leaning into him, gripping his shirt, inviting him to slide his tongue past my lips.

Just as common sense has very nearly evaporated fully from my head—*ding!*

It's over.

Or not.

Grant leads the way again, lifting me off that rail and setting me down gently on my feet. He slides his arm around my waist as he steps up behind me, his chest to my back. It's like he's a robber holding me hostage. His mouth is down by my ear when he tells me to walk.

I almost smile.

God, I like this. Like *him*.

"Or what?" I taunt.

He stops abruptly, tugging me back so I fall against him.

My butt is nestled right up against his hard length. We're feet from my apartment door, in plain view of the security cameras and my neighbors should they decide to walk out into the hallway. His free hand—the one not currently wrapped around my stomach—slides deftly up my inner thigh, confidently past the slit of my dress, until his warm palm covers my panties.

"I'll touch you here if you want me to."

He starts stroking me back and forth, his middle finger sliding *just* where he knows it'll drive me wild.

I nearly sag against him.

This is so wholly different from how I live my day-to-day life. Control, routine, precision. Everything has a place, a time, a set of instructions.

"*Grant,*" I beg.

"What, Tate?" he asks, all innocent, when in fact we both know he's proving to be a maniacal villain.

His fingers keep stroking me between my legs and my knees threaten to give out. My panties are askew and he takes full advantage, pushing them aside further. He can already feel how turned on I am, hot and needy. He drags his finger slowly up and down as a shiver of pleasure racks through me.

When it's clear I've lost the ability to speak, he tells me again, "*Walk.*"

I try to elbow him in the gut, and he laughs.

It's a dangerous game we're playing. Beneath the surface of our banter and barbs, it's a raging wildfire. We'll burn each other before this night is through if we're not careful. Hell, maybe he wants that. *Do I?*

He walks us both forward, keeping possession of my waist even as we reach my door.

"Key," he says haughtily.

"I hate you."

He tsks like I deserve punishment for that.

"What if my roommates are awake?"

I think this will earn me some reprieve. I brought my roommates up intentionally. They'll draw him back to the surface. He'll remember this can't continue. No way.

Instead, he tells me again to get the key.

My hand doesn't just tremble, it full-on shakes as I retrieve my key from my tiny clutch and try to fit it into the lock.

I expect him to laugh at my expense, but then I'm reminded who I'm dealing with when Grant wraps his hand tightly around mine and helps me unlock the door. "*Good girl*" is whispered against the shell of my ear as he takes the key and slips it back into my clutch.

I hold my breath as we walk into my apartment, but the living room is pitch black. Sophia and Daphne are either asleep or not here.

Grant releases me, and the sensation is so similar to that depressing moment when you first draw yourself out of a warm bath, all the luxurious heat gone in an instant.

I walk into my apartment on tiptoed feet, trying to be as quiet as possible.

Grant stalks in behind me. I didn't invite him in, but I also didn't shut the door in his face, so...

Once we're in my room, he closes the door. I take a step to turn on the lamp beside my bed, but Grant grabs ahold of me and pushes me back, back, back to the closet door. My purse falls to the floor along with his tuxedo jacket. My hands flatten against his chest. I feel his muscles working under his shirt.

Light seeps in from the street outside, but we're otherwise in the dark as his head drops and our foreheads touch.

"The stuff with Michael ends now..." he demands just before he starts to kiss me.

"Same with Lizzy," I bite out, then I kiss him again.

His fingers dig into my hips.

"I already told Michael," I admit, breathless. "*Yesterday.*"

You'd think this would make him happy to hear, but he doesn't say a word.

There's nothing to say. We're playing make believe here. We're pretending the only obstacles we have are Lizzy and Michael when we both know they were never really obstacles to begin with.

Grant kisses me again, sweeping my thoughts away as he gathers my dress in his fists. The sequins scrape my skin in a delicious contrast to his tender mouth.

I think he's going to keep pulling it up until he gets it all the way off me. Instead, he pauses when the dress is bunched at my hips. Then he reaches for my panties and tugs on the satin. They slide down my hips then fall the rest of the way down to the ground to pool at my feet.

I feel absolutely bare even with my gown still in place on the top half of my body.

When Grant breaks our kiss and peels back far enough to prop his hand on the door beside my head, he looks down and taps the inside of my high heel with his dress shoe. The intent is clear and pompous and I want to protest, and yet I have no choice but to move my right foot a few inches over, spreading my legs. His handsome face stays in shadow. If he likes that I complied so easily, I can't tell.

He's focused down on his hand as he watches his fingers tiptoe up, only this time, there's no satin separating him from my naked skin, nothing to stop him from sweeping his hand between my thighs and sliding his fingers through me. I arch my back, starting to shake with need. I want him to keep going so badly I hold my breath. His touch feels just as heady as it did out in the hallway, only this time I know I won't last. My body tingles as he works me up, higher, tighter, closer to the edge, and only then does he finally begin to press his finger inside me. My jaw drops at the feel of him starting to pump it in and out, stretching me so decadently I think I might pass away from the sheer bliss of it. But it's not enough.

He's incensed as he tugs my gown straps down off my shoulders, exposing my breasts. His nostrils flare. His eyes widen and then he bends, leaving open-mouthed kisses on my neck, collarbone...the center of my chest. I release a silent cry as his mouth closes over the tip of one breast, then the other.

Oh god.

I reach up to grip his shoulders, to secure myself to something as his finger works in and out of me, faster, hitting a deliciously wicked spot. I whimper and squeeze my eyes closed as my fingers dig into his shirt.

I drop my head back against the door with a heavy *thunk* and I know I'm in trouble.

"Show me," Grant says, pleading. "Show me what it looks like. I've imagined doing this to you so many times. You have no idea, Tate. Night after night on the road, fisting myself as a poor substitute because I knew I couldn't have you like this... I want you so badly."

His words combined with the feeling of his hand between my thighs is almost too much. I have to bite my lip to keep from gasping.

Immediately, Grant tugs on my lip to release it from my teeth. "No. Let me hear it."

Oh my gosh.

I want to push him to the ground, crawl up and over him, and grind down until we both lose our heads. I want to see him at a loss for words just like I am right now.

He starts to slip a second finger inside me when suddenly the front door of the apartment opens.

"Tate? You home?" Sophia calls out.

Keys clatter into the bowl near the front door.

"She's probably asleep already," Daphne adds.

"Does she work tomorrow? We were going to finish the second half of *Aftersun*. It's a 24-hour rental." Sophia's voice grows louder as her footsteps approach my door. "Tate?"

Grant shakes his head no, but I ignore him.

"Yes?" I call out, just as Grant steps away from me. In the dark, he glares.

What did he want me to do? Hide out from my room-mates? It doesn't work like that in this shoebox of an apart-ment. Let's say we tried to sneak around in here…if I flushed the toilet or turned on the sink, if I opened a drawer or even walked heavily, for that matter, they'd hear it. There's no privacy here.

I would explain that to him if only he wasn't looking at me like that. I fix the top of my gown and shift the bottom so my legs are covered again.

"Want to finish that movie we started yesterday?" Sophia asks. "The sad one?"

"Uh…"

A fist bangs on the door. "Why are you being weird?" It's Daphne now, impatient and suspicious.

"I'm not! I'm just naked."

"Oh, sorry. Finish putting on your pajamas and I'll make some popcorn. I want to hear all about your night. I heard Grant and Dustin were at the fundraiser. I bet Grant looked fine as hell in his tuxedo, don't even deny it."

I can't look at Grant to gauge his reaction to this. I'm so flustered and embarrassed, trying to work out how I'll possibly be able to sneak him out of here. My roommates can't know he's here because then this entire thing becomes real in a way I've been so careful to avoid.

If we were on friendlier terms, we'd be laughing about this. It's hilarious if you think about it.

"We messed up."

He shakes his head in disagreement. "No we didn't."

What?

Yes we did!

There's only one option. "You'll have to sneak out."

How though? The fire escape? Is he going to belay down the side of the building like a *Mission Impossible* wannabe?

Grant doesn't say anything. I peer over, worried, and my heart sinks as I see the disappointment clouding his expression. Whatever I should have said to smooth things over between us, it wasn't that.

"I'm not sneaking out—"

"*Grant.* What other choice do we have?"

"Jesus, Tate. I'm not your fucking secret." Each word arrows into my chest before he curves around me and opens the door to my bedroom.

"That was—" Daphne's voice abruptly stops when she sees Grant walking out of my room. "—fast."

He goes straight for the apartment door, flings it open, and leaves.

Sophia and Daphne are standing in the living room with mouths gaping.

"Was that Grant?" Sophia wonders aloud like she can't quite believe it herself.

Daphne shakes her head then turns slowly to look at me with eyes the size of saucers. "What the hell was *Grant* doing in your room?"

"Nothing."

That's all they'll get from me on the subject.

"Tate." Daphne turns to me with a *Get real* expression on her face.

"For once, just drop it!" I snap, losing all my patience with the situation.

I handled that poorly, I realize that now, but it's not like Grant and I had some preplanned strategy for how the night would go. I was thinking on my feet, and now I see I'm not very good at that. Noted. Next time I'll read off a script.

"Wait—what about Michael?" Sophia asks with a scrunched brow, looking to Daphne as if she hopes her sister will have answers to some of these questions.

All my energy is gone, zapped out of me. I walk to my bedroom door, grip the handle, and slowly push it closed until it clicks into place. Once they're on one side and I'm safely on the other, I drop my forehead against the door and squeeze my eyes closed.

I can't do it. I can't face them or anyone else right now. I mean for Christ's sake, my panties are still on the floor, my gown is barely covering me, and my heart is being carted down the elevator at this very moment, in the clutches of a man I just wounded with my careless words.

————

THE UNIVERSE IS TESTING ME.

That's the only way to explain the next forty-eight hours of my life.

I spend the day after the gala wallowing and periodically checking Instagram for messages from Grant, only to be disappointed time and time again, finding nothing waiting for me.

I have a horrible day the next day too. When my alarm goes off in the morning, I'm dead tired but mostly manage to get it together until I'm headed out the door. I go to grab my to-go thermos of coffee and realize too late that I forgot to screw the top on securely. Picture this: one idiot standing with her mouth gaping like a guppy as piping hot coffee drips down the front of her pristine scrubs.

After a quick change, I sprint to the hospital, where conditions only worsen dramatically. The whole atmosphere of the ICU is off.

Bianca shakes her head in warning when I arrive at the nurses' station. "Unless you're walking in with happy news, keep your head down. The surgeons are out for blood today."

"Why?"

She shrugs. "How should I know? Full moon? You know

how it gets around here. One of them has a bad case and they all start to tumble like dominoes. One of the cardiologists just had the nerve to ask me if *I* would take a note to Dr. Liota in the OR. Like are you *insane*? Deliver your own bad news and leave me out of it!"

I'm on tenterhooks all day, nervous and edgy, double-checking my work a thousand times over. Even still, I don't escape the wrath of one of the surgeons. It's just after lunch when I get laid into by Dr. Zhao because of a small abscess found on a patient's suture site that I didn't cause. I just have to stand there while he goes on and on about proper wound care and accountability, keeping my face as emotionless as possible, but as soon as he's done, I go straight into the bathroom and cry.

God, I'm so angry. I'm good at my job! I don't deserve to be yelled at. It makes me question everything—why the hell it's worth it for me to be here in the first place, if maybe I'm not as good of a nurse as I think I am. It doesn't matter that deep down I know logically, parents have off days, surgeons have off days, this has nothing to do with me. Even still, it feels like it does.

After a good little cry fest, I force a deep breath and walk out of my stall to see my eyes are red and puffy.

Just great. I still have three hours left to go on my shift.

Bianca isn't at the desk when I return to my chair, but she's left a little sticky note on my keyboard.

Hang in there.

Seeing it almost makes me cry all over again, but I suck it up, swallow down the last of my emotions, and get back to work.

Michael's here. I saw him around lunch time when he walked by the break room. He smiled at me as he passed, but he was en route to see a patient, I think, so we didn't talk. He comes to find me at the tail end of my shift though, which is surprising, because I thought we were mostly avoiding each other.

I'm closing out tabs on my computer, making sure I've put in the final notes so the nurses coming in are up to date on all our current patients when he says hi. Despite the slight awkwardness, it's actually really nice to see a friendly face.

I smile and stand, pushing my chair in. "Hey, Michael. Just leaving?"

"Yeah." He rubs the back of his neck, glances down the hall then back at me. "Actually, I stayed a little late hoping we could talk if you have a second."

I fight back a pained expression.

"Of course, yeah. Just…" I sigh. "Could I grab my stuff and maybe we go outside? I'd really like to be done in this ICU for the day."

I don't want to be in the hospital for one second longer than necessary. In fact, I was planning to sprint out of here.

He nods enthusiastically. "Yeah, of course. I get it. I heard it was a rough one today."

I shake my head and shoot him a look like he doesn't know the half of it.

He waits for me at the desk while I grab my lunchbox and uneaten snacks from the break room. Once I've got my bag slung over my shoulder, I nod toward the hallway.

"Ready?"

We walk in silence for a bit. I think we're both highly aware of the circumstances of our last encounter, the fact that we technically broke up, if you could even call it that.

Eventually, the tension starts to thaw out. Michael asks me about my day, and I explain it all, starting with the coffee incident. He's a good listener and actually makes me feel a lot better about the Dr. Zhao thing.

"I've heard him raving about you and the other nurses on

staff before. You have to know that had nothing to do with you today."

"I appreciate that."

"You're a good nurse."

I feel unwelcome tears prick the corners of my eyes. God, it's silly, but this job is important to me and I respect Michael's opinion, so his reassurance means a lot.

"Did you walk here?" he asks once we push open the lobby doors and break free out onto the sidewalk. I don't even mind that the setting sun is already hidden behind skyscrapers. I'm just glad to be out in the regular world again, done with that nightmarish shift.

"Yup. You?"

"Yeah. I can walk you home if that's okay? That way we can talk?"

I don't have the heart to tell Michael no, and more than that, I genuinely don't want to. Michael is someone I could see myself being friends with if the circumstances were right. It probably wouldn't work right now, but maybe if he finds someone else and settles into another relationship, boundaries would be clear between us and we could just be buds.

Michael doesn't launch into what he wants to tell me right away. He's probably just a little nervous, so I don't press him. If he wants to talk about the weather and what he's planning to eat for a late dinner and some new TV show he just started watching, that's fine by me. But we're getting closer to my apartment and I know he's going to have to say something soon. It's making *me* nervous for him!

We round the corner and I know my doorman is waiting for me up ahead a few yards.

I suddenly stop and take Michael's arm. "Hey, are we good?"

His eyes widen in shock.

"Just...is there something you wanted to tell me? Is that why you wanted to walk me home?" I laugh tightly. "Sorry if

I'm being a little too direct, but this day has been intense enough already. Let's just have it out, okay?"

I smile reassuringly, hoping that will help.

He chuckles a little and nods. "Yeah. Okay."

I let go of him and wrap my arm protectively across my waist, holding on to my other elbow for support.

He furrows his brows then looks down at the sidewalk. When he looks up at me, there's unmistakable conviction in his gaze. My stomach is already twisted into a tight knot as he launches into it. "So here's the thing. You're awesome, Tate, and I've been thinking a lot about what you said the other day, about how you're a little confused and you're in a weird place right now. But the thing is…" He takes a step closer to me and draws a hand through his hair, mussing the neat strands. "I'd be crazy if I didn't fight for you. I mean, I've seriously had a crush on you forever, even back when I was with my ex, if I'm being totally honest… I can't just let you slip through my fingers."

I was expecting something along these lines, but not *this*, not him bearing his heart so totally freely. I'm not sure what to say. I'm not exactly used to guys declaring their interest in me so blatantly.

I stay quiet as he continues. "This thing between us could be great. I know it."

Then he leans down and presses a light kiss against my lips.

I'm too startled to do anything but stand stock-still, then he steps back with a hopeful smile.

"I think this is what the teens call shooting your shot," he says with a silly wink.

I smile timidly, and just as I do, my gaze rises up past Michael's shoulders, toward the entrance of my building where Grant stands waiting for me.

EIGHTEEN
TATE

I PICTURE chaos raining down on the sidewalk as Grant loses his cool. I picture curses, uppercuts, split lips. I picture me crying like a fool watching these two men go at it over me.

In reality, Michael falls away, leaving to flag a taxi, wholly unaware that he's just tossed me a live grenade. Meanwhile, Grant stays where he is, his hands tucked into his pockets, his warm gaze steady on me as I approach. Emotions flood me; I'm a jittery scared mess. After the day I've had, Grant more than anyone else on earth has the capacity to absolutely wreck me. It's scary to realize how much I feel for him, how little control I have where he's concerned.

"Hi."

The word feels ineffective.

Hi and I'm sorry and I'm not sure what you saw or what you just heard but please accept this meek hi.

"Hi."

I look down the street, chickening out of holding eye contact. "Want to take a walk?"

He's here for a reason. If he's in a rush, he'll let me know. If not, well…

There's no vitriol in his eyes, no anger behind his nod

when he agrees. He even reaches out to take my hospital bag. He grasps it and we go another two blocks in silence until we arrive at a small neighborhood park with a smattering of benches, a playground, and giant trees. I love this park.

There's an empty bench we head toward. I sit on one end, Grant claims the other. I try not to notice the healthy distance, the fact that he tucks my bag safely between us. He takes care to ensure it won't tip over.

"Will you give me the chance to explain myself?"

He doesn't say anything, so I trudge right along.

"I told you the truth the other night. I talked to Michael the other day about ending things, though we were never really all that serious or exclusive to begin with, just to be clear." I sigh. "Anyway, I hadn't seen him since then, and today after work, he asked me if we could talk. Not so unlike what you and I are doing now."

I can't even look at him, which is fine because he's staring straight ahead too when he finally asks, "What'd he say before he kissed you?"

My stomach twists tight with anxiety. "That he has a crush on me. That he..." God, why does it feel embarrassing to admit this? "He thinks I'm worth fighting for."

I say the last part so quietly I'm not even sure he hears me. It doesn't feel good to admit the truth to Grant. I'd sugarcoat it if I could.

"Seeing him kiss you..." He shakes his head. "I'm surprised I kept my composure." He says it with so much conviction I nearly crumble.

"*Grant.*"

He sucks in a deep breath and leans forward, dropping his elbows to his knees. We stare out at the park, at the little kids passing us on scooters, the moms chasing after them, the guys playing a pick-up game of ultimate frisbee. The whole time I feel like I might be sick, like I might lean over and throw up everything in my stomach.

"You know, it's weird," he begins, his voice sincere and solemn. "I feel like in movies it's always some big sweeping thing that keeps two people apart—cheating, lying, scandals —but you know what's worse? A million tiny things. How can I conquer a million tiny things?"

He doesn't have to tell me I'm mostly in the wrong here. I know how badly I hurt him two nights ago when I insinuated that he needed to be hidden from my roommates. I don't have to imagine how I would have felt if he didn't want his friends to know about me, if he'd told me I needed to sneak out. Horrible. That's how I would have felt—absolutely horrible.

"I'm sorry."

He shakes his head, his attention down on the ground. "There's nothing to apologize for."

"The other night…"

Was amazing.

Spectacular.

Life-changing.

"I won't apologize for it. I can't pretend it never happened."

Is that what he thinks I want? To forget about it?

News flash: I'm going to be 99, still kicking it in some retirement home, and you'll find me regaling everyone in the buffet line about that one time *the* Grant Navarro put his hand down my pants.

Neither of us speaks as we sit, looking straight ahead, trying to pull a fix out of thin air. *What if we… Maybe we aren't… You and I could…*

The silence seems to expand like a gnarly twisted weed I'm ill equipped to fend off.

Then Grant pushes to stand and I think, *So that's it? You're giving up?* His departure will be so subtle. It makes me think of the T.S. Eliot verse: "This is the way the world ends, not with a bang but a whimper."

Where's the fight, Grant? Where's all that passion *now*?

"You're leaving?"

"I need to go. The guys are expecting me. I can walk you back?"

My jaw is clenched so tightly all I can do is shake my head.

He's about to walk away, just like that. I can't even look at him. I stare straight ahead, his tall figure shifting out of focus in my periphery, fading to abstract colors as he continues, "The thing is, Tate…just so we're absolutely clear…I'm dying to be with you. In fact, I would risk it all just to have you. I can't stop this, whatever it is…but I won't force it. Not anymore. So figure out what you want."

Then he's gone, walking behind the bench, crunching the leaves so that I can track every step as they grow fainter until they finally cut off altogether.

I whip around then, my mouth open, ready to speak, but he's gone.

I'd like to say realization dawns right then, his ultimatum shaking loose my stubbornness and illuminating everything I've been blind to up until this point, but in reality, I still feel like I'm at rock bottom, like there's no clear way forward. What's the point of standing up off this park bench and continuing right on with life as if everything is fine when it's not?

I stare straight ahead, letting my vision turn hazy as people cross in front of me on the path, nothing more than blurry blobs. Then a little boy on a scooter rolls past me, stops, and walks his scooter back to get a second look at me.

"Why are you crying?" he asks, tilting his head. "Did someone hurt you?" He looks around like he might try to apprehend the person himself.

I sniffle and swipe my hand under my nose. "Nope, just a bad day."

"Oh." This disappoints him; he really wanted to beat up a bad guy. Now, at a loss for what else to do in this situation, he offers up the only thing he has. "You want to borrow my scooter? It's my favorite toy and it makes me happy."

By this point his mom has hurried to catch up to him, shooting me a sympathetic smile. "Marcus, leave her alone." She mouths an apology as she prods him along.

I shake my head to let her know I didn't mind him talking to me. Not at all.

Now I'm just alone on the bench again, probably scaring everyone at the park. I could leave, but I'm stuck in limbo. If I stand up, I have to make a decision about how to move forward. I have to decide what I'll tell Daphne and Sophia when I get home and they see the evidence of my misery smeared all over my face: smudged mascara, swollen eyes, snotty nose. I have to decide if I'm willing to let Grant walk away from me so easily.

Then there's also Michael.

Ugh...

I'm not even mad at him about the kiss. How could I be?! He's ten times braver than I've *ever* been. He's pursued me from the start and managed to survive on mere morsels of my attention. Then when I tried to let him down gently, *no*! He had the guts to put it all on the line. I hope karma is real and at this very minute he's colliding with some gorgeous super-model out on the sidewalk. Oh, and you know what? She has a heart of gold. Yeah, she's one of those girls who likes all your Instagram posts and always comments encouraging things. "Yes, girl!" "Love the fit!" I hope he runs right smack into her and they laugh it off and he has to brush dirt off her knee and then she says her name is Christine and they're right by a coffee shop so Michael asks if she wants to go in and he buys her a drink to make up for running into her, and it's so weird, she was *just* craving a coffee...

Scooter kid goes home with his mom. The park empties out.

Putting a pause on my life and stalling here was nice, but I know it's time to leave when two punk teenagers walk by and loudly proclaim me "lame." *Okay well, who asked you?!*

I rise and mosey my way back to my apartment with slumped shoulders and a downtrodden curve to my spine. In the foyer, I kick my shoes off before I trudge into the living room. My two roommates sit side by side on the couch, their eyes wide with wonder at the sight of me.

"Before you ask, no, I'm not okay. Work was horrible. My love life is in shambles. And I've cried so much my eyes are burning."

Then, like that's all the strength I had left in me, I collapse dramatically onto the wood floor, letting my knees buckle and everything. My face *barely* makes it onto the carpet, and there I remain, splayed out like a sad starfish.

"That's quite a day," Daphne laments. "Can't top it, I'm afraid. On the plus side, your ass looks great in those scrubs."

Sophia sounds completely shocked when she replies, "I was *just* going to say that!"

"Like so good, right? I just want to pinch it."

I clench my butt instinctively and then reach back to cover my two cheeks with my hands. "Do *not*."

Daphne scoffs. "I only said I *wanted* to, not that I was *going* to."

Knowing I'm safe (for now), I let my arms flail out at my sides again.

"So are we problem solving or commiserating?" Sophia asks judiciously.

"Commiserating."

Without another word, they both get up. I don't turn my head to watch, but I listen to them head into the kitchen, pulling glasses out of the cupboard, opening a wine bottle, doing their roommate duty. *"When we sign on the dotted line on this here lease agreement, we agree to serve our apartment and our country, and by golly, we're sticking to that."* Popcorn is popped and some insanely overpriced chocolate bar we've been storing for just such an occasion is cracked open and split into three parts. Then I'm dragged up off the floor and propped between them on the couch.

In slow motion, as if accompanied by angels singing from above, Sophia bestows on me the gift of the remote.

"You get to pick any show you want to watch."

My dead heart beats anew.

"Current or old?"

Their heavy sighs tell me they already know where I'm heading with this question. *"Either..."*

And that's how we end up watching season four, episode seven of *Vampire Diaries* aka "My Brother's Keeper" aka exquisite television.

"Do you feel better?" Daphne asks when the show's nearly over.

Do I?

No, not really.

"Maybe after one more episode."

Alone in my room that night, under the cloak of darkness, I pull up Grant's Instagram. He hasn't posted a photo to his feed in days, but I entertain my misery by flicking back through older posts and reading the comments. Women are... creative and inventive, I will give us that. A few of the flirty one-liners even make me smile, they're *that* funny. Which makes me feel worse, actually. Because wait a minute, witty hot girls are going after Grant too? I'm doomed.

In his most recent post, the top comments discuss his appearance at the fundraiser two nights ago. Apparently, these savvy people have decided they can use the comment section on Instagram as an online forum for discussion of Grant in general, even if it doesn't pertain to the specific photo at hand.

Saw him in that tux last night. To DIE FOR! - 2,039 likes

Grate 4 life! - 1,688 likes

Is it weird that I hope G and T are actually dating? - 196 likes

I want them to get together so bad! They'd be like baseball royalty! - 1,334 likes

It's not until I read another comment: *They looked so cute leaving the fundraiser together! - 745 likes* that I realize they're talking about us! Grant and me!

I am "T"! I am the "ate" in "Grate"!

What?!

I panic. Of course I panic. I'm not a public figure, not at all. I cried on a toilet at work today, lest anyone need a reminder of my lowly existence on this planet.

I immediately search Google for images of Grant, looking for what the commenters could be talking about, but the top pictures are just professional shots from baseball games, headshots from the Pinstripes website, and old promos. I go back to the search bar and try a different strategy. I type in both of our names and hit enter, then *boom*, there they are, a whole treasure trove of pictures from the other night with a paparazzi watermark layered on top and everything like I'm Selena-freaking-Gomez. Wow.

My first thought? I'm glad I happened to be dressed to the nines with killer makeup.

My *next* thought? I wish I could call Grant.

It's interesting to look back on the pictures from this perspective because at the time, I didn't think we were doing anything even *semi*-inappropriate, but whoever took the photos knew just when to snap them. They caught us walking down the stairs toward the street, a hair's breadth too close for casual friendship. There's also one where Grant is looking over at me with a devastating smile—maybe when I made the joke about the Escalades—and his hand is reaching out toward me. I'm looking at him with, let's face it, unabashed love. Shiny hearts dazzle in my eyes.

We're *so* obviously interested in each other. It's blatant. We might as well have been full-on making out with how damning the photos are.

I'm expecting the phone call that comes the next morning.

Luke's name illuminates my phone screen at 8:01 AM, and he chooses to open with, "Want to tell me what the hell is up with you and Grant?"

"What?"

I'm pure innocence.

"Tate."

"Luke. Good morning. First, how's Harper?"

"Fever free. She's resting up in front of the TV."

"Great. Let me talk to her."

"Cut the crap."

"Wow, real polite. Mom raised you better than that."

"Fine. I'll just call Grant."

I sit up in bed. "Would you relax?! There's nothing going on. Are you talking about the pictures from the fundraiser? They were nothing. Just him escorting me home *like you asked him to.* Or did you forget that part?"

"You don't date baseball guys," he reminds me.

"Yes, I know that!"

"And you know what? I've always thought that was a great policy. They're assholes, every one of them."

"Including the one I'm talking to right now."

"You're funny. Here, Harper wants to talk to you."

My niece takes the phone from her dad and then her heavy kid breathing fills the phone.

"Sup," she says to me.

I laugh. "Hey Harper, how are you feeling?"

"A little better, but I still have to stay home today. Think I can get Chloe to make me some cinnamon rolls?"

"If I know Chloe, she probably already has something delicious baking in the oven for you."

There's rustling on her end and then I hear a door close.

"Harper!" Luke calls out after her.

"We don't have long!" Harper hisses. "I ran and hid in the coat closet. Now tell me, did you solve your boy problem? Last night, Dad was looking at some pictures on his computer with Chloe and they didn't think I could see them, but I could! And Grant Navarro is so handsome! Chloe said something about you being a really cute couple and then Dad just grumbled like he was real angry. Do you like Grant? Is he your boyfriend, Aunt Tate?!"

Luke's fist pounds on the door of the closet. "HARPER, if you're downloading Barbie apps again, you're grounded! *Worse* than grounded!"

The closet door swings open. Luke must have remembered there's no lock on it.

"What's 'grounded'?" Harper asks.

"Hand me my phone."

Luke's voice has no venom behind it.

"I'm sick, remember." Harper coughs *Mean Girls* style then there's more rustling as she shouts, "Bye, Aunt Tate! I love you!"

The line goes dead.

———

I'M DISAPPOINTED by how easily life continues on. The people in front of me in line for coffee the next day have the audacity to laugh as if this is *any* time to be jovial! We should be sulking, collectively, as a nation. I want mourning attire and funeral dirges trumpeting sadly on every radio station.

Back at the apartment, I've run out of wine. I'm low on ice cream. The last tissue went a few days ago so now I'm relying on toilet paper.

Sophia, Daphne, and I have discussed the situation from every angle, carefully examined and peeled it back layer by layer with a fine-tooth comb like we're trained anthropologists. I know their patience with me wears thin, the expiration date for this dilemma looming. I have to throw them a bone, so when the Pinstripes have a home game scheduled on Friday and I find out Luke is pitching, I know I have to put on a cheery face and attend. It'd be crazy if I missed it.

I go through the motions of dressing in jean shorts and a Pinstripes t-shirt (*not* Grant's jersey), and I do my hair and makeup like it's any other day. At the stadium, I take my seat near the dugout sandwiched between my roommates and my family. We're so close, we're basically *on* the field. We can see the sweat dripping down the players' faces as they hustle to and from the dugout. Hence my problem—WE CAN SEE THE SWEAT DRIPPING DOWN THEIR FACES. I haven't seen Grant in days, not since our conversation on the park bench. I want there to be visible signs of distress like the ones I've been sporting all week, but that magnificent tan hides everything. He looks good as new. Handsome, sweaty, ready to conquer the world.

When he goes up to bat for the first time, I can't even watch. He makes it two steps toward the plate and I stare down at my feet, relying on the sounds of the stadium, the chants and squeals of excitement, the booming voice of the announcer over the loudspeaker telling me what's going on.

Harper takes my hand and tugs. "He's batting, Tate. Your boy!"

"He's not my boy," I admonish.

She frowns. "But I thought…"

STRIKE ONE.

My heart drops.

I squeeze Harper's hand tighter.

"Oh no, oh no, oh no." Harper's antsy on her feet, watching Grant prepare to take his next swing.

STRIKE TWO.

Oh god.

"GO GRANT!" Harper screams with every fiber of her being. He *had* to hear it.

Then the stadium holds its breath as Grant's bat cracks against the ball.

"It's going, going, *GONE!*"

Before I realize what I'm doing, Harper and I are screaming and jumping around, going wild like everyone else.

"HOME RUN FROM GRANT *NAVARRO*," the announcer declares, stretching his last name out in that fantastic way they must learn in announcer school.

"He's the best! Right after my dad!"

I laugh and shake my head, but it's true. He's really something.

The game ends up being one of the best I've seen in a while. Dustin gets a home run in the ninth inning that sends two guys home, clinching the win for us. The stadium erupts again. Daphne merely shrugs as if she's thinking, *What? Like it's hard?*

After the game, we head down to the field to congratulate Luke and the guys, but I purposefully keep my distance from Grant. He's at work right now. I don't want to distract him from his job. Per usual, he's getting a lot of attention. He gets tugged in front of a camera for a postgame interview alongside Luke, then another with Dustin. When he wraps up the last one, he props his hands on his hips and turns to search the crowd of faces like he's hoping, hoping, *hoping*… He looks relieved when his eyes land on me. Warmth blankets me as I smile tentatively, unsure of what else to do. He freezes for a moment, then he looks me over. It's not malicious or cruel, but it's also not friendly or welcoming. It's like he can't even help himself; his drawn-out inspection of me feels innate. He wants to see how I'm doing. I want to walk up to him so badly I feel a physical tug in his direction that's almost painful to resist. He nods, keeping his expression aloof, and he hesitates for a moment—a glorious moment—before he turns in the opposite direction, heading toward the locker room.

I almost keel over as something finally shakes free in that moment, likely the last shred of control I thought I had. Realization first began to grow when Grant and I sat on that park bench together. Longing and despair have poured over me like rain, helping to feed all the complicated feelings I've been fighting tooth and nail to stamp out. I didn't want to end up here: exposed, raw, needy, scared…hopelessly, miserably, endlessly…*in love*.

Every choice in my life has always been carefully measured and assessed, and I foolishly thought I could do that with love too. I thought I had the power to conquer it, and then it showed me.

Resist all you want, it said. *We'll win in the end.*

The team leaves the next day for a three-game series against Seattle. From there, they go to Los Angeles. I don't see Grant again until the following Sunday, when our group is at a neighborhood bar, having a drink. The weather's nice so we've claimed a table outside. We've been here for an hour already. I'm on my second glass of wine. Nick's on my left, sandwiched between Daphne and me. Josh and Sophia are across the table. For the better part of twenty minutes, we've been scrolling through Nick's Raya account, arguing over the pros and cons of a particular blonde woman like our lives depend on it. Then Josh looks up and waves at someone behind me. I glance over my shoulder and my heart swells as Dustin and Grant walk up the sidewalk to join us. I wasn't sure if they'd come tonight, and I wasn't gutsy enough to outright ask.

There's a vacant seat beside me and I push it out for Grant, but he doesn't take it. He loops around the table without so much as a *blink* in my direction and claims the seat by Sophia. It's as far away from me as he can possibly get while still sitting at the same table.

Subtle.

Dustin at least greets me with a side hug. Grant doesn't bother. Is this how it's going to be between us? So awkward he can't even look at me?

No. Not if I can help it.

I pick up my wine glass and sip, then sip some more. Everyone's relaxed, talking and laughing, and I'm staring at the dwindling contents of my glass as they disappear down my throat.

I motion for someone to pass me the bottle so I can top myself off.

Sophia frowns, but she hands it over. She's probably aware of the same thing I am: I'm not a heavy drinker. It's not part of my normal routine. Ope! There's that word again —*routine!* Can't wake up and run nine miles if I've had a bunch of wine the night before! Can't carry out all my perfectionist tendencies if I'm slurring my words! My routine can kiss my ass. Tonight, it's just me and this lovely sauvignon blanc.

Down the table, Grant says something to Dustin, and my body instinctively takes note. *Why does he do that to me?! Why does he get to have that much control over my body?!* I don't shiver when Nick or Dustin or Josh talk. Hell, I don't even listen to them half the time. But Grant could whisper something a mile away and my ears would prick like, *What now?*

I'm doomed.

Or...maybe not.

"Will someone tell Grant he doesn't have to ignore me?"

The words slip out of their own accord.

The table goes dead silent. Every head swings in Grant's direction, then to me, then back to Grant.

His heady gaze captures mine, and he has the audacity to

look amused. God, he's handsome tonight. Miserably beautiful.

"Oh you *can* look at me! That's good, because I have a lot to say to you."

Nick's grinning from ear to ear. Everyone else looks like they're watching a slow-motion car wreck as I continue, "I just think it's funny how much you *say* you want me, but where's the fight?" I demand, sounding angrier by the second. "Where's the conviction? You haven't even reached out to me all week!"

"*Tate...*" Dustin is trying to warn me.

Too late.

"Don't stick up for him, Dustin!"

I want Grant to slam his fist on the table, shatter his beer glass, throw his hands up, curse...I want him to get angry like I'm angry.

His composure only riles me up more. He's dignified and I'm crazed.

With an air of coolness, he slowly pushes his chair back and circles the table to come for me.

I gulp as he tugs my chair out. "Up. Let's go."

"I'm not done here," I protest. "Not with my drink *or* this discussion. You just let Michael kiss me! *Michael!* I don't want Michael!"

I reach for the wine glass, but Dustin lifts it up before I can get it. Then Grant hooks his hands underneath my armpits and lifts me up despite my protests.

Oh. Okay.

We're leaving.

"My roommates can get me home just fine, thank you very much."

I look at them expectantly, but neither of them volunteers. Just great.

They're abandoning me. It seems loyalty is dead these days.

"I have plans to go out," Daphne explains.

"Yeah, same," Sophia says, sounding completely put out. "I was going to go to Josh's…"

"Fine then, forget both of you. I can get home fine. Watch." I turn toward the street and whistle as loud as I can. Then I wave my hand up over my head like a seasoned New Yorker. "Taxi! Taxi!"

Long seconds pass and nary a taxi arrives. No cars even. In fact, if we were in a desert, a tumbleweed would roll by nice and slow, coming to a standstill right in front of me.

Okay. Not a *great* start.

"Well, never mind. That's why they have apps! I'm just going to request an Uber right now and it'll be here before you know it."

My phone is yanked out of my hands before I can get the app open. Grant towers over me, holding my phone up out of reach. I arch a brow then jump up to try to take it from him.

He doesn't let me.

"Ha ha. I get it—you're tall. Now hand me my phone."

I jut my hip out and hold my palm up impatiently.

He doesn't comply. Instead, he slips my phone into his back pocket, takes my shoulders in his sturdy grip, and pivots me around. Then he points over my shoulder, speaking low, so I feel his words cascade down my back.

"You live two blocks that way, Tate. No Uber needed. Now let's go. *March.*"

"Are you serious? Do you guys see how bossy he is?"

But when I turn to the group for backup, they're all looking away like they don't even know us. In fact, Nick's whistling a cheery little tune! It seems they're all siding with Grant on this.

Fine.

"Let's go," he prods. "I'll carry you if I have to."

He thinks I'll make a big stink about this, but instead I

fling my arms out wide. "Don't make promises you can't keep, buddy boy." I start to tip back in a trust fall...

So that's how I end up getting a piggyback ride from Grant down the streets of New York City at midnight. In this position, with little ol' me riding along on his back, I get full access to his bangin' body, and you know what? I go for it. I rub his biceps and get a good feel for their size (big), I tiptoe my fingers along his sloping shoulder muscles (*ooh la la*), and then I even wrap my hands around his neck and squeeze like, *Mwahaha finally, here's my chance to kill you.*

"Would you knock it off?" He laughs.

Fine.

I lean forward and loop my arms around his neck, letting my head fall against his shoulder. I love the scent of his shampoo so much I close my eyes and inhale.

"Why are you being nice to me? I thought you were done with me."

He shakes his head. "Not in this lifetime, Tate."

"Oh yeah? You didn't even look at me once all night."

He snorts. "I couldn't *stop* looking at you."

I don't lift my head. I just smile and keep my eyes closed.

"Was it fun to watch me wallow all by my lonesome?"

"Why were you sad tonight?"

I tighten my arms around him, but there's no need. He has a firm grip on my thighs beneath the hem of my shorts. I'm not going anywhere.

"*You know why,*" I say in a hushed whisper.

Then, because he stays quiet and because maybe now is as good a time for honesty as any, I admit, "I almost wanted to cry when you didn't take the seat by me at the table. You walked right by me and my heart just sank straight into my butt."

Grant almost doubles over with laughter at this. It isn't exactly what I was hoping for, but then I'm laughing too.

And then I'm admonishing him in what I hope is a

punishing tone, but mostly it's just filled with laughter. *"Do not drop me, Grant Navarro.* I might not be some fancy baseball player with hands that are insured for a million bucks, but I still don't want any broken bones tonight!"

Somehow, we make it to my apartment building in one piece.

I tip my head to Howard, the doorman. "Good evening, Howard," I say, as if this moment demands extreme pomp and circumstance. If I had a top hat, I'd doff it in his direction.

"Good evening, Ms. Tate."

"A fine night for a piggyback ride, wouldn't you say?"

He laughs and shakes his head. "Need me to call the elevator?"

"I've got it," Grant assures him, and in we go.

While we wait, I lean in to whisper in his ear. "Last time you accosted me in this very elevator. Do you remember?"

He adjusts his hold on my legs, innocently sliding his hands higher up my thighs. "Of course I remember."

The doors open and we step inside.

"My butt cheeks were on that very rail, right there."

"Keep talking about it and I'll do it again."

My heart thunders with the threat, but I don't back down. I'm half human, half wine at this point; he doesn't scare me.

"Remember what I said earlier about promises?" I taunt.

Suddenly he drops me and turns on me. I've done it now… Every ounce of playfulness is gone. His eyebrows are furrowed, his jaw is set with tension. I audibly gulp.

"I don't like this game you're playing," he tells me. "I've been doing the best I can here."

He pushes the number for my floor, and then the doors close and we're enclosed in the small quiet space. This feels dangerous. We should have opted for the stairs.

"I've stayed away, haven't I?" he continues.

I nod as he descends on me, crowding me into the side of the elevator.

"I haven't messaged you, haven't stolen your number out of Josh's phone..."

I tremble. His eyes don't seem so warm and welcoming in this light.

"I walked right past you at the table tonight instead of taking the seat beside you so I wouldn't do something rash, like this."

He's got me backed into a corner now. I'm as small as a mouse. He takes my hips in his big hands and he grips them so tight I nearly wince. God, I love it. Then he tugs and I sway toward him.

"You don't want me fighting for you, Tate. So, I've stayed away. I've been playing baseball and keeping my head down, but...you know what?" He gets a wicked gleam in his eyes, a cruel tilt to his mouth. "Tonight, if you weren't drunk, I'd finish this game."

We arrive on my floor just as I shake my head, assuring him, "I'm not drunk. Never have been. Don't believe in it. There was actually water in that wine bottle. I'm Jesus in reverse."

He rolls his eyes, cups me around the neck, and prods me out into the hallway like he's my jailer.

"Keep moving. Come on."

I'm already panicking over the thought that he's about to leave me. *Again again again.* We get so close and then he's ripped away from me. I can't take it anymore. "So that's it?! You're not going to take advantage of me even though I wholeheartedly agree to it?! I'll put it in writing. Hand me a piece of paper. I'll sign whatever you want. You got a pen?"

"Tate, unlock the door. *No*—actually, hand me the key. I don't have all night here."

"Oh really? Got somewhere to be? Someone else you'd rather be toying with?"

He ignores my taunt and pushes the key into the lock. Inside, the apartment is pitch black. It's déjà vu, only this time, Grant's not going to haul me up against my bedroom door and kiss me senseless. He's going to leave. Right now.

I can't let that happen. I whirl around and clasp my hands together. "Help me get to bed?"

He frowns.

"What?" I sound surprised. "*You* yourself just said I'm drunk. I can't even walk straight. Ahhh, I'm falling." I'm not. "Help me get ready for bed and tuck me in." I don't even wait for him to agree. I head for my room and pray with every fiber of my being that he follows.

My plan of seduction takes a sharp left turn when I flip on my light and get a good look at my bed. I just washed my sheets earlier this afternoon. The bedding is crisp and fluffy and I'm running toward it before I can help myself.

I let out a guttural moan of pleasure when I get a whiff of detergent. Heaven is a freshly made bed, let me tell you.

I could go to sleep just like this, but Grant walks over and slowly turns me over then motions to my feet. "Left one."

I lift up my left foot, and he takes off my shoe. When he drops it, I lift my other foot for him.

His eyes rove over my face as he admits, "You know your brother gave me an earful this week. All sorts of threats about staying away from you."

"He interrogated me too."

He sets my shoes neatly in the closet and then walks over toward my dresser.

"Pajamas?"

"Top left drawer."

He tugs it open. "It seemed so cut and dry when we first met. I couldn't pursue you. You didn't want me pursuing you. It was better for both of us if I just kept my distance."

"And here you are, picking out my pajamas. I like the ones with little lambs on them, by the way."

He finds the pair I'm requesting and tugs them out.

"Sit up."

I do as he says, dutifully lifting my arms. He comes to sit on the edge of my bed, and I smile at him with a dopey lovesick smile. *Lean in and kiss me, Grant. I'll rock your world, you just wait.*

He doesn't return my smile though. His eyebrows are furrowed so deeply they're almost touching. He doesn't look angry, exactly...

He tugs my shirt up and off gently, like he's taking care not to hurt me as the collar slips over my nose and ears. Then he sets it down on the bed and, with reverent care, slips my pajama top on to replace it. No monkey business. No staring at my chest. God, how can he be so good? I want to be bad, *bad* I tell you!

"Can you take off your shorts?" he asks.

I can, but I shake my head. Why would I when it will be so much more fun to have him do it for me?

He shoots me a deadpan look and I bite down on my bottom lip, not because I'm trying to be sexy—*hello*, that ship has sailed—but because I'm genuinely trying not to laugh. This is all too funny. Grant Navarro is sitting on the side of my bed, larger than life, with a surly expression and that handsome face and those kissable lips and I would trade my entire life savings to know what he's thinking right now as he unbuckles my jean shorts and shimmies them down my legs. I lift my butt to help him out a little bit and then they're gone, whisked away.

He puts my pajama shorts on much too quickly for my taste. It only takes him half a second and then he's off to my bathroom, returning with my pre-loaded toothbrush and a cup of water. It occurs to me then that I might be taking advantage of the situation a little.

"Now I feel bad for making you do this. I only wanted to keep you here a little longer. I'll make it up to you, I swear. What do you want?"

"For you to finish with that toothbrush so I can put it

back."

"Fine."

I brush and brush while he sits down on my bed and watches me.

He's trying so hard to be annoyed, I can tell. I let my eyes cross just to poke at him. He yanks the toothbrush from my mouth and then takes the water cup from me while I'm still drinking it.

"Hey!"

"Lie down, Tate."

"So grouchy."

"Says the pain in the ass."

I burrow down beneath my comforter wearing an ear-splitting smile. "Oh please! You're the one who almost accosted me in the elevator! You...you..."

I forget what I was going to say as he flips off the bathroom light and stands there, leaned against the doorframe, watching me as I dig deep in my psyche for something to say that will set us perfectly back on track. Only, I can't think properly when he looks at me like that.

There's a prolonged charged moment of staring. It's so intimate I could cry. He surveys me with a reverent longing, dragging his gaze from the top of my head where all my hair spills out across my pillow, down to my toes wiggling underneath the comforter.

When his eyes meet mine again, a fissure of awareness passes through me like a cascade of goose bumps.

Oh Grant, you've done it. You've made me fall in love. Good going, you fool.

The thought is so terrifying I have to make light of it. "We have a celebrity name, you know."

He nods and stays put in the doorway. "I was wondering if you'd caught wind of that."

"Oh yes. We're famous. I think that's why Luke suspects something. Pity when you think about the fact that there's nothing to be discovered. We aren't dating. We're not even hooking up…"

"I'm tucking you in bed," he points out like this is absolutely damning.

"Yes, like a dutiful babysitter. Don't worry, I'll tell my mom to tip you."

He very nearly smiles.

"I want you to come lock the front door after I leave."

He's leaving.

NO.

No.

Panic spikes through me as painful as a bolt of lightning.

"Don't leave. Come lie down with me," I plead.

The invitation exhausts him. He rubs the back of his neck as his expression turns weary. Then he shakes his head. Is he staying away because he doesn't want me or because he's trying not to take advantage of me in my current state? Either way, rejection is a searing knife straight through my rib cage. I can feel it like it's really there, wedged in the center of my chest.

"*Please.*"

Reluctantly, he pushes off the doorframe to walk into the room. Like it's the most important thing he's ever done, he slowly takes a seat beside me on top of my comforter.

It feels so good to have him here with me. I reach for his hand and bring it up to my lips so I can kiss his knuckles, then I turn it over and kiss his open palm, his wrist. I clamp down like if he suddenly gets the idea to stand up and flee, I won't let him.

I watch the change come over him. It's so quick I would have missed it if I'd blinked. His light brown eyes turn lethal, a growl of indignation slips past his lips, and then he takes my wrists in his and crushes them against my pillow on either side of my head. He hovers over me with a look bordering on insanity. "You undo me, Tate…"

"How do you think *I* feel?"

He looks almost sorry when he adds, "I can't make myself stay away from you. I can't..."

There's no more fight or flight. I've chosen fight. I've chosen Grant. I'm breathing hard now as I desperately reply, "Then don't. Please, god, don't stay away. Not anymore. Whatever it is, we'll work through it. I can't keep...I can't—"

His lips crush mine as he kisses me hard enough to steal my breath, my thoughts, my soul. Every ounce of despair we've felt in recent days gets poured into our kiss. His fingers bite into my wrists as he holds me still, and I arch up off the bed, almost angrier now than ever. *How dare you deprive me of this? How dare you give me time to come to terms with us? You could have just taken me.*

So take me.

Now.

His mouth breaks away and I'm speaking, trying to give him the truth as fast as I can. "I was wrong—about baseball players, about *you*. I'm... I was prejudiced and stubborn and I thought I needed something, *someone* different. I couldn't see what was right in front of me."

"It's okay, Tate. We're okay." He kisses me again, silencing my apology. Maybe he already knows. Maybe we both have regrets, things we'd take back in a heartbeat.

My hands fist his hair as I grow hotter. I could cry big fat tears as he strings a line of kisses down my neck, showing me how much he adores me with his touch and his groans. His soft lips travel down my chest, skimming the edge of my collarbone, and I shiver with excitement, with need, with complete bliss.

I start to reach for the hem of his shirt, and he sucks in a breath and grabs my hand to stop me.

"*No*. Please don't, Grant. I can't keep doing this. I can't have you one second and then have you ripped away the next."

He hushes me with his lips, reassures me with kisses until I'm putty again.

"I want this *so* bad," he murmurs, his voice so filled with conviction it sends a shiver through me. "I'm not going anywhere. Just let me kiss you, okay?"

And I do.

I let him kiss me until my lips feel swollen and my limbs feel weak. I could do it forever, could fall into him and never resurface. Eventually, he has the good sense to stand and turn out the lights, to crawl into bed beside me and hold me while I close my eyes. I'm so tired and all that wine has taken effect. I can't keep my eyes open even as I beg him not to leave.

"I'm not going anywhere," he promises, kissing my temple and pulling me closer.

―――――

GRANT'S DRINKING coffee with Daphne and Sophia when I rouse myself from my bed the next morning. Minutes ago, I woke up alone and assumed Grant left at some point in the middle of the night for one reason or another, but here he stands with my two roommates, casually talking.

His hair is a little mussed, but he looks no worse for wear, really. I wish I could say the same.

"Morning," I croak, feeling like walking death as I approach them. I can barely pry my eyes open.

My roommates laugh, but Grant just smiles cheekily as he hands me his cup of coffee. "Need this? I just poured it."

"*Yes.* In an IV, preferably, but this will do. Thank you."

I peer up at him with a shy smile, testing the waters. Last night was...*hot*, but I'm not sure where we stand this morning.

Turns out, I'm worried about the wrong thing. Grant isn't looking at me with regret in his eyes. Oh-ho, *no no no*. His expression is downright dangerous. He looks like he knows

I've behaved badly and he not only approves, he *likes* it. I get the impression that if Daphne and Sophia weren't standing here right now, he'd haul me up onto the kitchen counter to continue what we started last night.

In fact, he steps closer and bends down to kiss me even while they watch. It's not on my cheek or my temple—it's square on the lips. A searing claim.

"How'd you sleep?" he asks quietly just before he pulls away.

"Good." I blush, flustered. "You?"

He smiles knowingly. "Good."

"Oh my god. Will you two just get it on already?" Daphne makes a big show of airing out her t-shirt. "This is like watching porn."

Sophia snorts, but Grant doesn't even look ashamed as he keeps his gaze pinned solely on me. He lifts a single brow, teasing as he asks, "*Should we?*"

OH MY GOD.

Daphne lets out a commiserating sound that's half gasp, half groan. "Some of us haven't had sex in ages! This is NOT FAIR!"

Grant laughs and reaches out to grab my waist so he can move me toward him. He leans down and kisses me again, just like that. It's easy as pie now that we've given in to our feelings for one another.

"I'm joking. I mean, I would love to…" He grins at my wide-eyed expression. "But I was just telling Sophia and Daphne that I have to get going in a second. I was going to come wake you, actually…"

My hand grips his shirt before I know what I'm doing. "*No!* Don't leave."

He frowns dejectedly. "I have to. I have a few things I need to do before our team workout."

I try on puppy dog eyes. "Before breakfast?"

He looks truly pained that he can't give in to me. "What about later? Do you have work?"

"I go in at 3 PM so I won't be out until late."

"All right. Get your phone so we can exchange numbers. That way you can call me as soon as you leave."

I smile at his overt bossiness. "Okay. One sec."

Then his phone rings and he checks it. "Again, *seriously*?" he mutters under his breath.

When he realizes we're watching him expectantly, he shakes his head. "It's nothing. Baseball stuff. Go get your phone."

NINETEEN

GRANT

IN TRUTH, that phone call was one of many I've received from Josh today. We've been at his apartment all day. Over the course of the last few days—or hell, it could have been several weeks by the looks of things—Josh has turned his place into a full-blown command center for his proposal to Sophia tomorrow night. There are detailed schematics scattered on the ground and the coffee table. On a previously blank living room wall, he's pinned maps and coordinates of where we're meant to be at exactly what time. He's even hung up a blueprint of the inside of the restaurant where he's planning to do it (he drew it to scale *by hand*, mind you) and we're each accounted for, tiny stick figures with laminated names. Nick drew a penis on his when we first got here, which sent Josh into an absolute tailspin.

He's flustered. Close to losing his shit if you ask me.

"I fucked up, I think. I've been so busy planning the proposal lately. I know Sophia suspects something."

Nick, Dustin, and I sit on his couch, watching him pace back and forth in front of us. None of us says a word until Nick leans in—keeping his wary eyes on Josh—and whispers to me, "Think he's about to puke?"

To be fair, he does look sickly pale.

Josh abruptly stops pacing and pivots, sheer panic draining the last vestiges of color from his face. "Where's the ring?!"

We all sigh. Same thing happened about ten minutes ago. And ten minutes before that too.

It's my turn to assuage his fears. "It's in your suit jacket pocket, on the inside."

He pats around and his shoulders slump with relief once he feels it in there. "Right." Then he continues his pacing and waves his hand in a fast circle. "Someone walk me through the plan again. I'm losing my head here."

We've been through everything half a dozen times. Tomorrow night, Josh is taking Sophia back to the restaurant where they had their first date. He's going to wine and dine her and then the restaurant staff is going to bring the engagement ring out on a dessert plate at the end of the meal.

Nick was confused when he first told us this earlier. "It won't be like *in* the food, right? Didn't that happen in a movie once and the person choked on it?"

"No," Josh confirmed. "The ring box will be on the plate. Nothing else." He tugged the box out of his jacket pocket. Apparently, he's been carrying it around with him for a while. "You guys want to see it?"

In less than a second, we were all huddled together while he tipped the black velvet lid open.

"Oval cut, just like she wants," he explained. "Five carats."

"*Damn*, dude," Dustin commented. "I don't even want to know how much that cost."

"I do," Nick argued.

"It's great," I assured him.

He closed the lid and tucked the ring back into his jacket. "Yeah, I think so. Anyway, I'm hoping you guys can sneak into the back room of the restaurant along with some of our family. Sophia thinks they're all flying in to watch the game tomorrow afternoon, but I want to do a little surprise engagement party right after I propose. I ordered a cake and the restaurant will have food and champagne for you guys."

"Be pretty awkward if she says no and we're all there with balloons and party favors…" Nick said. When we all glared at him, he held his hands up in innocence. "What? It's the truth!"

That was the beginning of the end for us. Once Nick put that little seed of doubt in Josh's head, there was no coming back from it, even now, hours later.

Josh wipes sweat from his brow.

"Okay, first, you need to calm down," I tell him, slow and patronizing.

Josh ignores me. "I think I should go through it from the top one more time with the mannequin."

"Bro, I think you need to burn that thing. I feel like her eyes follow me when I move," Dustin says, which tracks, considering what happened when we first arrived. None of us knew about the mannequin until we walked in here for our "mandatory" planning session with Josh after our afternoon game. She/it/*the thing* was just standing there in the living room wearing a Pinstripes t-shirt with a fire-engine-red wig and a plastic smile. She looked like she came straight from a department store display case *in hell*. When Dustin saw her, he let out a girlish shriek. "What is that, man?!"

"Oh, that's Sophia," Josh said with a tone that made it clear he didn't think there was anything weird about having a fake doll he was using as a stand-in for his girlfriend so he could practice his proposal speech.

Nick took one look at it and inquired mildly, "So you fuck that thing?"

Josh doesn't think we're allowed to make fun of how he's handling this. After all, in his words, "None of you have had the balls to propose to a girl before."

"*Au contraire*," Nick says, holding up a finger. "I have to stop you right there, bud. I asked Megan Scott to be my wife in kindergarten. There was a ceremony by the sand pit and everything."

"Noted," Dustin says, rolling his eyes before trying to get us back on track. "The point is, Josh, Sophia is crazy about you. You guys have been together for years. Hell, you're practically married already. You have nothing to worry about."

Josh looks to me for backup, and I give him a reassuring nod.

Then without a word, Dustin stands, picks up the mannequin, and stuffs her into the hall closet. He wipes his hands as if it's a job well done. "There, that's better."

I'm anxious to wrap this up so I can get to Tate. She's already off work. We've been texting all day. Josh apparently called her around lunch time to tell her his plan for his proposal to Sophia so I don't have to keep it a secret as I text her back.

Grant: Not looking good over here.

Tate: Is he still losing it?

His pacing is worse than ever.

Grant: We're about to have to find a tranquilizer gun. No idea how he's going to manage to sleep before our game tomorrow.

Tate: It's an afternoon game, right?

Grant: Yeah, I need to be at the stadium first thing.

Tate: So...no late-night sneaking into my apartment?

Oh jeez.

My blood travels south.

Dustin looks over at me, suspicious. "You good? What's Tate saying?"

He knows, without having to ask, that's who I'm texting.

I just ignore him.

Tate: Because I just slipped into bed and I would realllyyy love to see you right now...

I push to stand.

"You're leaving?" Josh asks, his voice pitched high.

"No, man. I just need to use the bathroom."

In truth, I would love to leave, but I understand Josh needs me. This is an all-hands-on-deck situation, and I can't abandon him. More than that, I can't leave Dustin and Nick to keep things under control. I just know they'd screw this up somehow. I can imagine Nick chiming in with, "You know what will calm your nerves? A night in Vegas. Yeah, let's do it. I got a plane on standby."

Down the hall, I pass the bathroom and head toward the guest bedroom instead. I shut the door and lock it before immediately dialing Tate's number.

She answers quickly. "Grant? Hey."

"I'm not leaving," I reply to the question in her tone. "I just snuck away for a second."

She laughs. "You're crazy. What's going on over there?"

"Oh just..."

Out in the living room, I hear Dustin's voice. "Do NOT get that thing out again, man! *I swear to god!*"

The mannequin is making a reappearance it seems. I barely restrain a groan.

"You don't want to know," I tell her.

"That bad?"

"How much did Josh tell you about tomorrow?"

"Just that he's going to"—she lowers her voice—"*propose*

at the restaurant where they had their first date and he wants us all there to surprise Sophia afterward. Sophia thinks her parents are coming in to watch the baseball game. I don't know anything else. You can't break away?"

I drag my hand down my face, annoyed at the situation. "I'd feel like an asshole."

"I get it. Yeah."

"And I have to be at the stadium at 6 AM tomorrow…"

She groans, and as innocuous as the sound is, I still feel it low in my stomach.

Every part of me wants to pry open the window across the room, shimmy out, and dash over to Tate's house. We could spend the rest of the night in her bed, forgoing sleep and all our commitments.

I think back to our kiss this morning before I left her apartment. At her door, I stalled as long as possible with a shoe I was pretending wouldn't go on right. "*Damn laces.*" Then I stood to find Tate hanging there, waiting for me.

She had her lips rolled between her teeth, trying to fight back her smile.

"All good?" She was pointing to my shoe.

I approached her and nodded. "All good."

I stood there for a moment, looming over her. I watched her swallow, those delicate muscles working in her neck. Then I lifted my gaze to her lips and I kissed her.

When I pulled back just enough so our lips were still barely touching, I told her I'd see her later. She sagged back against the door, looking like I'd just dosed her with a love potion. I liked her bewildered smile, the happy sheen in her eyes. I would have kissed her again if Josh hadn't called me *yet again*.

"I missed you today."

I can hear the smile in her voice. "Oh yeah? *How much? Enough to come visit me after you're done there?*"

Dammit. I want to, I do, but I have no clue when we'll

wrap up, and I have to get at least a few hours of sleep tonight before our game tomorrow. I can't jeopardize anything with the team. All I have to do is think of my dad sitting in his apartment back home in Phoenix, tuning in on his small TV, waiting to see his son take the field and make him proud. I can't chance it all for a late night with Tate when I know we're going to have a million more nights to come, at least we will if I have anything to say about it.

Besides, there's something to be said about anticipation. Tate and I met at that party just before opening day back in March. It's June. A lifetime has passed between then and now. I've suffered my fair share. I hung back and let Michael swoop in and I managed to not throw blows. I watched her in the stands at my baseball games and fought the urge to wave and smile. On a dozen sleepless nights, I've resisted the urge to message her on Instagram both long paragraphs outlining all my feelings for her as well as the occasional impulsive *You up?*

Now I have her begging me to come over and I'm standing here like a shmuck in Josh's apartment?

Fuck it.

"I'll come right after I leave," I tell her suddenly. "I'll come straight there."

Screw a taxi. I'll run if I have to.

She laughs. "Grant, *no*. You have your game tomorrow, and I agree that it's not a good idea. Josh and the guys need you. We'll just have to wait and see each other at the restaurant tomorrow. I'm trying to get someone to cover my shift at the hospital, but if I can't get off, I might be a little late."

"Tate…" I sound anguished.

"*Grant.*"

"I'll make it up to you tomorrow."

"Swear it," she demands.

I smile. "I swear."

TWENTY

GRANT

"SIR, ANOTHER BROWN BUTTER RADISH CROSTINI?"

I accept the waiter's offered hors d'oeuvres and thank him. He passes me a napkin then moves on to another guest. I have no doubt he'll be back by soon. I'm an easy target for him, especially if he's trying to meet some kind of appetizer quota. This is my third crostini, and I can't be stopped. I've never been a big radish guy. My single dad wasn't regularly garnishing my dinner plate with vegetables unless they could be easily tipped out of a can and nuked for thirty seconds in the microwave. These crostini are so damn good though. The brown butter glaze, the lemon, and the thyme all come together so nicely on the thinly sliced baguette.

The appetizers are only the beginning. Everything in the banquet room has been executed perfectly in accordance with Josh's plan, down to that potted plant in the corner I remember seeing on his blueprint. He's gone all out, spared no expense, and left nothing up to chance.

All of Josh and Sophia's family has arrived in the city, and not just the relatives Sophia knows about, the ones who went to our game this afternoon. Josh has secretly flown in *all* their aunts, uncles, and cousins too. We've got "Memaw" from Arizona, "Pappy" from Mississippi, Sue and Bob from Florida —the list goes on. The room is packed with people.

Josh was smart to hire professionals to handle the decorating. There's a balloon arch in front of a photo backdrop and a big sign that reads CONGRATULATIONS hanging up over the buffet table. Overflowing floral centerpieces perch on every available surface. There are custom napkins and cups printed with a logo Josh had designed that interlock the letter S and J like the two of them are about to launch not just a life, but also a small business together. I'm starting to understand why Josh was so nervous. This is nicer than most weddings I've been to. Scratch that, *all* the weddings I've been to.

Nick comes over with a plate overloaded with little chicken nuggets shaped like dinosaurs.

"Pretty sure those are for the kids," I tell him.

He shrugs and dips one in ketchup. "Why should they get to have all the fun?"

I nod toward the double doors that separate the banquet room from the front of the restaurant. "What's happening out there?"

"Nothing. I don't even think they're here yet."

We can't see into the restaurant because Josh's party planners made sure to cover the glass windowpanes with drapes. Every so often, someone (i.e. Nick) breaks protocol and peeks out to get the scoop on the proposal.

Daphne is the one leading the show back here. Josh didn't trust any of us with the job, which seems fair. Dustin hasn't been at his assigned post near the doors all night. He's too busy annoying Daphne as she circles the room, taking head counts, making sure everyone knows their part. "Now remember, when I give the cue, we're going to sweep the doors open and surprise them. No one go out into the main restaurant before then or the surprise will be ruined and Josh will quite literally *kill* me. There are bathrooms down that hall over there, and if you have any questions or need a drink or a napkin or another plate of food, talk to this guy."

She's referring to Dustin, who's forced to smile and wave at everybody.

The restaurant's manager comes rushing into the room. "They're here!"

"Oh shit! It's happening!" Nick says, starting to scarf down his food faster.

Everyone starts chatting excitedly, worrying over where they should stand, what they should do with their arms. "Are we saying surprise and like jumping out at them or what?"

Fortunately, the restaurant is big and can handle the uptick in noise. Besides, it doesn't really matter if Sophia suspects there's a party going on back here. There probably always is.

The side door to the banquet room swings open and a waiter escorts Tate inside. She's late, but we knew she would be. She couldn't find anyone to take her shift so she had to dash here straight from work. God I'm happy to see her. More than that—*ecstatic*.

She's still wearing her scrubs, which I happen to like. They're fitted and cute. I'm already headed in her direction and I will her to look over at me, but Daphne's on her first, scooping her up and taking her straight to her parents. They're excited to see Tate, which makes sense. I'm sure they've met her before. After that, Daphne keeps ahold of Tate and leads her around the room to introduce her to various aunts and uncles. It's nice and all, but some of us have been waiting all day to see Tate. Do I need to get in line or something?

Tate has to know I've been tracking her every move. She finally peers over her shoulder, scanning the room, looking, looking, *looking*. Her hazel eyes lock with mine and her mouth spreads into a slow smile. It's astounding what that smile does to me. Before I think of the consequences, I tilt my head toward the door she just came through.

The gesture says, *Follow me.*

In the hallway, there are two separate bathrooms. They're each formal and fancy, with decorative wallpaper, moody lighting, and burning candles on the marble counters. I stand at the door of the far one as I watch Tate turn the corner into the hallway wearing a perplexed expression.

"Showing me around?" she teases as she approaches.

I don't steal a kiss from her then even though I want to. I take her arm and lead her inside the bathroom before closing the door behind us. That heavy thud is ominous. The swipe of the lock makes her gulp.

I'm not a villain, but my feelings for her almost feel villainous, extreme, all-consuming.

She still has her hospital bag slung on her shoulder, always too heavy for her to be lugging around everywhere. I take it and set it up on the counter.

"Did you bring clothes to change into?"

She doesn't take her eyes off me. She's tracking my every move. "They're in my bag."

"Get them out."

She frowns, trying to figure out my angle. She wants me to put her fears to rest, but unfortunately, I can't. She and I have been circling each other for weeks now. Finally, we're alone in this bathroom.

When she doesn't move, I reach into her bag and reverently lift out her folded black dress and heels to set them down on the counter, then I walk over to Tate and, without asking first, take the hem of her scrub top and start to slide it up to reveal her toned stomach. We've been here before. I helped her undress after the bar, but that was different for a million reasons. I was still holding back then, not only because I didn't want to take advantage of her after she'd had a few glasses of wine, but because we hadn't finished coming clean about our feelings.

I push her top up and then peel it off. She stands before me wearing a black bra with frilly lace adorning each cup. It's too sexy for work. *Jesus.* She wore this all day, expecting to see me here after. I imagine her picking it out this morning with the intention of driving me wild.

I trace the edge of each cup first with my eyes and then with my pointer finger.

"Someone will need the bathroom soon," she says with a breathy voice.

I watch how swiftly her chest rises and falls. Erratic, excited, *scared*.

Her hands fist by her sides.

"There's another one," I say with an indifferent tone and a shrug before bending down and kissing the swell of each breast. I feel her heart there, pounding hard with anticipation.

God, she smells good.

I stand back up and she lifts her eyes, watching me through her dark lashes. I reach for one of the dainty straps of her bra and slip two fingers underneath it like I'm going to tug it off. Instead, I run my fingers from her shoulder down over her collarbone and then back. Her skin is so soft, her breaths so short, even from this.

I decide to leave her bra in place as I untie her scrub bottoms. Her panties are also divinely, *heavenly* black. They cut up high over her hips, making it so her legs stretch on forever once she finishes stepping out of her pants and shoes. She wiggles her toes in her white cotton socks, and it makes me smile.

"Are you going to dress me now?" she asks, tipping her head to the side as her gaze roves over me. "Don't we need to get back to the party…?"

She's presenting me with the responsible option, but it sounds like she's hoping for the exact opposite.

I casually lean back against the counter. "Do *you* want to go back to the party, Tate?"

She folds her arms across her stomach while she looks back over her shoulder, at the door, as if to listen for what's going on out there. Josh and Sophia only just arrived. Because he went over his plan with us a thousand times, I know they're going to eat their dinner first. It'll include cocktails, an appetizer, entrees, and then *finally*, they'll get to dessert. We have a good while to stall before then. We could go back out, Tate could chat with Josh's Memaw, or...*not*.

She seems to come to the same conclusion I do because she lets her arms drop to her sides. Then there's a subtle change about her, in her expression mostly. That innocent, scared look morphs into a determined sort of wickedness that sets my body on fire as she reaches behind her back and unclasps her bra. The black straps and all that sweet frilly lace slip off her chest, and then she dangles her bra on one finger, holding it out for me to take and put with the rest of her clothes.

I don't know if I breathe as I take her in, all that bare skin, tan and pink, pert and quivering. I watch her stomach squeeze tight with nerves. I know I have to act, but I could stand here and stare forever like she's my last sunrise, my life's work.

"Grant?" she asks, her voice shaky.

My throat is tight. I can't speak.

I push off the counter and walk toward her. Without a moment's hesitation, I sweep my hands up to cup her face and I kiss her. Not hard, not demanding—tender and coaxing and loving. *Loving.* The word sideswipes me. I pull her to me and part her lips. Our tongues touch and we're backing up against the wall. I have her pinned there as our kiss deepens.

Her hands were down, forgotten at her sides, but now they're on my hips, creeping under my sports coat and shirt to get to my bare skin. She shivers and then I lift her, forcing her legs around my hips, keeping her in place against the wall. I hold her there securely. She's kissing me with enough abandon to let me know she's not scared of falling.

"Touch me," she begs, and I release her face, pulling back to look at her.

Red lips. So red I take them again in an instant, biting down on her bottom lip and tugging until she whimpers. Then my mouth descends on her neck, the top of her shoulder, her naked breast. I take the tip into my mouth and I adore her, taste her, suck until she's rolling her hips against me and digging her fingers into my coat. She rubs herself on me in a hot steady rhythm, trying to ease her suffering.

I'm entirely too dressed for what we're doing, but the idea of stopping to sling off my coat and shirt and jeans pisses me off. The moment feels too precarious, too tender to let it slip away, so I stay put, recapture her mouth, steal her good sense.

Stay here, stay here, I plead as our tongues roll together. *Let me have this.*

Quickly, before she even realizes what's happened, I set her down and drop to my knees. Not slowly, in a rush, I tug her panties down her thighs until she's completely naked above me. Another shiver. A cascade of goose bumps over all that wonderfully bare skin. I grip the back of her thighs then let my head drop to her navel, breathing her in. Her hand caresses my hair. There's a sweetness to it that almost doesn't belong here. I close my eyes and try to get a grip on my own desire, but it's useless. We're on the cliff of insanity. The only thing left is to leap.

I've never thought of love as crazy before, but then, maybe everything before this was a poor substitute for the real thing. What's sane about kneeling in a restaurant bathroom, staring up at Tate with her blown-out pupils and trembling bottom lip? What's normal about feeling like I would do whatever she asked of me in this moment—slay, conquer, fight, love, *plead*. It feels like a thousand lifetimes have brought me to this moment on the floor, on my knees before a woman I love.

I understand then the feeling my dad must have had when he walked away from his entire family—life as he knew it in Mexico—to pursue a future with my mom.

"Do you regret it?" I asked him once, when I was young and couldn't wrap my head around his decision.

He caught me by the chin and looked me square in the eyes as he replied sternly, "Not for a single second. I loved your mom with everything I had."

It looks like Tate can barely breathe, but then neither can I.

I use my grip on her thighs to peel her further apart, opening her up for me. She looks down at me with flushed cheeks as I kiss my way between her legs, coaxing her sweetness out of her as I drag my tongue over her center, right in that perfect spot. A groan tears through her like it's painful to have me here, in possession of this intimate part of her. I'm so gentle at first, but then I can tell she needs more. My tongue swirls around and around, and then I back away. She whimpers and presses her hips closer to my face. I smile, which she hates. I feel it in the way her fist tightens in my hair. I bite her inner thigh, and she growls.

"*Grant*," she says, her voice thick with desire. "Please."

I'm teasing her and I should feel bad, but no. We've both been left wanting these last few weeks. There's a certain kind of torture in drawing out the inevitable. I press my forearm against her stomach, pushing her flat against the wall again as I lift her leg over my shoulder. Then I drag my thumb through her wetness, and as she quivers, I bury my face between her legs again. This time, I'm relentless with my tongue as I slide two fingers inside her. She thrusts her hips, rubbing herself back and forth over my mouth as much as my arm over her stomach will allow. She's taking from me the same way I'm taking from her. I love how desperate she is, not shy in the least, not now.

My name slips from her lips in a hushed, desperate whisper as she clenches around my fingers. I continue to work her up as she starts to shake and tremble. Her back arches off the wall and her lips part as she gasps harshly.

It's like I've taken a pickaxe and shattered her. Watching her come apart is the sexiest thing I've ever seen.

The bathroom is utterly silent as I rise to my feet. Her eyes open and she surveys me with an awed expression. I take it as a compliment. Then I check my watch and shake my head.

"Time to head back out there."

A laugh bursts out of her like the idea is utterly absurd. "You can't expect me to go out and join everyone *now*!"

I walk to the sink and turn on the water as I meet her expression in the mirror. "We have to."

"I'm naked in this restaurant bathroom, Grant Navarro!" Then it's like the realization *really* dawns on her. "Oh my god! *I'm naked in this restaurant bathroom...*"

I can't keep from laughing as she suddenly leaps into action.

"You just completely hijacked my senses, by the way. I can't *believe* I let you do that."

"I'd do it again if we had time."

She stops unfolding a linen hand towel and looks at me, her jaw dropped, mouth wide open. "Grant! You can't keep on like this! I won't be able to look you in the eyes the rest of the night!"

Over the course of the next few minutes, I help her get dressed and make sure she feels put together enough to join everyone again. She was smart to pack a dress that wouldn't wrinkle in her hospital bag. Once she has it on and she's touched up her makeup with some products she brought with her, you'd never suspect a thing. Well, except for every time she meets my eyes in the mirror and blushes bright red.

"Would you stop?!"

"I'm just watching you get ready."

"Yes, well...it feels like a lot, okay. I've never done anything like that. I mean—wait." Her eyes grow wide. "*Have you?*"

I shake my head. "Not at a restaurant..."

"Grant!"

I come up behind her and drop a kiss to her bare shoulder, just beside her dress strap. I want to tell her the truth, that there were women before her but this feels markedly different. Scary in a good way, but also in a bad way. This fear is new and unfamiliar. The worry about how much I've already given her. The helplessness that comes with trusting another person with your heart.

She finds my hand and gives it a squeeze. I think we both understand the gravity of the situation we've found ourselves in, but there's not time to discuss it now.

"C'mon, let's go. Hand me your bag. We need to hurry or we're going to miss the big surprise. You and Josh will both kill me if that happens."

As luck would have it, we return to the banquet room just as the double doors are swept open. We rush over to the group and peer into the dining room as Sophia glances up from staring admiringly at her new engagement ring to find us all waiting for her.

Everyone throws their arms up. "*SURPRISE!*"

A beat later, Nick asks, "Did you say yes?"

Sophia freezes then looks at Josh. "*What?!* Are you kidding?!"

Her hands cover her mouth as she starts to cry.

Josh immediately looks horrified. "Oh god, did I do the wrong thing? I can send everyone home. Pappy, get your cane."

I know he'd make good on the threat if Sophia wanted him to. That's how much he loves her.

Sophia laughs and shakes her head, throwing her arms

around his neck as she hugs him tight. "It's perfect. It's exactly what I wanted."

There's a collective sigh across the crowd. Even the other patrons in the restaurant are relieved to know the engagement went off without a hitch. No one wants their dinner with a side of heartbreak.

Josh tugs Sophia to her feet to lead her toward the banquet room. She takes in everyone he thought to invite, all the details he included: the flowers, the balloons, the decor. Meanwhile, she fires off a million questions.

"How'd you keep this such a secret?!"

"How long have you had this ring?"

"Oh my god! Is that my cousin Lucy?!"

Dustin catches my eye and laughs. I know we're both thinking of Josh pacing at his apartment like a madman last night. All that worrying for nothing...

Then I hear a sniffle, and when I peer down, I realize Tate's crying at my side. Tears trickle down her cheeks as she laughs and brushes them away. She looks up at me with wet eyes, her brows tugged together as she smiles. "It's just so sweet. They love each other so much."

It's then, staring down at her, that I realize I'm a total goner. No better than Josh.

I wonder if he'd let me borrow that mannequin.

TWENTY-ONE

TATE

GRANT and I leave the engagement party arm in arm around 8:30 PM. Most of the gang planned to stay and hang out at the restaurant bar, but Grant had somewhere he wanted to take me. The whole group seemed interested in the fact that we were leaving together.

"I don't see why you guys have to go," Nick said. "Party's just begun! If you want to make out, just sneak off to the bathroom again…"

I reached out to playfully slap his arm. "*NICK.*"

"*What?* You guys were so obvious!" He continued with an impersonation in a high-pitched voice. "*Oh hey, Tate, follow me out into the hallway for no reason at all. I definitely don't look like I'm about to hump your leg as soon as I get you alone.*"

"It wasn't like that," I insisted, looking at Grant for backup.

He gave an amused shrug. "It was a little like that."

I tossed my hands up in defeat.

I guess the cat's out of the bag there. At least they think our bathroom activities were PG compared to what really happened. I'd pass away from embarrassment if they found out the rest.

I won't lie…I sort of thought Grant would whisk me straight back to his apartment as soon as we left the restaurant for some sweet, sweet lovemaking. Instead, we head back toward my place. Only, we don't turn when we're supposed to. He's the one who called the Uber. I didn't even think to confirm our final destination with him, so when we arrive outside my brother's house, I'm speechless.

"Do…" I look between the house and Grant then back again. "Do you live close by here?"

Grant shakes his head, already unbuckling his seatbelt and preparing to get out. "That's your brother's place, right?"

"Yes…"

He thanks the Uber driver then gets out to open my door. My mouth is still hanging open in shock as we ascend the stairs and ring the doorbell.

Harper answers and immediately gets reprimanded for it.

"Harper Allen, you do not answer the door on your own! What if there's a crazy person on the other side?" My brother sees me and decides to be funny. "Oh look, there *is* a crazy person."

I would flip him off if not for Harper. I settle for a mocking "Ha ha."

My brother grins, and then finally he puts the pieces together: I'm standing on his doorstep beside Grant Navarro, his teammate. We're here alone, just the two of us.

"Is he expecting us?" I ask Grant out of the corner of my mouth. Before he can answer, I repeat the same question to my brother. "Were you expecting us?"

"Who's there?!" Chloe calls from the kitchen.

"Aunt Tate and *Grant Navarro*!" Harper shouts back.

"What?! Really?" Chloe comes peeling around the corner. "Huh. I assumed you were kidding."

"Nope. Look, it's him. You're taller up close," Harper says to Grant, leaning her head back. "More handsome too."

Luke's already massaging his temples. "*Harper.*"

"*What?* I have eyes, you know. He looks like my Ken doll, the one with brown hair and a tan."

"You're eight!" Luke and I say at the same time, further solidifying that as much as we want to be different, we are, in fact, *the same.*

"All right, all right, can you two move aside so they can come in? I swear. Were you just going to leave them on the doorstep all night?" Chloe pushes Luke and Harper out of the way so Grant and I can walk into the foyer.

I ruffle Harper's hair and wink down at her.

"That's him, isn't it?" she whispers (loudly) to me. "The *boy.*"

I nod and she squeals, drawing the attention of all the adults.

"I...thought I saw a mouse." She comes up with the lie almost too fast and points to the corner. "Over there."

By now Luke and Chloe know not to believe any of her nonsense. In fact, Luke doesn't even look in the corner. His attention is on Grant.

"It's good to see you, man," Luke says with a stiff tone. Clearly, he's confused by our appearance at his home, which tells me Grant didn't give him a heads-up that we were on our way over. I wonder how he got the address. Dustin or Josh, probably.

"Yeah, sorry for the intrusion. I was hoping we could talk for a second."

Uh-oh.

"All of us?" Luke asks, meeting my eyes.

I subtly shake my head to let him know I have no idea what this is about.

Although...I do have an inkling, a tiny fear-slash-hope of what this could be.

"Just you and me if that's okay."

Chloe immediately starts prodding us out of the room.

"Oh! Yes. Harper, Tate, come to the kitchen. Let's have a midnight snack. You girls want some popcorn?"

Harper says, point-blank, "I want candy."

She's too smart for her own good. She knows Chloe's trying to get her out of the room and she's using the opportunity to her advantage. If there were a CIA for children, Harper would have already been recruited.

"Fine." Chloe rolls her eyes. "Come on. I'll let you have something from my secret stash."

"Secret stash?! I *knew* you and Dad eat candy after I go to bed every night. What is it? Huh? Peanut M&Ms? Skittles? Starburst? Oh my gosh, *do you have Hershey's Kisses hidden somewhere?*" Chloe neither confirms nor denies her suspicion, and Harper gasps like she's never heard anything more hurtful in all her life. "You *know* those are my favorite."

Chloe is wholly unfazed by Harper's theatrics. "Uh-huh, come on. You can have whatever you want."

I hate to leave Grant to fend for himself. Before I head into the kitchen with Chloe and Harper, I glance back one more time. He meets my gaze and nods reassuringly before Luke claps him on the shoulder and points down the hall toward his office.

"So is this what I think it is?" Chloe asks me as soon as we're out of earshot.

"It could be."

She stands on a barstool to reach a bag of contraband candy hidden in a cabinet above the refrigerator.

"So *that's* where you hide it!" Harper exclaims.

"Yeah, well, not anymore…"

I motion for Chloe to throw me a Hershey's Kiss. Then she heaves the overly filled bag down from the cabinet and slaps it onto the counter. It's filled with what looks like Halloween, Christmas, and Easter candy from the last year, at least.

We all go digging.

"Should we be eavesdropping?" Chloe asks, tearing into a mini bag of Skittles with her teeth.

"It's probably better not to, right?"

"It'd be dishonest," Harper chides, looking affronted that we would even consider the idea.

"Things are getting more serious with you two?"

Aware of the tiny ears in the room, I simply nod. I can give Chloe details later. "Serious enough that we're here right now."

"You really like him?"

I nod, too embarrassed to even meet her eyes. I more than like him. *Ugh.* What a horrible spot to be in—this feels so fragile and new and horrifying and wonderful and before I know it, I'm rooting through that bag of candy again because it seems like sugar is the only thing that's going to help get me through the foreseeable future.

While we wait for the boys to finish up their conversation, I regale Harper and Chloe with the details of Josh's proposal to Sophia. It was a really sweet night, and though Josh kept the engagement party to just family and a few close friends, I'm sure Luke and Chloe will be invited to the actual wedding, so that will be fun.

"I want to go to the wedding too!" Harper says.

"Maybe you can be my date," I tell her.

I mean…she might have to be if it's not going well with Luke and Grant.

"What could be taking them so long?" I ask now, my impatience growing.

Chloe smiles at me, recognizing something that I don't. "It's sweet, what he's doing. I don't think it was totally necessary. Quite frankly, Luke had already started to come around to the idea of you guys dating, especially considering the kind of guy Grant is. But it's still a nice gesture if you ask me. It makes me like him all the more."

"So you approve?" I ask, knowing how much her opinion matters to me.

She grins. "Absolutely."

A door opens down the hall and I go hurtling out of the kitchen with Harper hot on my heels. Grant and Luke walk out of Luke's office, and I swear to god, there are tears in my brother's eyes. *What?*

Before he says anything, he walks over and pulls me forward into a tight hug.

Okay...

"Um, what's going on?" I look between my brother and Grant as my brother's arms tighten around my shoulders. I only manage to return the gesture with a light awkward tap on his shoulder, like, *There there, now get off me.*

No one answers my question.

Luke steps back and shakes his head, smiling wistfully. "You'll have to bring Grant over for breakfast on Sunday."

When I look at Grant, he's smiling. "You ready to go?"

"I guess?"

We say our goodbyes. Harper makes me promise to come over Sunday, and then she tugs on my arm so I'll bend down and she can whisper in my ear, "*I think your boy problems are over!*"

Yeah, maybe so, kid.

Once we're alone out on the sidewalk, I make a show of stopping Grant and turning him to face me so I can inspect him for bodily harm. I lift his arms one at a time, spin him around, pat his thigh, and tell him to "spread 'em."

He doesn't. Instead, he laughs and grabs me by the shoulders so he can redirect us toward my apartment. It's not far from here, only a few blocks.

"No cuts? No bruises?"

He laughs. "No. Your brother and I were just talking."

"Did he threaten your life or anything? Because I swear he

takes his job as my big brother too seriously sometimes. It's just that our parents are so far away—"

"Tate, no. We just talked, I promise. And most of it wasn't even about you and me. We were just shooting the shit in there after a while. He's a good guy."

"Shooting the—" I exclaim, only half-serious. "I was *sweating* in that kitchen! I mean, I was really losing my head in there!"

"Oh yeah? You have a little chocolate on your lip."

Dammit. I wipe it away.

"So…what'd you tell him?"

Grant shrugs.

My jaw drops. *"Are you serious?* You aren't going to tell me?"

He narrows his eyes and looks off into the distance like he's trying to recall. "You know? It eludes me. It all happened so fast."

I jostle his arm. "Grant!"

He laughs and shakes his head. "It was nothing, Tate. I just wanted to smooth the path forward for us."

*"So…what does that mean?"

He turns and levels me with a sincere, heart-clenching look. "It means I'm going to ask you to be my girlfriend."

THE G WORD.

"Seriously?"

He nods, taking my hand and squeezing it with reassurance.

"Like right now?"

I'm just trying to prepare myself for it. Practice my facial expressions, my cool-calm-and-collected *sure, okay, whatever*.

He shakes his head. "Nah, when you least expect it."

His mischievous smile tells me I'm really in for it. As we keep walking and slip into conversation about other stuff—his game schedule later this week, the desserts they had at the engagement party—he really lets me have it.

We turn the corner toward my apartment building and we're about to pass a magazine stand.

Grant cuts in front of me and takes my hands. "Hold on."

My mouth immediately goes dry. This is it! It's happening!

"Tate, do you want to…" He pauses for dramatic effect. I'm already imagining calling him my boyfriend for the first time. I'm going to work it into every conversation I can for the next three months. Then he drops the axe. "…pick out some gum before we head up?"

I growl and cut past him toward my apartment. He laughs and chases after me, but the torture's not done.

When we reach the elevators in my building, he stops and looks at me with a completely earnest and reverent expression. "Tate, do you—" Heavy pause. Soaring hope. Racing heart. Then he points beside me. "Want to press the button for the elevator?"

"I hate you," I say once the doors sweep open.

He laughs and grabs my hips, tugging me back against his chest.

"No, no," I tell him. "You go stand over there, in timeout."

He relegates himself to the opposite corner of the elevator, the whole time fighting back his self-satisfied smile.

Then just before the doors open at my floor, he says, "Be my girlfriend."

Just like that!

Is he joking!?

"No!"

He laughs, completely blindsided by my response.

"Absolutely not."

My voice has a lot of heat, but it's for dramatic effect only. I want him to suffer.

He follows me toward my apartment, right on my heels, but he doesn't touch me. Knowing he wants to is half the fun.

"Be my girlfriend," he pleads, grabbing my hips while I'm unlocking the door.

I push it open and shimmy out of his hold. "*No.*"

Another laugh, but then we're inside the apartment, sliding off our shoes. He takes my hospital bag into the kitchen so he can empty my lunchbox and start to clean it out. *INFURIATING!*

While he busies himself with that, I go into my room to shower. It's been a long day and I feel like I still smell like the hospital.

I drop my clothes on the floor like a Hansel and Gretel breadcrumb trail. My dress gets tossed here, a high heel there. I turn the water on and listen to him moving around in the kitchen.

I leave the bathroom door open on purpose. I step inside the shower and start my usual routine as the glass turns foggy. I hear my bedroom door close and my nerves skyrocket. I try to play nonchalant when in fact I am chock-full of chalant. I reach for my shampoo and squirt some into my hand, lathering it up into foamy suds. Like I'm being watched by unblinking lust-filled eyes, I try to apply it as seductively as possible, only to realize once I'm done that Grant isn't even *in* the bathroom.

I rub a little circle to clear the glass at my eye level, and dammit, he's over on my bed, flipping through the book on my nightstand, *Klara and the Sun*. It's not a big deal that he's found my current read except for when he catches the bookmark tucked inside it.

For the Pinstripes home games, they print photos of the players on the tickets. Each fan gets a different player. Sometimes you might get Luke, sometimes Nick, etc. It's a nod to baseball trading cards, and fans really go crazy over them. When I went to the game with Michael a few months ago, I happened to get a ticket with Grant's picture on it. I kept it, and now he's looking down at it.

Is it hugely telling? I hope not. It's not like I've drawn hearts all over it or superimposed an image of myself beside him to see what we would look like as a couple (though the thought *has* occurred to me).

Even still, it's not nothing.

He tucks the bookmark back into *Klara and the Sun* then rests it gently back on my nightstand. His gaze rises and our eyes lock, and even though I'm the one standing naked in my shower, I feel like of the two of us, *I'm* the voyeur. I look away quickly and grab my conditioner, finishing up as fast as I can.

After I turn off the water, I'm careful to crack open the glass door only enough that I can wrench my towel off its hook and yank it inside. I manage to do it all while staying mostly concealed in the shower. I think I hear a faint chuckle from my bedroom, but I can't be sure and I'm too chicken to look up and confirm if he's watching me right now as I fumble with my towel in this confined space.

I'd love to put my clothes on in here too, but I forgot to bring them with me. I don't usually have a man waiting on my bed while I shower...so I wrap my towel around my middle, concealing the important bits: everything between upper chest and midthigh. Then I throw my shoulders back and stroll out of the bathroom as confidently as possible.

Grant sits on the edge of my bed, watching me like a predator. He doesn't speak, but his gaze follows me as I head toward my dresser.

I don't want to, I really thought I could avoid it, but I lose the battle and glance over at him at the last second. Our eyes meet and that familiar awareness tingles down my spine, settling like a warmth in my lower belly.

He cocks his head to the side. "Should I try to convince you to be my girlfriend?"

I stay quiet, but he can see the little quirk of my smile I'm trying to hide.

He doesn't let me reach the dresser where my pajamas are waiting for me. He pushes up off the bed and cuts in front of me, blocking my path, as impenetrable as a concrete wall.

I swallow my nerves and look up, but I don't make it all the way to his face. I can't. I settle for his broad chest, which, quite frankly, feels difficult enough on its own.

He takes a step closer, and I stand stock-still. I hold my breath when he lifts his hand to feel my towel between his fingers. He rubs the cotton at the center seam that runs down my chest and stomach. He's not even touching me yet and I still shiver.

Damn. This isn't a fair fight.

I clutch the two ends of my towel with a fiercely tight grip, white knuckles and all, as he slowly slips his hand past the opening. His hand smooths over my naked waist, gripping it firmly.

"Should I?" he asks again as I sway toward him. "*Convince you?*"

"You had your chance by the magazines," I argue, completely annoyed that my voice has lost all conviction now. I'm hopeless.

"Ah, so we're doomed already..." he quips, rubbing his thumb up and down the front of my hip bone.

Doomed is one way to put it, for sure. I certainly feel like whatever this is, it's inescapable, for better or worse.

His hand moves higher in the towel and my breath hitches. My mistake. I should have thrown on an oversized robe or a zip-up onesie. I'm ripe for the taking in this cotton towel, and he uses it to his advantage. His hand slides around my back, parting the two sides of the towel even more as he bends to take my mouth. He kisses me soft and sweet, gentle and tender. For a few moments, we stay like that, with his strong arm banded around my back as he holds me tightly. There's a sweeping swell of emotions building as our kiss turns desperate. He backs me up toward the bed as our tongues explore each other. We're taking our time, and yet I feel how much he wants me. It's in the firm grip of his hand, his whispered

"Fucking hell" as he breaks the kiss and stares down at me.

I'm unsteady without him, tipping back onto the bed. He doesn't help me. He lets me fall and then he hauls me higher so there's room for him to climb up and over me. His knees rest beside my hips as he tugs his shirt off, tossing it over the edge of the bed. He doesn't make it to his jeans before he impatiently bends down to kiss me again. We get swept up in it. I think it was only meant to be a fleeting pause in the middle of him undressing, but now my fingers are tangled in his hair and the towel is slipping off me. He pushes the two sides apart so his hands can cover my bare skin wherever he'd like. Tightening around my bicep, skimming over my breasts, pressing down my navel, peeling apart my legs. He takes his time, and I grow more and more restless.

My hand tightens in his hair, and he looks up. Our eyes lock.

Grant.

Save me here.

He sits up on his knees and reaches for his jeans. God, let me. I do it faster. I have that zipper down in a flash, and all the while, he watches me with a lust-filled gaze like he's trying to decide his best plan of attack for devouring me. *Start with her head or her toes?*

I have his boxer briefs pushed down and his hard length in my hand before I've even registered what's happening. He hisses as I tighten my hold. I love it, *love* it. He's silk in my palm. He squeezes his eyes closed and I turn wicked, starting to drag my hand up and down, loving the way he responds as I do. I pump harder and watch him unravel. Mwahaha, I'm maniacal. Then his eyes blink open and the darkness there sends a shiver of fear across my skin. Goose bumps bloom everywhere.

He knocks my hand off him in a manner that's just authoritative enough for me to realize I'm not the only one with magic hands. He slides his fingers down the center of me, spreading me open, dipping inside. Oh how the tables have turned. Now I'm panting, losing my head, grabbing his wrist and keeping him there as I buck my hips and use him to satisfy my every whim. "I'm so close," I tell him with my eyes squeezed shut and my head tipped back. I feel the first tingles starting to sweep through me, the promise of what's to come. Then his hand is ripped away and I could scream.

My eyes open to find he's getting a condom from his wallet.

THANK GOD.

I'm impatient, grabbing fistfuls of my comforter as I watch him tear that foil. He's looking at me while he does it, arrogantly taking in my naked body. It's like my belly button interests him as much as my breasts as much as my knees as much as my fingers, wrists, toes. My towel still covers a portion of my leg, and he pushes it off with an annoyed flick as if he can't stand the thought of not having access to every inch of me.

I want him to know he can continue full steam ahead. I'm giving my hearty consent. Once the condom is on, I reach forward, grab his butt (it's DIVINE) in both hands, and smile.

"Please, please have sex with me and do not stop until the sun comes up. Do you understand the assignment?"

He laughs and returns his hand between my legs. *God, that feels good.*

"Think you can handle that, Tate?"

"Think *you* can handle that, *Navarro*?"

He smirks and shakes his head, bending over me. I love his weight, the way the mattress dips as he covers me. His mouth is on mine, sealing our fate as he kisses me. My legs fall apart and he positions himself there, sliding into me slowly for the first inch, then another. Finally, he finishes with a deliciously painful thrust.

Holy hell.

I arch up off the bed and I must have cried out because he holds himself steady as I adjust, *barely*. He tilts my chin, asks me something.

I blink up at him, and he's staring down with so much adoration I could cry. I nod and smile to let him know everything is okay. Intense, but okay.

He starts to move in me with hard, deep, powerful strokes, one building upon another, upon another. Grant is no amateur. Me? I have no control over anything. The sounds coming from my mouth? That lust-filled heady moan tearing through me as his finger rubs soft circles over my sensitive skin? What am I doing with my hands again? Oh right, gripping his butt, digging my nails in, demanding more when, in fact, I cannot handle more. I'll break, sir.

I'm gasping for breath, *for sanity*.

He asks if I'm okay as I turn my head against my comforter and bite my bottom lip.

No I am not okay, MR. NAVARRO, and you're to blame for that.

When I don't answer, he moves like he's going to pull back.

I turn back to face him and wrap my arms around his neck like I'm going to try to hold him against me. "No! I mean, *yes*. I'm okay, just…"

He doesn't make me finish my sentence, which is good because it was going to sound like incoherent gibberish at best. He rolls his hips and thrusts in me as he closes his eyes. It's like he's in a state of absolute nirvana. *Me!* I'm the cause of that!

He confirms this with a sexy *"Christ*, Tate" that sounds like it was ripped from deep inside him, not of his own volition, and already I know my ego will know no bounds after this. Good luck trying to convince me I'm not some kind of seductive goddess.

His hand stays where I need it, creating that perfect

amount of friction. He strokes me, and each time, I tip closer to that feeling like a bomb is detonating inside me. I'm there with him one second, and the next I'm crying out as my back arches off the bed and stars dance behind my closed eyes.

As tingles spark down my limbs, he never stops thrusting, pumping, rubbing until I feel him jerk inside me. He lets out a low, guttural moan, his hips meeting mine as he sinks into me as deeply as ever. He continues sliding in and out, slowing down after each time until we've finished fluttering back to reality like two little exhausted feathers.

Our eyes open at the same time and our gazes meet. I smile a secret smile, which makes *him* smile.

"So? Did I convince you?" he asks, surveying my flushed cheeks and wrung-out features.

I shrug playfully. "Maybe. I mean, that was round one. Let's get some hydration and see if we can't do a bit more convincing. I really want to be sure I know what I'm getting myself into here…"

He just shakes his head and bends down, sealing the challenge with a kiss.

TWENTY-TWO

TATE

A WEEK LATER, I walk to work beneath a cloudless blue sky. A little animated robin lands on my shoulder and tweets a cute-ass song in step with my stride. My coffee is exactly the temperature I like. My hair has never been shinier or healthier. My mood? Fan-fucking-tastic.

Grant and I are boyfriend and girlfriend.

HAVE YOU HEARD, EVERYONE?! I'm dating Grant Navarro!!

I expect life to be different, like people will stop me on the street and ask me about my skincare routine. "Girl, you're *glowing*!"

Much to my disappointment, work is still work, and animals aren't any more drawn to me than they would be otherwise. But it doesn't matter. My smile can't be dulled.

Every night since Josh's proposal to Sophia, we've stayed together either at his place or mine. In the shower, against the closet door, propped up against a dresser, hanging off the side of the bed, propped precariously on a kitchen stool —we've done it. A lot. I'm surprised I haven't pulled a muscle or sprained my neck. Grant's not really one to go easy on me. In fact, I'm blushing just thinking about the

ways he positions my body for maximum, *erm*...effective-
ness. Wink.

Everything's perfect except that yesterday, he had to fly
out with the team to Boston for a series of away games. I was
with him at his apartment while he finished packing his bag.
He keeps most everything he uses on the road pre-packed in
a carry-on, but he still needed to toss in a few changes of
clothes. I tried not to be sad as I sat on the bed, watching him,
but he could tell something was up because I hadn't been
talking much.

"Still tired?"

I nodded, trying to get out of having to tell him the truth.

"Yeah, same," he continued. Then he shot me a sidelong
glare. "I'm definitely not sad about having to leave you
today..."

His wistful smile was too much. I almost had tears in my
eyes, *almost*. Thank god I looked away.

"I'll be back next Monday. That's only six days."

I nodded, still not looking at him.

Even though he was fully dressed and about to head out
the door to meet his team, he crawled back up on the bed and
started littering kisses across my cheeks and neck until I
finally broke and laughed, forcing myself to look at him. I'm
sure he could see too much in my expression; I wasn't doing a
very good job of concealing how I felt about him leaving.

"We can do this, okay? Look at Luke and Chloe, Josh and
Sophia."

"They've been together forever. It's different."

He frowned, and I hated myself a little in that moment.
This wasn't some unforeseen circumstance. I knew this
would happen. I knew his travel schedule would be a
problem for me, and layered within that is the professional
athlete lifestyle too. I've just seen how different it is to normal
life. When these guys are on the road, they're offered a veritable buffet of willing bedmates, and the temptation is just

too hard to resist sometimes. Nick and Dustin are single and no doubt take full advantage of all the *perks* while they're on the road.

"It's not that I don't trust you…" I started, trying to figure out a way to explain to him how I was feeling without forcing him to be on the defense. I didn't want to make it seem like he was the problem.

But he shook his head, already understanding where I was headed. "I know the stereotype about professional athletes, and Jesus…" He sighed. "I know how many of us have lived up to it. I've just never been that guy, Tate."

"I know. It's—"

"No, listen. I don't expect you to trust me one hundred percent from the get-go." He was drawing his thumb back and forth across my cheek, trying to ease my furrowed brows. "This is new, and as your boyfriend, it's my job to prove myself to you, okay? If you stick this out with me, if we just take it day by day, I promise I won't disappoint you."

I couldn't say anything after that. I was so prepared to have to play it cool and act like I was fully on board with everything. *Oh yeah, going to a bar with a bunch of girls? That's so fun and exciting! Let me know who desperately wants to hook up with you tonight!* I didn't expect him to understand where I was coming from, to accept me where I was at rather than trying to make me feel like *I* was in the wrong. It choked me up.

He leaned down and kissed me again. "Do you work today?"

I shook my head.

"You can stay here as much as you want while I'm gone. There's a spare key in the junk drawer in the kitchen. Take it."

"Okay."

He pushed off the bed to finish gathering his stuff. "The building has a great gym and a sauna. I know you run outside, but there's a pool here too if you want to give it a try.

Oh, and down in the lobby there's a complimentary coffee bar, barista included. You'll love it."

As nice as his offer was, I didn't linger at his place for long after he left. It made me feel inexplicably sad. His pillow smelled like him and his toiletries were arranged so neatly on his bathroom counter and the picture of him and his dad framed on his dresser was just too sweet. *Why am I like this?!* I showered and changed and grabbed the spare key like he told me to, then I tried to go about a regular day. I went grocery shopping and then out for a run. I surprised Harper in the afternoon with an armful of art supplies and we painted pictures on canvases in her playroom.

"Oh, that's really good, Aunt Tate. Is it supposed to be a whale?"

"A butterfly."

"Right! *Yes!* I can really tell!" she said, lying so she wouldn't hurt my feelings.

I sent a picture of it to Grant.

"Cool butterfly," he wrote back.

We'd been texting off and on all day. I wasn't sure how it was going to work. I'd planned on giving him space—after all, I know he's a busy guy—but within an hour of leaving for the airport with his team, he was already giving me updates. It was just little stuff, like a picture of his bagel, which he said was the best one he'd ever had; the view of his hotel room; a funny part of the book he was reading. We settle into a nice rhythm over the six days he's gone. My phone isn't glued to my hands or anything, but I'm also generally aware of what he's up to and I like that we both seem to want to stay in contact throughout the day. He calls me when he can. Sometimes it doesn't work, like if he doesn't get home from the stadium until really late and I have an early shift at the hospital the next day, but the night before he gets home, he has one of the best games of his life against the White Sox and I stay up waiting for his call.

It's a little past midnight when my phone vibrates on my nightstand. I jump for it and answer it straight away.

"Grant?"

I don't know why I say it like that, like someone else might be using his phone.

"Hey, Tate."

I love hearing his voice. I could talk to him all day every day if our schedules allowed.

"Your game..."

He laughs.

"I can't believe how good you played! That double play in the fourth inning! Talk to your dad yet?"

"Just got off the phone with him. He, of course, had some pointers for me. Areas where I can improve..."

I smile. "Parents keep us humble, don't they? I'm sure if my mom watched a broadcast of one of my shifts at the hospital, she'd have a list a mile long of exactly what I'm doing wrong. Never mind that she's not in the medical field..."

He chuckles, then I hear "Oh! Talking to Tate?"

It's Dustin in the background, followed by Nick. "Tate! Can you hear me? You have this boy *in love*!"

Dustin cuts in again. "Yeah, tell her how much you've talked about her this week, Navarro. Tell her you're *obsessed* with her. God it's sick. Tate!" His voice gets louder like he's fighting to get the phone out of Grant's hand. "*It's all I've heard.* He's been such a baby about it. I'm surprised he doesn't have a countdown or something ticking away until he sees you again."

"Who says I don't?" Grant laughs, and the guys lose it.

"At least he's self-aware!" Nick says.

There's a muffled conversation on their end of the line, then finally Grant's voice returns. It's quieter now. He's found somewhere private to talk. That, or he's killed his friends.

"Sorry about that."

I laugh. "It's fine. They're just being silly."

"To be clear, I talk about you a normal amount," he assures me, trying to play it cool.

My grin stretches from ear to ear.

"It's okay. Sophia said if I bring you up again, I have to find a new place to live."

He laughs. "That's fine. Move in with me."

"*Not funny.*"

"I wasn't really kidding."

Tell me why I'm embarrassed by how hard I'm blushing even though he can't even see me.

"What time do you get in tomorrow?" I ask, changing the subject.

"Flight leaves at 6 AM."

I hiss. "That early?"

"None of us mind. We have people we want to get back to…"

Me.

ME!

"Unfortunately, I work until 6 PM tomorrow."

"Let's plan to meet after."

"Ugh, wish I could…I'm busy. I'm going—"

"*Tate,*" he cuts in with a sharp warning.

"What!? I was kidding. You didn't even let me finish my joke. It was going to be funny, I'm sure." I sigh like I'm really put out. "Now we'll never know."

"I'll see you after work."

He says it with so much conviction I shiver.

I'm extremely relieved by how light my workload is the next day. My focus is admittedly shot, but I take my time with the few important things I need to get done and double-check my work a dozen times just to be sure I don't let anything slip through my fingers.

I'm in such a rush to leave at the end of my shift that I make it all the way downstairs to the main lobby before real-

izing I forgot my hospital bag upstairs—phone, keys, wallet…
yup, I was just going to walk out without any of it.

I race back toward the elevators and press the up arrow
about a hundred times in a row. Just in case it wasn't already
broken, it is now. The elevators are notorious for taking
forever, but one finally comes just as two nurses from another
department join me.

"What floor?" I ask.

"Six," one of them says before turning to her friend and
whispering (not all that quietly), "Oh my gosh, that was
really him. Did you get a picture?"

"Yes, but I didn't want to be too obvious…" She angles her
phone so her friend can see what she got.

"Girl, why not?! Everyone else was being obvious! They
were getting him to sign autographs! Man, that picture is
blurry as hell—you can't even tell who it is! No one's going to
believe you if you share that."

"I know! I froze. It's not my fault. He was so much hotter
in real life. Should we go back out there?"

"We'll be late for our shift."

Her friend acts like she's tipping scales back and forth
with her hands. "A paycheck versus a once-in-a-lifetime
chance to meet Grant Navarro."

I freeze.

The nurse laughs and shakes her head. "Leave it. We had
our chance, now we'll just have to regret it for the rest of our
lives."

I'm smiling so deviously I'm surprised they can't tell, but
they're off in their own world. Back on my floor, I race over to
grab my bag from the desk. Kara, the nurse on duty after me,
winks. "I was just trying to figure out how to call you to let
you know you left your stuff here."

"Cell phone and all," I say with an eye roll.

"Knew you'd be back."

I laugh and grab my bag, hauling it over my shoulder as I

race toward the stairs rather than relying on the elevators this time. I have absolutely no chill as I take the steps two at a time. I only slow down after I nearly wipe out not once, but twice. On the ground floor, I whip open the door so fast and with so much force I nearly take out a man walking with his head down.

"I'm sorry!" I shout over my shoulder as I walk-run through the front lobby.

My heart soars even more the moment I see Grant. There's a swarm of people around him. I can't believe he's here! Is he crazy? With the way he's been playing this season, he's too conspicuous for public life. It's not just him either. Dustin, Luke, Josh, Nick—they need disguises and aliases at this point.

I love how nice he's being to everyone. I highly doubt he planned on taking pictures and chatting with strangers like this, but he's not the least bit rude about it. That is, until he looks up and catches me walking through the revolving door out onto the sidewalk. I smile, but I don't step any closer. I'm not sure of the protocol here. In the two weeks we've been official, we've somehow neglected to discuss how we were going to deal with being in the public eye. For all I know, Grant wants to keep things under wraps, which is fair. There are a whole host of reasons why that could be the better option for us, but seeing as how Grant politely extracts himself from the group and confidently makes his way toward me, I don't think we're aiming for subtlety.

I'm helpless when it comes to my responding smile. He's so damn sexy I could just rise up onto my toes and kiss him long enough that I'd pass out from lack of oxygen. He's so cute in his jeans and blue Henley t-shirt. He has the audacity to look reserved, almost bashful, as he approaches me. He rubs the back of his neck and then gives me a shy smile.

"I thought we were planning to meet at my apartment," I say once he reaches me.

He shrugs. "Yeah, that was the plan, and then I thought, you know what? Why do that when I can stand on the sidewalk in front of your work for thirty minutes and humiliate myself, all for the honor of walking you home."

My head tips back so I can meet his gaze as we inch closer to each other. People call his name, but now he ignores them. Now, he only has eyes for me.

My gaze falls to his mouth, and he wets his bottom lip. That physical tug is back. That need…

"Can we kiss, or—"

The second half of my question is cut off when his lips meet mine.

Well then…I guess we're kissing.

I'm faintly aware of the crowd of people going crazy around us. There are one or two camera flashes and plenty of iPhones recording this moment, I have no doubt. In fact, maybe I'll ask someone to send me the footage so I can watch it on a loop from now until the end of time.

Grant pulls back and takes my hospital bag, then my hand.

"How was work?"

I laugh and shake my head. "We're just going to pretend this is normal?"

"Unfortunately, it is. Haven't you been around Luke when he's been swarmed by people?"

"Yes, but it always felt different somehow."

I wasn't in the limelight alongside Luke, not like this. I'll have to ask Chloe and Sophia how they handle it. Neither one of them complains about living life alongside a professional athlete, and in large part, they go about their days completely unencumbered by their partners' celebrity status, which is a huge relief.

We turn the corner and already, the crowd is gone. The people gathered there weren't professional paparazzi or anything, just eager fans.

Now, it's just Grant and me, hand in hand. I look up to see him staring down at me curiously, likely trying to assess if I'm about to bail on him or not. I squeeze his hand tighter.

"I'm so glad you're home."

"Me too," he says, staring down at my lips then belatedly meeting my eyes with an air of mischief. "Have you had dinner yet?"

"No. I'm starved."

"Good. Let's go eat."

"And after?"

Excitement dances like butterflies in my stomach with his reply. "After…where should we go? *Your place or mine?*"

TWENTY-THREE

TATE

IT'S funny the way life never works out the way you expect it to. I had a rule about dating baseball players that was very cut and dry. There were no special circumstances, no "in case of" scenarios. Simply don't do it, plain and simple. Now here I am, not just casually dating a baseball player but hopelessly in love with one. I'm the girlfriend in the stands with all the matching gear: hat, jersey, foam finger, koozie—you name it, I'm rocking it. When I'm at the games and Grant walks out to bat, I am so obnoxious, so uncouth I'm surprised I don't get an official sealed letter from the league asking me to kindly refrain from "all that annoying shit". It's better when I can watch the away games at home, frankly, because there at least I don't have to worry about embarrassing myself and others (sorry to everyone within five rows of me).

Grant and I both agree that while we're young and kidless, it'd be fun for me to travel with him as much as possible. I work with the hospital to stack my shifts so I can occasionally work one week on, one week off. I don't go on the road with him for every series, but I like the flexibility. Sometimes I even load up on shifts during the weeks he's gone so when he's back in New York City, I have as much free time as possible to, you know, bang his brains out.

In the first few weeks of our fledgling relationship, I'm embarrassed to admit my moods oscillate wildly to and fro based solely on Grant's schedule.

Is he about to leave town for a week on the road? Okay, well then everything is bad and we should just keep the lights off in the apartment. Don't open the drapes.

Is Grant flying home? OPEN THOSE DRAPES. Thaw me out, baby! My boyfriend's back!

I feel out of whack and so unlike myself that it scares me a little. I've never been this beholden to a rollercoaster of emotions in my entire life. I'm self-aware enough to know I'm being a version of myself I never wanted to be. I wouldn't even put it past Sophia and Daphne to kick me to the curb in those weeks. *I'd* kick me to the curb. But they stick it out and eventually, by late September, I've mostly acclimated to my new normal.

Those initial feelings of crazy love slowly morph into something steadfast and, dare I say, calm. God it's good. Better than I could have imagined. A kind of love you can depend on day in and day out? Kids, it does exist, I swear.

I make a concerted effort to not become so focused on Grant that I lose sight of the other relationships in my life, namely my relationship with my brother and his family and my friendships with Sophia and Daphne. Grant would love nothing more than if I moved in with him ASAP, but I hold off. I love this time I have with my friends, and I know it won't always be like this. Sophia's getting married soon, and we've already talked about ending our lease before that. And by "talked about", I mean we've absolutely hysterically cried about it as if the three of us were getting shot by cannon to three different parts of the world. *Write me from Antarctica!*

There's something about living with roommates in your early 20s. The absolute shitshow of an existence that can only happen when three girls find themselves in "silly goofy" moods at 2 AM and we decide Sophia definitely needs high-lights in her hair, and then I try to do it for her with a hair dye kit I find under her bathroom sink only to realize halfway through that I have absolutely *no* idea what I'm doing, but it seemed easy enough when I read the instructions. The moment she looks in the mirror and screams and then starts laughing, and *I* start laughing, and *Daphne* starts to laugh so hard she starts to cry—that is the stuff of legends. I want to take advantage of every second we have together, just the three of us.

In late fall, the Pinstripes make it deep into the post-season, and they're favored to take it all in the World Series. Unfortunately, things begin to unravel at the end of October. Nick has a season-ending injury when he breaks a bone in his wrist, and Dustin can't seem to connect the bat to the ball with the same magic he was conjuring during the regular season. A string of bad luck culminates in a game seven loss that turns the city on its head. Collectively, we'll mourn. Restaurants and shops will proudly leave up their Pinstripes flags and posters in the windows for weeks to come. Bill-boards and signs will belatedly show support for a team that's out of the running for the year. I'm so disappointed for Grant, for Luke, for all the guys.

I'm with Grant that night. As soon as the ninth inning ends and we're cleared to access the field, I walk to him with tears gathered in my eyes. I watch him clap Nick on the back then shake his head at something Josh tells him. The team-mates and friends hug and console each other, and then Grant steps back, alone as he waits for me to reach him. He stands near the dugout, shoulders slumped, frustration written across every line of his face.

I don't say a word because what is there to say? I let him reach out and grab me. I sway toward him as he wraps his arms around me in a punishingly tight hug. There, I cry against his chest. I squeeze him to reassure him. I tell him how much I love him, how proud I am. His tears are mostly held back, though I understand how much anger seethes under the surface. It must feel like an entire season wasted even though logically that's not the truth.

That night, he takes longer to get home from the stadium than usual. I didn't want to rush him, so I left with Sophia and Daphne.

I can only imagine him and the guys in the locker room, rehashing every moment of the game, talking through what could have been if only *this* play had worked out or *that* out had been counted or *that* ball had just cut a few inches to the left—had it all gone their way. I'm asleep when he slides into bed behind me, wraps his arms around me, and draws me to him. I give in so easily when he starts to kiss my neck and wrap his arm possessively around my middle, pushing my pajama top up in the process.

It's obvious how much he needs this, *needs me*, as I shake off the last vestiges of sleep and turn to face him, kissing him back. It's slow and tender. We keep the lights off, but there's no fumbling. He knows my body as well as I know his. His rough hands run gently down my stomach until he reaches my thighs and spreads them apart so he can sink into me, bury his problems there with a heady groan.

"I love you," he tells me a dozen times.

I kiss him and hold him tight, splaying out first underneath him, and then on top of him, stealing his sorrow with my touch. It feels like we're trying to burrow into one another. In the end it feels like we're a shared heart pulsing together.

I try to take away every ounce of anguish he feels, though I know it's futile. I've grown up with Luke. I know how dejected Grant feels right now, and I also know in a few days, he will resurface, recharged and reinvigorated for next season. For now, I commiserate with him because he needs it, and he'd do the same for me. I tell him I'm sorry a million different ways, and we end up falling asleep together sweaty and tangled in the sheets.

One Saturday in spring, I spend an afternoon with Harper. We get hot chocolate at Serendipity and then walk around the city bundled in hats and long coats. We get our nails done sitting side by side in massage chairs. "*Ah! It's punching my back!*" she cries when she accidentally turns her spa chair up to its max speed.

Once we're sporting matching Barbie pink nails, we eat a late lunch at Dim Sum Palace and she tells me she kind of wishes Grant were with us.

I smile. "He's fun, isn't he?"

"Yeah, and you're always so happy when he's around."

"I'm happy now," I tell her, reaching over the table to steal one of her dumplings. "I'm spending the day with *you*."

"No, I know. It's just different. I really like him too. So does Dad, but he probably doesn't say so. I'd be sad if you two broke up. You won't, right? You're gonna marry him, aren't you?"

I choke on my bite of food. "Uh...well..."

"Dad thinks you're going to marry him. He and Chloe were talking about it last night at dinner. They did bets. Is that what it's called? Bets?"

I laugh. "Yes. That's what it's called."

She shrugs. "Anyway, I would like that. Having him as an uncle, I mean. He's really nice to me even if no one is paying attention. Chloe says that's important, how people act when other people aren't watching. I forget why, but anyway, when you aren't looking, he's still nice to me. He plays Legos with me and he brings me my favorite candy even though Dad says it'll rot my teeth out of my head."

"That's...descriptive."

"Also I think you really love him."

"Why do you say that?"

"You just…you look at him like he's your favorite person you've ever met. Can you pass the soy sauce?"

I had no idea I was so transparent or that Harper was so astute. "He is my favorite person—besides you, of course," I add with a wink.

"So just marry him already."

She says it like, *just* take out the trash, *just* brush your teeth, *just* do your homework. What's the problem?

"Okay, yeah. I just might."

"Good because I was already thinking about how we should do it. I stole one of Chloe's wedding magazines and I tore this out." Harper reaches into her coat pocket and extracts a crumpled piece of glossy paper. "I think you should wear something like this."

She points down to the dress in the picture. It's…large. I'll give her that. It looks like one Cinderella dress gorged itself on *another* Cinderella dress. You can barely make out the bride's tiny face among all the layers of tulle, beading, lace, and glitter.

My silence is audible.

"Or if that's not what you like, how about this?" she continues, drawing out another crumpled magazine page.

The needle has swung in the opposite direction with this one. The bride is wearing a barely-there tube top paired with a low-slung mermaid skirt. She could be going clubbing.

I barely manage to keep the judgment out of my voice. "Those are certainly…options."

She taps the page. "Good. Okay. I'm glad we agree. Also, I'm the flower girl, right?"

"Obviously. Though to be clear…Grant and I aren't getting married." I worry she somehow missed that part.

To her this is a minor issue. "Eh, we'll see."

Will we?

I narrow my eyes.

"What do you know, Harper Allen? *Spill it.*"

EPILOGUE

Tate

IT'S GETTING REALLY LATE, and I'm bored of sitting in this private lounge at the stadium. I've scrolled through my phone to my heart's content, and you know what? I found the end of the internet. We can pack it up now.

I check my phone again, but there's no new call or text from Grant. I'm really antsy to see him, not only because I've missed him all day and it's getting late and I'd like to go home now, but because I had the strangest thing happen to me at work today and I *need* to tell him about it.

Michael has found love, and not just with anyone.

"I actually met someone," he told me when we bumped into each other at the hospital and were forced to do the obligatory small talk.

He and I haven't had much of a friendship since I broke the news to him that I was officially dating Grant after our awkward sidewalk kiss. For a few months, we meticulously avoided talking to each other outside of the occasional work question, so I was surprised to hear this answer when I asked how he was doing.

"Oh really?"

"Yeah." He laughed, sounding bewildered. "It was the strangest thing. I ran into her outside a coffee shop. I mean, I literally *ran* into her. I spilled her drink all over her shoe on accident, but she let me replace it—her coffee, I mean. Not her shoe. Anyway, we got to talking while we were standing in line. Her name's Christine and she's—"

"What?" I asked, sounding accusatory. "Did you say her name is *Christine*?"

He looked at me with a puzzled expression. "Yes. Christine."

I almost laughed, then recovered quickly. "That's...that's awesome, Michael."

Now if you'll excuse me, I need to go purchase a winning lottery ticket.

I can't wait to tell Grant this story, though I know he's going to be skeptical. *"I wished for the universe to set Michael up with someone and it actually happened exactly the way I intended it to! Down to her exact name!"*

I can almost see his arched brow now. *"Uh-huh."*

"I swear it's true! I'm a witch! Or clairvoyant or something!"

Now, I check my watch, trying to figure out how long it could possibly take Grant to finish up in the locker room. I don't usually wait for him after games; there's no point. I'd be here all night. There's always postgame press, a catered meal, physical therapy, and more. I even know some guys who prefer to get their workouts in right after the games rather than the next morning.

Tonight though, Grant promised he'd skip everything he could and get out fast.

"Wait for me. It won't take me long."

So I agreed, but it's been over an hour and a half, and I

can't stay holed up in this lounge much longer. The cleaning crew needs in here, I'm sure.

Another wave of annoyance threatens to send me over the edge. Why am I here? Why couldn't I just wait for Grant at home like usual?

Worse, I don't even know the security guard standing at the door, tapping his foot. He just showed up a minute ago with a haughty attitude I don't much care for if I'm being honest.

"Ma'am, I need you to follow me now. We kindly ask that you vacate the premises. As of ten minutes ago, the stadium is officially closed to all non-personnel."

He makes it sound like I'm loitering!

Which…I guess technically I am.

Before I go with him, I try to call Grant again, but it goes straight to voicemail. Whatever. I'll text him that I had to leave; he'll understand. It's either cooperate with this big burly suited man or wind up on the morning news. I'd prefer the former.

"Right this way," he says with a gruff voice, motioning out into the hall. Clearly, he's annoyed to be dealing with me. He probably just wants to go home.

"You don't have to escort me—I know how to leave the stadium on my own. I'm sorry for the trouble. My boyfriend wanted me to stay so I was just waiting around for him."

"Boyfriend?"

"Grant Navarro."

He snorts. "Right."

He clearly doesn't believe me.

"It's why I was up in the private lounge," I say, feeling a bit defensive. "The one for league families."

He nods again like, *Whatever you say, lady.*

I've never seen the stadium so empty. All the vendors are shuttered and closed. You'd expect a cleaning crew, at least, but it looks like the floors have already been swept. Trash cans are emptied and ready to go for tomorrow's game. Maybe I was in there waiting longer than I thought.

The security guard speaks into the walkie talkie mounted on an official-looking shoulder holster. I don't catch what he says though.

"This way." He points to the left when I had planned on continuing straight.

"Isn't it faster if I—"

"Ma'am, this way."

Well all right then. Who am I to argue with a guy wearing an earpiece?

We go into an elevator I've never used before, and as the doors sweep closed, I have a few belated thoughts. A) I don't know this man, which is odd, because I know a lot of the security guards at the stadium, most of them by name. B) He's not dressed like regular security guards, i.e. black slacks with a coordinating polo that says SECURITY in bold white script across the back. C) The stadium is creepy as hell now that everyone's gone.

I hope Grant's happy when he realizes I've been good and stolen because of him. I chance a peek at my kidnapper. He looks gruff and mean, but maybe he has a chink in his armor I can exploit, a strained relationship with his mother or a love of chocolate. I might have something in my purse I could tempt him with…

I'm about to check when the elevator doors open. I was expecting to arrive on the ground floor, somewhere near an exit. There, an unmarked van would be waiting to whisk me away to an airstrip. I'd be out of the country, untraceable, in half an hour, tops.

I gulp as he motions that I should leave the elevator.

"Wh—where are we going?"

No answer, just a curt, "Go ahead."

It takes me an obnoxiously long time to get my bearings for where we are. I didn't recognize the entrance to the field at first. We're walking through a tunnel, the same one the guys usually use when they go to and from the locker rooms and clubhouse.

Okay...

Maybe the kidnappers have a different strategy for getting me out of here. The stadium roof is open tonight because of the nice weather, which probably means they'll land a helicopter on the field instead of taking a van.

I'm so ensconced in this absurd idea that it takes me a second to register the scene laid out before me.

The stadium lights have been cut, save for a spotlight aimed directly over the pitcher's mound. Grant stands in the warm glow, waiting for me. He looks freshly showered. His short hair is styled handsomely, and he's dressed to the nines in a black suit, no tie. He nods to the security guard, who abruptly turns, leaving me on the edge of the field all by myself.

"What is this?" I ask with a nervous chuckle.

Grant's response is a winning smile, but nothing else. I look around me, searching. The stands are empty. The place is ours.

"What are you doing?" I ask with a shake of my head.

It's the shock that keeps me from understanding right away what this is. Not until I shake off my stupor and start to walk toward him on trembling legs as he slowly bends down onto one knee does realization dawn.

This is a proposal happening *exactly* one year to the day since Grant officially asked me to be his girlfriend. We had plans to eat a late dinner together. That's why I thought he was asking me to hang back at the stadium for him. We'd been going on all week about where we could go and how we could celebrate our anniversary. We could do a spa day! We could do a stay-cation! We could stay in bed for twenty-four hours *straight*! He just let me run my mouth, and all the while he knew this was going to happen. This!

I'm crying before I reach him. Happy tears trickle down my cheeks as I laugh and swipe them away.

"You're crazy!" I say as I stand before him. "Insane!"

He smiles and waits for me to get it out.

"You let me go on and on about getting Chinese food tonight! You were *so* convincing!"

He tips his head, watching me.

"*Grant.*"

"Tate…"

His voice slays me. That steady calm timbre seems connected to every nerve ending inside me. He plays me like a fiddle.

"I'm sorry about the Chinese food, I am," he says with a teasing smile.

I laugh as he continues.

"But I had an important question to ask you tonight, and I couldn't wait another day."

In his right hand, he holds up a small diamond ring. Its gold band is ornate, antique, beautifully delicate as it glistens in the spotlight. I recognize it right away as having once belonged to his mom. When did he ask his dad for it? How long has he…

"Tate…" His voice trembles now. "Will you marry me?"

Emotion tightens my chest as the past year flashes through my mind. The high highs and low lows. The week we spent in Phoenix with his dad over the holidays. The way Grant spoiled him in subtle ways his father couldn't argue with: a home-cooked meal, a few new flannel shirts wrapped up with a bow, not letting him lift a finger to wash a dish or clean up while we were there. The way when we're together, he's just Grant. He doesn't care about the fame. He could be a damn mailman with the way he treats people. No one is beneath him, no one is less worthy than anyone else. I think of the time he was at the grocery store and I begrudgingly asked him if he could pick up some tampons for me since I'd just run out. There was no huffing and puffing about running the errand. He showed up at my apartment with two bags full and made sure to ask if he'd purchased the right brand so he'd know for sure for next time. I think of how once, offhand, I mentioned that it would be fun to take a cooking class, and a month later, he surprised me with a date at Sur La Table. I think of how when we have a free Saturday, he asks if I want to swing by and pick up Harper so we can spend the day with her. He's so sweet with her, tender and silly. He wants her to like him so bad, which is absurd because Harper likes everyone, but the fact that he cares that much makes me love him all the more.

When his schedule allows, he rides his bike along my route while I do my runs. He keeps his distance behind me, but he knows I like the company and he likes to know I'm being safe. After we're done, without fail, we always stop for bagels and coffee.

When my dad had wrist surgery in February, Grant came down to Texas with me and stayed by my side at the hospital the entire time. When I got a bad case of strep and felt like I couldn't drink, much less eat, for three days straight, Grant nursed me back to health. When we fight, Grant is the apologizer, the one who breathes peace and calm into every situation.

He's shown me that love is less about the overt acts of passion and more in the daily details: how he always texts me back, never making me wonder about his intentions or his feelings; when he gives me the last bit of ice cream in the pint; his willingness to be a good sport with Sophia, Daphne, and me on our wildest nights out; the way, without fail, he wakes up before me, but instead of going out into the living room, he'll stay in bed and read quietly beside me or scroll on his phone until I wake up. I asked him about it once and he shrugged and said, "I just like being with you," as if it was the most simple thing in the world to him.

I'm surprised how easy it is to love Grant. The night we met, when I saw him standing across the room at that random party, I took one look and thought, *This guy is trouble. Run for your life.*

Now, here he is, bent down on one knee, waiting patiently to marry me.

I smile as the tears keep coming. My first nod is so small it goes unnoticed. When I nod again, it's harder. Absolutely resolute.

His smile widens and he leaps up to slip the ring on my finger and then envelop me in a bone-crushing hug.

"I love you," I say, inhaling his familiar scent as I squeeze my eyes closed.

"I love you too."

How many times can you tell someone you love them before they realize there is only peace so long as they're by your side, before they realize in the simplest way possible, their mere existence in your life has changed the shape of you forever so that any other heart, any lips, any hand will forever feel wrong. Words don't feel strong enough at the moment, so I'm left to string a line of kisses across his cheek until our mouths meet and everything I'm feeling gets conveyed in that simple touch.

I love you and I would marry you a million times over.

He laughs, so overcome with happiness and relief. He tilts back and cups my face, flitting his gaze between my eyes, taking me in. I smile and hold my hands over his.

Then his eyebrows furrow. "Do you remember when we went to Luke's house exactly a year ago today? The night I asked you to be my girlfriend?"

I nod. Of course I remember.

"When we left, you asked me what I told Luke when he and I went off into his office to talk in private. I wouldn't tell you then…"

Right. In the beginning of our relationship, I often

wondered about that conversation, but less so in recent months. Luke and Grant have developed a real friendship. I don't have to worry whether my brother approves of Grant—he's told me he does himself—but still, I chuckle thinking about how awkward that night must have been for them both.

I shrug. "I sort of assumed he did a good deal of threatening and that was that. Oh god, was it bad? If he threatened you—"

Grant shakes his head and steps back, taking my hands in his as he explains, "I went there that day with the intention of asking for Luke's permission to date you, though that's not exactly how it went." He clears his throat and adjusts his grip on my hands before he continues, "I told him that even though I'd only known you a few months, even though we weren't officially dating yet, I already loved you.

"I told him he could approve or not, could argue against us all he wanted, but I would love you anyway. By that point, there was no stopping it. At first, I think he was annoyed. Here I was saying 'I don't really care about what you have to say,' but I told him I was there because if I was going to love you the right way, that meant coming to his doorstep and telling him the truth. I wasn't going to treat you like a secret. You were never someone I wanted to hide."

My bottom lip trembles as he speaks. Then, before I can stop myself, I throw myself at him again, wrapping my arms around his neck and holding on for dear life. I don't even have full coherent thoughts, so I'm sure the things coming out of my mouth make absolutely no sense.

I'm really sniffling then, a blubbering mess. It's a good thing no one's watching us.

Then I realize…

Of course they are.

OF COURSE THEY ARE!

I rear back, eyes widening in horror before they narrow again with playful accusation.

"Where are they?"

Grant's devious smile is slow to spread. "For what it's worth, I did consider having it just be you and me. And rest assured, I'm not mic'd up or anything. They can't hear us."

I shake my head, turning to survey the stadium. They aren't on the field and they aren't in the stands. They could be in the private boxes with those tinted windows...

Grant leans down so we're shoulder to shoulder, and then he points toward the dugout.

Sure enough, at that precise moment, our friends and family jump up and start whooping and hollering. Nick's the first one out on the field, running in front of the rest of the pack.

"DID YOU SAY YES?!"

"Yes." I laugh as he nearly bowls us over with a hug.

He turns and shouts to everyone. "*SHE SAID YES!*"

It's a whirlwind as our family and friends reach us. Grant clearly took a page out of Josh's book, though on a much smaller scale. He didn't fly in any of my extended family, no second cousins once removed, but my parents are here and so is Grant's dad, along with our tight-knit group of friends.

Harper takes my hands and twirls me around, screaming on repeat, "Another wedding! Another wedding!"

Sophia and Daphne both rush over to hug and congratulate me. Daphne even swipes tears from her eyes, and just behind her, Dustin watches curiously. I wait for him to make some jokey comment, something that will rile her up, but he holds off. I'll consider his silence an early wedding gift.

Something gets Grant's attention back near the outfield. He nods then and gives me a slightly apologetic grimace. "Harper talked me into this. If you hate it—"

"She won't hate it!" Harper insists.

"I promise to make it up to you."

"What are you—"

Before I can finish my question, there's a loud BOOM and an explosion of purple and blue sparks cascade across the sky. I jump out of my skin only to realize a second later how silly I am.

It's just fireworks.

"*FIREWORKS!*" Harper exclaims, jumping up and down just as more whistle and then explode in the sky, perfectly in sync one after another. There are enough of them to rival a city-funded Fourth of July show.

My jaw drops as I look at Grant.

"Too over the top?" he asks with a self-conscious smile.

I can't stop shaking my head in disbelief. I'm at a loss for words.

Fortunately, Harper says everything I wish I could say as she runs over to grab his hand.

"Thank you, thank you, *thank you*, Uncle Grant! I love fireworks!" The sparks dance in her gaze as she looks up at the sky, wide-eyed. "It's *amazing*..."

I never thought I was someone who wanted a fireworks show put on in my honor, but here I am totally in awe of the fact that he's gone to the trouble to coordinate all of this.

It's so special we all end up a little teary-eyed. Grant hangs on to Harper as his dad comes over to loop his arms around his shoulders. I go over to my mom and dad and kiss them on the cheeks before pulling them close. For a few minutes, I take it all in. All my family and friends are here to support us. Even Daphne and Dustin stand close together, staring up at the sky. Apparently, they've called a truce for the evening and set aside their weapons, which is really something, let me tell you.

Just before the grand finale, Grant grabs me and makes his apologies as he pulls me to the back of the crowd, away from everyone else. When it's just the two of us, he cups my face between his hands and looks me over as if wanting to memorize me in this moment.

Then he kisses me with so much joy I start crying all over again.

"I can't wait to make you my wife," he says as he pulls back. He lifts my hand and we both look down at the antique ring nestled perfectly on my finger.

Sparks rain down atop Pinstripe Stadium, and I can do nothing but smile—incandescently, wildly, endlessly *happy*.

Made in the USA
Monee, IL
23 August 2024

64392826R00163